"Serenity *place, Karen.*

"No one chooses to be here," Jamey said.

"Except you," she observed. "You choose to be here."

For a moment he was silent. She was right. It had been a long, long time since he'd *had* to live here. But the simple fact was that Serenity was his home. He might not have family or much in the way of friends, but he still had neighbors. Somebody had to look out for them, and for the past eight or ten years, that somebody had been *him*.

But damned if he wanted to look after Karen Montez, too.

Karen spoke softly. "Why do you find it so hard to believe that I choose that, too?"

"It's my home."

"I intend to make it my home. I intend to spend the rest of my life here."

"Darlin'," Jamey said cynically, "let's hope it's a long one."

Dear Reader,

Any month with a new Nora Roberts book *has* to be special, and this month is *extra* special, because this book is the first of a wonderful new trilogy. *Hidden Star* begins THE STARS OF MITHRA, three stories about strong heroines, wonderful heroes—and three gems destined to bring them together. The adventure begins for Bailey James with the loss of her memory—and the entrance of coolheaded (well, until he sees *her*) private eye Cade Parris into her life. He wants to believe in her—not to mention love her—but what is she doing with a sackful of cash and a diamond the size of a baby's fist?

It's a month for miniseries, with Marilyn Pappano revisiting her popular SOUTHERN KNIGHTS with *Convincing Jamey*, and Alicia Scott continuing MAXIMILLIAN'S CHILDREN with *MacNamara's Woman*. Not to mention the final installment of Beverly Bird's THE WEDDING RING, *Saving Susannah*, and the second book of Marilyn Tracy's ALMOST, TEXAS miniseries, *Almost a Family*.

Finally, welcome Intimate Moments' newest author, Maggie Price. She's part of our WOMEN TO WATCH cross-line promotion, with each line introducing a brand-new author to you. In *Prime Suspect*, Maggie spins an irresistible tale about a by-the-book detective falling for a suspect, a beautiful criminal profiler who just may be in over her head. As an aside, you might like to know that Maggie herself once worked as a crime analyst for the Oklahoma City police department.

So enjoy all these novels—and then be sure to come back next month for more of the best romance reading around, right here in Silhouette Intimate Moments.

Yours,

[signature]

Senior Editor and Editorial Coordinator

Please address questions and book requests to:
Silhouette Reader Service
U.S.: 3010 Walden Ave., P.O. Box 1325, Buffalo, NY 14269
Canadian: P.O. Box 609, Fort Erie, Ont. L2A 5X3

Marilyn Pappano

CONVINCING JAMEY

Silhouette®
INTIMATE™ MOMENTS®

Published by Silhouette Books
America's Publisher of Contemporary Romance

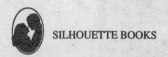 SILHOUETTE BOOKS

ISBN 0-373-07812-9

CONVINCING JAMEY

Printed in U.S.A.

Books by Marilyn Pappano

Silhouette Intimate Moments

Within Reach #182
The Lights of Home #214
Guilt by Association #233
Cody Daniels' Return #258
Room at the Inn #268
Something of Heaven #294
Somebody's Baby #310
Not Without Honor #338
Safe Haven #363
A Dangerous Man #381
Probable Cause #405
Operation Homefront #424
Somebody's Lady #437
No Retreat #469
Memories of Laura #486
Sweet Annie's Pass #512
Finally a Father #542
*Michael's Gift #583
*Regarding Remy #609
*A Man Like Smith #626
Survive the Night #703
†Discovered: Daddy #746
*Convincing Jamey #812

Silhouette Books

Silhouette Christmas Stories 1989
"The Greatest Gift"

Silhouette Summer Sizzlers 1991
"Loving Abby"

*Southern Knights
†Daddy Knows Last

MARILYN PAPPANO

After following her career navy husband around the country for sixteen years, Marilyn Pappano now makes her home high on a hill overlooking her hometown. With acreage, an orchard and the best view in the state, she's not planning on pulling out the moving boxes ever again. When not writing, she makes apple butter from their own apples (when the thieves don't get to them first), putts around the pond in the boat and tends a yard that she thinks would look better as a wildflower field, if the darn things would just grow there.

You can write to Marilyn by snail mail at P.O. Box 643, Sapulpa, OK 74067-0643.

Chapter 1

Not much happened on Serenity Street that Jamey O'Shea wasn't well-informed about, but the activity across the street on a lazy August Monday came as a surprise. Leaving the bar with the twenty-four-hour news channel droning on the TV, he made his way around the tables to one of four sets of French doors that spread across the front of O'Shea's, braced one shoulder against peeling white paint and watched.

One rusted iron gate leading to the house across the street was propped open and a car was parked in the driveway. A moving van was in the process of backing into the driveway, the driver concentrating on a figure in the rearview mirror as he inched back closer to the car. A glance at the fence showed that the For Sale sign still hung there. It had been there so long that its words were obliterated by rust and graffiti. Jamey vaguely remembered when the sign had appeared, when the last owner had moved out some ten or twelve years ago. No one had wanted to buy a beat-up old house in a beat-up part of town. He had always figured it

would stay empty until it fell in on itself or until one or
another of the kids who hung out there got careless with a
cigarette and sent it up in flames. He had never figured that
someone would actually buy the place, that anyone would
ever move in.

Satisfied with his position, the driver shut off the engine
of the truck and climbed out, taking a look around him as
he did. He didn't look impressed with the neighborhood,
Jamey noted with perverse humor. Serenity wasn't a place
for good impressions. It was the sort of place the Chamber
of Commerce wished didn't exist. The sort of place the
surrounding neighborhoods were, at the same time, scornful
of and grateful for. No one wanted to live close to a dump
like this, but at the same time, since gangs and thugs found
such easy going on Serenity, they tended to gather there
instead of elsewhere.

Hell, even the cops hated the fourteen-block district. Call
them for anything less than murder, and you weren't likely
to get a response. Even on murder calls, they waited until
they could come in force. You never saw a lone police car
on Serenity Street.

You didn't often see a lone woman.

She came around from behind the truck, carrying something large, light and wrapped in paper. After talking to the
driver for a moment, she started toward the walk. The or-
nate gate that led out of the yard and onto the sidewalk
fronting the street hung askew on its hinges, one end resting
on the cracked concrete, the top corner wedged at an angle
between two iron bars. That didn't stop her from trying the
gate, from tugging on it, trying to lift it up and into proper
alignment. She almost managed, but it slipped from her
hands and fell with a dull clang, wedging even tighter.

With a shrug, she turned to the side, set her package
down and climbed onto the crumbling bricks that supported
the fence. She had to stretch onto the tips of her toes to
reach the For Sale sign that was hung by thin wire loops

over the top of two iron rails, had to stretch even higher to slide the wires free of the rails; then, sign in hand, she jumped backwards from the brick, landing lightly on the dirt where grass had once grown. She dropped the sign, retrieved her package, tore the paper loose and climbed onto the bricks again.

It was another sign, a big, rectangular one. Jamey could make out a painting of a house, an elaborate Victorian that looked much like the one in front of him must have eighty years ago. Underneath it in graceful script was a name, Kathy's something-or-other. A yellow-and-red banner across the upper left corner proclaimed Opening Soon.

He shook his head in amused disbelief. A business? This redheaded stranger intended to open some sort of business on Serenity Street? She must be crazy. She only had to look down the street to see shop after empty shop. The markets were gone, the five-and-dime, the barber shops, the Laundromats, the restaurants, the doctors. The only retail businesses left on the entire six blocks of Serenity were the bars, including O'Shea's, and one lone liquor store. There wasn't any money on Serenity. His own pathetic business records attested to that.

She was stretching onto her toes again, trying to slide the plastic loops on her sign over the iron bars. Impulsively Jamey stepped out onto the sidewalk, crossed the street without looking in either direction and stopped in front of her. He reached over the fence, took the sign and slid it into place. Kathy's House, it said, and the house in the picture bore more than just a resemblance to the old house in front of him. It was exactly the same place, as it must once have looked. As she hoped to make it look again?

"Thanks," the redhead said, jumping to the ground once again, wiping rust from her hands to her jeans. "Hello. I'm Karen Montez."

He corrected the angle of the sign before looking at her, automatically assessing her. She wasn't any great beauty.

Redheads weren't his type, especially redheads with skin as delicate and pale as milk glass. Petite wasn't his type, either, and sure as hell neither was foolish. And this woman had to be foolish.

"Jamey O'Shea," he responded at last.

Her smile was the slightest bit uneasy. "From O'Shea's, I assume." She gestured toward the bar behind him, but he didn't waste time looking. He knew exactly what she was facing: a run-down, narrow, two-story building that hadn't been much brand-new and was nothing now. The brick was old and crumbled in places. A broken pane at the bottom of one of the French doors, courtesy of old Thomas's over-indulgence and size-thirteen shoes, had been repaired with a piece of plywood and nails. The sign was faded and hard to read, the screens over the upstairs windows rusted and torn.

It was a shabby place on a shabby street. Her place was also shabby, but while he belonged in his place, she obviously didn't. She looked too hopeful. Too well-bred. Too comfortable. She was as middle-class as they came, so what was she doing slumming?

"Yeah, from O'Shea's." He glanced toward the van. A helper had materialized from somewhere, and he and the driver were carrying a wood sofa with brightly striped cushions onto the veranda. "You're not moving in here," he said, as if saying it could make it not true. She didn't belong here, and he didn't want her here. No one would want her here.

She looked around, too, and smiled in that nervous way again. "I am. I bought the place."

He gave the house a brief visual exam. Peeling paint, broken windows, rotting wood, piles of debris, years of neglect. It made his place look downright homey. "And no one tried to have you committed?"

The smile came again, more natural this time. Almost dazzling...if he were the sort of man to be dazzled. "My family considered it. They wanted me to stay in Landry. The real estate agent was appalled when I told her I wanted to look at this place. And the bank..." She laughed and simply shook her head.

He could well imagine what the bank's response had been. They weren't in the business of throwing away their investors' money. They didn't believe in taking risks—and counting on this place to be standing another year was a risk. Investing money in any way on Serenity was most definitely a risk. Moving into one of the roughest, toughest neighborhoods in the city of New Orleans was more than a risk. It was outright lunacy.

Gesturing to the sign, he asked, "What *is* Kathy's House?" It sounded like a cutesy shop, one that would sell locally made crafts, stale pralines, postcards and other souvenirs of New Orleans to tourists. Or a bed-and-breakfast, meticulously refurbished in true Victorian style, providing those same tourists an alternative to big, impersonal hotels. Or maybe a restaurant, some sort of upscale, designed-to-appeal-to-society-class-matrons—

"It's a women's center," she replied, interrupting his thoughts. "At least, it will be once I get it open." His expression must have been blank, because after a moment's hesitation, she explained, "You know, a place where women can get help—if their husbands are abusing them, if the system is taking advantage of them, if they need medical care or legal advice or just a safe place to stay. We'll be their advocates."

That told him more about her than he needed to know. She was a do-gooder, an idealist—and a nosy one at that. She was naive, unrealistic, gullible and foolish enough to be dangerous, to herself if no one else. She thought she could come down here and solve problems that had been taking shape for generations. She thought she could teach these poor ignorant women—these nobodies who were obviously inferior to her, or else they would never have wound up on Serenity Street—how to resolve their troubles and run their lives. She—Ms. Middle-class-small-town-never-had-a-trouble-in-her-life—thought she could *make a difference,* hallelujah!

"There aren't many husbands on Serenity Street," he said, allowing only a shade of sarcasm to creep into his voice.

"Excuse me?" She looked a little puzzled until she remembered her own words:...*if their husbands are abusing them...* "Husbands, boyfriends, pimps, strangers on the street—whoever. The point is it doesn't have to happen. We'll help them make it stop."

"We," he repeated. "Who is in this besides you?"

"I've lined up a number of volunteers—nurses, teachers, a psychologist, a nutritionist."

"No social worker?"

She smiled. "I'm the social worker."

Of course. How could he not have guessed?

The smile slowly faded. "You seem skeptical."

"Darlin', I've lived on Serenity Street since I was born. I've seen people like you come and go. They don't make a difference. They don't solve any problems. They don't do anything but waste their time and their money. They stay a few weeks, maybe a few months, and if they're lucky, they leave with only a little less than they came in with. If they're not lucky..." He shrugged expressively. "The last one died trying to save the soul of a fifteen-year-old punk whose only concern was finding where she kept her money."

He expected fear to come into her clear blue eyes, but it didn't. Obviously she'd heard about the failed mission down the street and had convinced herself that it didn't concern her. She wasn't force-feeding religion the way that woman had been. She didn't intend to be caught late at night in an empty storefront with a vicious little bastard like that kid. She would reach the kids, would earn their respect along with their mothers' respect. She would be *different*.

To these kids, these people, there was no difference among outsiders. There was no respect and no reaching them. Those were lessons she would have to learn.

"I'm sorry you feel that way, Mr. O'Shea."

"Doesn't matter how *I* feel, Ms. Montez. I'm not one of the souls that you've come to save."

"Don't underestimate me. I'll start with the women and the children. I'll move on to the others," she said, with a smile that was at once innocent and full of promise. "So…you've lived here all your life. Any advice for Serenity Street's newest resident?"

"Yeah. Get out while you can."

"I'm serious, Mr. O'Shea."

"So am I…but until you go, you can call me Jamey."

She acknowledged his grudgingly offered concession with a nod. "I'm Karen. Seriously, what does it take to live on Serenity Street?"

"Despair. Having no place else to go. No common sense. A death wish." He gestured down the street with a sweeping movement. "Look around. It's the middle of the day. School doesn't start for two more weeks. It's hot, humid and miserable in all these unairconditioned houses and apartments, but there's no one out. There's no one on this street but you, me and your movers, who are paid to be here. The park's empty. The porches are empty. Look." He pointed to a house across the street and down thirty feet. Once a single-family home, it had long since been converted to apartments, two per floor, each with its own small porch. "The doors are closed. The windows are closed. People are scared to death around here. They'd rather swelter inside than risk their lives for a cool breeze."

She looked—not only at that house, but at all of them within her field of vision. Then she fixed her gaze on him again. "And your point is?"

"Serenity Street is a dangerous place. People born here work long and hard to get out. No one chooses to be here."

"Except you," she pointed out. "You choose to be here."

For a moment he was silent. She was right. It had been a long, long time since he'd had any ties to the neighborhood. His parents had died years ago, and his friends had moved away. Everyone he'd grown up with was gone— moved on to a better life, in prison or dead. The only thing holding him here was O'Shea's. He couldn't sell the place. Who would buy it? He couldn't even torch it for the insurance money, because there wasn't any. With his meager profits, who could afford insurance? All he could do was pack his bags and walk away. That was what most of the other businessmen on the street had done.

But where would he go? Someplace safer? He didn't worry about his safety here. The punks pretty much left him alone. He wasn't as easily intimidated as the other residents of Serenity. Like typical bullies, they never hit anyone who might hit back, and Jamey had demonstrated over the years that he would hit back, and hit hard.

The simple fact was there was no place he would rather be than on Serenity. This was his home. He might not have family or much in the way of friends, but he still had customers and neighbors. Somebody had to look out for them, and, for the last eight or ten years, that somebody was him.

But damned if he wanted to look after Karen Montez, too.

"You choose to live here," she repeated. "Why do you find it so hard to believe that I choose that, too?"

"It's my home."

"I intend to make it my home." Her smile was cool, confident, determined. "I intend to spend the rest of my life here."

Hearing his phone ring through the open doors, he started across the street, then stopped in the middle to glance back at her. "Darlin'," he said cynically, "let's hope it's a long one."

Karen watched until he was out of sight, then gave the street a long, intent look both ways. She'd known something was a little odd before she'd driven more than a block down the street, but she hadn't put her finger on it until Jamey O'Shea had mentioned it. Where *were* the people? Why weren't the kids outside playing in the park? Why didn't someone turn on a hose so they could cool off and have a little fun? Why weren't the mothers sitting on their shady porches, talking back and forth?

Because they were scared. Because Serenity *was* a dangerous place. Sure, it was quiet right now, but it was an eerie quiet, a sort of calm-before-the-storm quiet. At any moment a car could come tearing down the street, its occupants shooting everything in sight. Rage could erupt in any one of the apartments. Violence could flare from any source.

That unnatural tension was why she was here. Jamey O'Shea might not think she could make a difference— heaven knew, her parents and her in-laws were convinced that she couldn't—but she knew she could. Not by herself, of course; no one was that good. But with the staff she'd lined up and with even the slightest cooperation of the mothers on the street, she knew she could help turn the neighborhood back into the community it had once been. She *could.*

And who was she trying to convince? a dry little voice inside her asked. The rest of the world? Or herself?

Fortunately, one of the movers commanded her attention before she had to answer that. "Ma'am," he called from the veranda, using the formal address with the familiarity of a man who spent too much of his time working with strangers to remember names. "Where do you want all this stuff?"

Giving the sign on the fence one light touch for luck—for reassurance—she started across the yard to the steps. "Upstairs," she directed. "Everything goes upstairs except the boxes marked 'Kitchen.'"

She didn't miss his grimace or his grumbling as he went back inside. The poor guy had probably thought he'd picked up an easy job when she'd hired him. All he'd had to do was load her furniture—two rooms full, maybe three—from a storage locker in Landry, drive the four hours to New Orleans and unload it. He hadn't counted on a destination right smack in the middle of the city's worst neighborhood, or on carrying everything up a narrow staircase to the second floor on what had to be one of the hottest, muggiest days of the summer.

That was what she was paying him for, she thought as she followed them up the stairs. Still, she felt a little guilty. After first being turned down by a mover familiar with this part of the French Quarter, she had deliberately withheld from this one even the slightest hint that their destination was considered no-man's-land. In all the years she and Evan had lived in the city, she had never known this place existed. She had thought they'd covered every nook and cranny of the Quarter in their explorations, but they'd missed these crannies. That had probably been Evan's doing. A New Orleans cop, he had tried his best to shield her from the city's dark side.

Too bad he hadn't been able to protect himself as well as he had protected her.

The stairs opened onto a wide hall that ended at the left in front of a tall window that faced the brick building next door. On the right it traveled thirty feet before making a turn toward the front. At its end was one of the turret rooms, a perfect octagon with windows on five of its sides. It would be a lovely room for a study or a nursery—not that she would ever have need of a nursery. She'd found that out only three days after Evan's death. It hadn't been

enough that she'd lost her husband of nine years so unexpectedly, so violently, but she had also lost a part of herself.
She would never be a mother, would never know the joy
of holding her own baby in her arms. It would have broken
Evan's heart if he'd known, but he would have tried to hide
it. He would have assured her that it was all right, that they
could adopt, that they could love *any* baby, not just their
own, and with him at her side, that would have been true.
They could have made a family anyway.

She couldn't do it on her own, though. She had lost too
much in the last few years—Evan, the chance to have her
own child, Kathy. She couldn't lose any more.

So what the hell was she doing here?

Forcing a smile to counter the dampness in her eyes, she
wandered into the center room, back to the windows that
looked down into the narrow backyard. She had wanted
one of the front rooms for her bedroom, one of them with
the big bay windows and the broad seat underneath, but
common sense had voted against it. Drive-by shootings on
Serenity occurred with more frequency at night. For safety's sake—at least until things had begun to change—the
rooms facing the street would be used only during the day,
when violence still erupted but usually with some small
warning.

The room was dusty and musty. She should have delayed
the move a few days to give herself a chance to come in
and give the place a thorough cleaning, but instead she had
arranged to move in immediately following this morning's
closing. If she had waited, she had been afraid she would
never do it. She might have let her parents and Evan's
parents influence her, let them persuade her that this was
sheer folly. She would have thought about the horror stories
the real estate agent had related, and given second and third
thoughts to the woman murdered in the storefront mission
less than a block away. She would have considered what
advice Evan would give if he were here, or Kathy if she

could, and she would have been cowardly. She would have
given up her plans, written the money off as a loss and
stayed in Landry, forever grieving, forever sorrowful, forever guilt-ridden.

She would have died there.

So instead of cleaning empty rooms, she would clean
around her furniture. She would vacuum and dust one room
at a time until the house was properly spotless. She would
unpack and straighten up and settle in…and then the real
work would begin.

Bending and pulling, she opened every window except
the one in the middle, painted shut or swollen closed thanks
to the humidity. Across the hall in what would be her living
room, she opened those windows, too, even the ones without screens. They gave her a view of just a few feet or so
into O'Shea's Bar, tempting her to lean outside and call to
Jamey O'Shea to notice that *her* windows were open. Naturally, she resisted the temptation and instead knelt on the
wooden seat and studied the bar's façade.

Why did a man like Jamey O'Shea stay on Serenity? He
was young enough—surely not much past forty—and apparently bright enough to make opportunities for himself
elsewhere. He must have some business acumen to keep
the bar in business long after almost everything else had
shut down. He wasn't making a tremendous profit, obviously, but he was getting by. Why would he choose to get
by here when he could most likely be fairly successful elsewhere?

Someday, as soon as she was settled, she would ask Jolie.
A former reporter, Jolie Wade—now Kendricks—had covered the police beat for the *Times-Picayune*. She'd been
friendly with all the cops, but had become good friends
with Evan and his partner, Michael Bennett. More important, she was *from* Serenity Street. She was one of those
people Jamey had talked about who'd worked long and
hard to get out. She'd gotten an education and made a name

for herself as one of the best reporters in all of the South. Maybe she would know why Jamey was still here. Maybe she could give Karen information and advice about everyone down here.

Once she got over her shock that Karen was here.

Realizing that their arguments against this venture were falling on deaf ears, her parents had finally offered acceptance with one condition: if Karen discussed the move and the women's center with Evan's three best friends. Their intention had been so transparent, she thought with a faint smile. Could there be any doubt at all what Evan's friends would say? Michael, a narcotics detective with the New Orleans Police Department? Remy Sinclair, an FBI agent? Smith Kendricks, Jolie's husband *and* the newly-appointed U.S. Attorney for the Eastern District of Louisiana? They were all so straight, so law-and-order, so right-or-wrong-black-or-white-no-shades-of-gray. Of course they would be as vehemently opposed to this move as her family was.

And so she had refused. In fact, in the times she'd come house-hunting in New Orleans, she had guiltily avoided any contact with them. Eventually she would let them know she was here—maybe now, with the closing past, the papers signed, the house legally hers. Or maybe when she'd sunk much of the rest of Evan's insurance money into the remodeling and repairs. Maybe not until Kathy's House was open for business. Maybe she would send them invitations to the grand opening.

She hoped there *was* a grand opening. She fervently hoped that Jamey O'Shea was wrong, that she didn't last only a few weeks or a few months before leaving with less than she'd come in with. She prayed that she didn't end up like the woman down the street.

She wouldn't, she silently promised herself. She had good sense. She wasn't naive, merely hopeful. She believed in what she was doing and in herself. That was half the battle, right?

Movement on the street below caught her attention. A car was creeping down the center of the street, riding low to the ground, an old Chevy Impala that sounded as bad as it looked. The driver came to a stop right in front of her house, and three young men climbed out to take a closer look. The one in the front passenger seat was handsome, with the type of tall, dark and tough looks that had made her hormones rush when she was a teenager. Standing beside him was a blond, also tall, also handsome, displaying a world-class scowl. The man who had been seated in the back seat on her side wasn't so dark as the first or so handsome as the second, but he looked tougher than either of them.

They stared at her, and, arms folded across her chest, she stared back, refusing to flinch or back away to the safety of the corner. She simply stared until the blond man took a look behind him, then gave the man beside him a tap on the shoulder.

Standing behind him, leaning in the doorway, arms crossed and looking as if he didn't have a care in the world, was Jamey O'Shea. The three young men got in the car, though not without some posturing from their leader, then it continued its slow, rackety journey down the street.

When they were gone from sight, Jamey moved to the middle of the street. "There are two rules for staying alive and unharmed on Serenity Street, Ms. Montez," he called. "Don't stand in front of a window, and don't draw Ryan Morgan's attention."

She didn't say a word, didn't ask who Ryan Morgan was. Without ever having heard his name before, she knew who he was. Mr. Tall, Dark and Dangerous. The leader of that ragged little gang. The man who controlled the men who controlled Serenity. The man who was probably going to make getting rid of her a top priority.

Leaning forward into the open window, she braced both hands on the old wood sill and answered in a far cheerier

tone than she actually felt. "Thanks for the advice, Jamey."
She waited a beat before continuing. "Don't be surprised
if I don't take it."

The look he gave her in response was long, steady and
very clearly annoyed. "I won't. And I won't be surprised
if I find you dead some morning." Then he smiled coolly,
carelessly. "Welcome to Serenity Street."

Nighttime in O'Shea's was always a quiet time, whether
the bar was virtually empty or, on rare occasions, filled to
overflowing. Jamey's customers weren't the raucous sort.
They didn't get into arguments, didn't fight or break up the
place. They hardly even talked, not even to order. Hell,
he'd known all of them for so long that he knew what they
drank, when they were ready for another and when to cut
off the flow and send them staggering home.

He stood behind the bar, a towel slung over his shoulder,
a toothpick between his teeth. There was a baseball game
on the television, but it could have been opera for all anyone cared. It was a miserably hot night, the ceiling fans
overhead doing little besides stirring the damp, heated air
in circles, but no one cared about that, either.

Leaning both elbows on the bar, he glanced around the
room at his regulars. Someone like the social worker across
the street would probably look at them and see sick souls
in need of treatment, losers in need of her help, but they
weren't—at least, not all of them. They were unhappy people with more sorrows than the world's deepest shot glass
could drown, people with no place else to go, no family
and no hope. Old Thomas over there in the corner had lost
his wife of forty years in a drive-by shooting. Eldin, near
the door, had lost a nine-year-old daughter in the same way.
Ray had lost his wife when he'd lost his job. She had
packed up the kids and moved back home to Mississippi
with her sister, and he had moved in here.

Everyone had a sad story, and Jamey knew all of them.

Sometimes it seemed that was his role: Serenity Street historian. Keeper of sorrows. Caretaker of broken lives.

For a man who had witnessed so much sorrow, he'd been remarkably untouched by it himself. He'd had disappointments—what man hadn't?—but none he couldn't live with, none that could turn him to a life of crime or drive him to drink. He regretted that he and his parents had never been much of a family, that James O'Shea had been a drunk, that Margie O'Shea would have been in the running for world's worst mother if his buddy Nicky's mother hadn't already clinched the title. He regretted his teenage romance with Meghan Donovan and the brief marriage that had left her so bitter. He had a hundred regrets about the son who had prompted the marriage—that he'd been raised without a father, that his mother hadn't been any more maternal than Margie, that she'd abandoned him when he was fifteen, that he'd grown into such a punk.

He regretted all those things, but he lived his life in spite of them. He hadn't let them destroy him. He hadn't gotten so bogged down in sorrow and misery that he'd crawled into a bottle and refused to come out.

But he understood people who did, people like Thomas, Eldin and Ray, and he looked out for them. He fed them when they'd forgotten to eat and checked up on them when they didn't show up at their usual tables.

Historian, keeper, caretaker and guardian.

Leaning down as he was, he had a good view through the open doors of the house across the street. Lights were on both downstairs and up, bright and yellow in the dimly lit night. He had watched the moving van drive away this afternoon, its occupants looking relieved to be leaving it behind, but he hadn't seen Karen Montez again since Morgan had stopped outside.

She hadn't taken his warning about Ryan Morgan seriously, he suspected, but she would learn. It wouldn't take any time at all on Serenity to learn that Morgan was the boss around here. He pulled all the strings, although, of course, he was only pulling them for someone else—for Jimmy Falcone, New Orleans's wiliest and slipperiest crook.

The feds had thought they had Falcone cold over four years ago. Hell, with the evidence and testimony provided by Nicky Carlucci—Falcone's attorney and personal adviser, and Jamey's closest friend since childhood—Smith Kendricks had blown away the jury and walked off with a whole string of felony convictions in hand. Falcone, of course, had appealed, and, damn the son of a bitch, he had walked. Amid talk of threats, coercion, bribery and blackmail, the appeals court had overturned all but the most minor of his convictions, and the bastard had paid a fine, then walked away a free man.

Nicky wasn't free. He was on the homestretch of a five-year sentence at the federal penitentiary over in Alabama. Practically everyone involved with Falcone had gotten locked up or fined in addition to being fired or—in the case of the politicians in his pocket—run out of office. But not the old man. He was still living in his big house, driving around in his black limousine and doing business as usual. In the last year the scope of his business had expanded to include Serenity Street. He ran the drugs, the gambling, the hookers and the loan sharks that had moved onto the street. He had his finger in every pie except O'Shea's.

He wasn't going to be thrilled by Karen Montez's plans for his territory.

As if summoned by his attention, the ornately carved door at the house opened, and light flashed out onto the veranda before it closed again. For a moment she was just a shadow moving across the yard; then she stepped into the light that came from the nearest streetlamp. He slowly straightened as she crossed the street, disappeared into shadow, then reappeared in his doorway. She stopped just inside, glancing around more than a little disapprovingly at his clientele before making her way to the back. She climbed onto a stool directly in front of him, folded her hands together on the bar and waited for him to acknowledge her.

He did so after a moment, removing the toothpick from his mouth. "Rule number three: stay locked up tight at night."

"Your customers come out."

"No one's interested in messing with my customers, not even Ryan Morgan."

She moved, getting comfortable on the vinyl seat, making her hair sway and shimmer. It was long and heavy, falling past her shoulders in corkscrew curls, and about the same color as a dirty new penny. He wondered if either the curls gone wild or the coppery color were for real. She definitely had the coloring for a natural redhead—all pale, from her forehead across her face, down her throat and all the way into the deep V of her T-shirt. Of course, there was only one way to tell for sure: get rid of those jeans that fit too snugly and whatever little bit she might be wearing underneath them.

His smile was tight and humorless. Strip her down naked, and he wouldn't care if her natural hair color was red, green, purple or yellow. No man would.

"Ryan Morgan is the tall, dark kid, right?"

"He's tall and dark," Jamey allowed. "But he was never a kid, not from the time he was born."

"I take it he's the man to fear around here."

"You got it."

"And the blond kid beside him this afternoon?"

The muscles in Jamey's jaw tightened. "That's Reid. Stay away from him, too."

"Is he dangerous?"

"He's a punk." The explosive beginning and ending of his last word were emphasized by his disgust. All of them, from Morgan on down, could have turned out better than they had. Even if they'd fallen in with the wrong people, at some point they could have made a conscious decision to go straight, to learn the meaning of "law-abiding," to not make the whole world suffer just because their little corner of it stunk. Reid could have made that decision, and might have if he'd had a decent influence in his life somewhere along the way. If he hadn't been raised by a mother undeserving of the name, if he hadn't been abandoned by a father who knew better.

"And the others?"

"The ugly little bastard is named Marino. The driver is Morgan's kid brother."

"So Ryan Morgan is the person I should watch out for."

"He's the worst of the bunch, but any one of them would hurt you. Any one of them wouldn't think twice about raping you or beating you. Marino wouldn't feel a moment's regret about setting you on fire and listening to you scream while you burned." He waited a moment, then softened his voice. "He's done it before."

She didn't blink, didn't reveal a hint of fear or revulsion. "Then why isn't he in jail?"

"And who's going to testify against him? Marino works for Morgan. Morgan works for Jimmy Falcone. You ever hear of Falcone up there in Landry?"

"I lived in New Orleans for nine years. My husband was a cop. Narcotics." She offered that cool smile of hers. "I've heard of Falcone."

Her husband, she'd said. Not *ex*, but simply husband, as in current. So where was he? What was he doing letting her move onto Serenity? What the hell was he doing letting her spend one night down here alone?

Drawing back, he opened the cooler and pulled out an icy can of soda, setting it on the counter in front of her. She looked at it for a moment, then smiled. "I'd rather have a beer."

"It's on the house. Take it."

"If I pay, can I have a beer instead?" But she reached for the can, popping the tab with one neatly manicured, pale peach nail and taking a long swallow. "Thanks."

"So where is he?"

"Who?"

Damn it, he hadn't meant to ask that. It wasn't as if it was any of his business, wasn't as if he cared. "Your husband."

For a moment the light disappeared from her eyes. When the moment passed, she was quieter, more subdued, less...vibrant. Yeah, that was a good word. "He's dead," she said flatly.

He considered asking how it had happened, but decided against it. Cops got killed. *People* got killed. It might have been something as innocent as a heart attack or an auto accident—or, considering New Orleans's more-than-one-a-day homicide rate in the last few years, it could have been as sinister as murder. Either way, she obviously didn't want to talk about it, and he didn't want to know. "Sorry," he remarked with little emotion.

"So am I," she responded with just as little—which meant, he suspected, that she felt more sorrow than she knew what to do with. She took another long drink, then glanced around the room. "Are these your regulars?"

He nodded.

"Tell me about them."

"Why? So you can learn their problems and come up with neat, easy solutions that they're not capable of seeing for themselves? So you can save them from themselves?"

Her gaze was chastening, but he didn't feel chastened. "So I can get to know my neighbors."

He stubbornly shook his head. "You do that on your own. I'm not helping you screw up anyone's lives more than they already are."

For a long time she studied him, her expression thoughtful enough to make him want to squirm; then she sighed. "You really don't want me here, do you?"

"People like you come in here and stir up trouble. They disrupt everyone's lives. They might even create a little hope. But when the going gets tough, they get going, and for a while, things are worse than before they came. These people already have enough trouble and disruption in their lives. They don't have much hope to lose. They don't need your Band-Aid solution to their life-threatening problems."

"You know, there's a variation on that saying. *When the going gets tough, the tough get rough.*"

"That's right, darlin', and you haven't seen tough *or* rough until you've seen Ryan Morgan. You interfere with him or his business, and he'll have you for breakfast."

For another long, uncomfortable moment, she simply looked at him; then she slid off the stool to the floor. "All right, Jamey. You've done your duty. You've warned me. You've scared me. Now can we get past that to whatever comes after?"

Whatever comes after. And what might that be? Exactly what was it she thought she wanted from him? Assistance? When New Orleans's finest and richest claimed Serenity for their own. Friendship? He wasn't much interested in friendship or anything else with a naive, idealistic, sure-to-be-disillusioned social worker—not even if she was pretty and slender, with hair so fiery that a touch might burn. Protection? He had enough people to look out for already, people who truly needed him. If she felt the need for protection, let her go someplace else, someplace safe. Let someone else take care of her.

When he didn't answer, she gave a little sigh, then stiffened her shoulders and lifted her chin. "Thanks for the hospitality," she said, her tone not quite icy enough to create a chill but close. "I'll see you around."

She left the bar, drawing no one's notice but his own. She crossed the street, slipped through the wide, creaky gate and, a moment later, went inside. A moment after that, the downstairs lights went off, then all but one or two lights upstairs.

Crumpling her empty can, he tossed it into the trash, then yanked the towel from his shoulder and wiped the ring it had left on the bar. He didn't need this, he thought with a scowl. He didn't need one more person to look out for, didn't need to feel responsible for one more person who was ill-suited to life on Serenity Street. Let her go back to Landry, back to her home and her family and her husband's memory, and let her go soon.

Before it was too late.

Karen lay awake in bed the next morning, gazing out the window at the brick wall of the house behind hers that formed the rear property line. That house, like so many on and around Serenity, was empty, long ago abandoned by anyone who cared. In the wildest of her dreams, she envisioned all the houses cleaned up and fixed up, providing not just shelter but real, welcoming, loving homes to their residents. She imagined the neighborhood an inviting place to live, once again with schools, churches and businesses of its own. She pictured children playing, watched over with nothing more than the average mother's concern, with no fear, no threat of death, no risk of injury more serious than a skinned knee.

Jamey O'Shea would call her a dreamer, and he would do it in that tone that made clear the word's insult. For an Irishman, he was surprisingly down-to-earth. She would bet he'd done little, if any, dreaming in his years on Serenity Street. Of course, the street as he knew it wasn't conducive to dreams, only nightmares.

She'd had more than a few of those herself. She hadn't slept well last night. Every sound had been new and out of the ordinary, worthy of awakening to determine if it signaled danger. She had heard that old Impala drive by a time or two, had fancied the second time that it had stopped out front again, just as it had yesterday afternoon, although she couldn't say so for a fact. She hadn't found the courage to leave her bed and creep across the hall to the living room to look out the window. Instead, she had lain there and thought about the young men who had subjected her house—and her—to such hostile scrutiny a dozen hours earlier. Ryan Morgan, tall, dark and dangerous, never an innocent child, now, no older than twenty-five, a name to frighten an entire neighborhood. Reid, a punk who wouldn't think twice about hurting a woman, and Marino, who *had* hurt someone before—a woman, no doubt, though Jamey hadn't said. Men like that were always more likely to prey on women, who were physically weaker and less able to defend themselves. Maybe she was weaker, but she would fight back. The sooner Morgan and his flunkies understood that, the better. The sooner Jamey understood it, the better.

By the time she'd gotten the resident thugs out of her mind, the street had been quiet again. Had the car driven on while she was otherwise preoccupied? Or had she only imagined it stopping in the first place?

With a sigh, she leaned over and shut off the alarm before it could go off, then sat up, swinging her feet to the floor. All in all, it hadn't been a bad night, considering that it was her first night alone in a new house, in a new neighborhood. The house made lots of noises, but she would grow accustomed to them. She would learn which creaks and groans were normal and which were cause for concern. She would become comfortable with the night sounds and the night disturbances. She would learn to belong.

Leaving the bedroom, she shuffled down the dusty hall to the bathroom. Seven bedrooms on the second floor—with room for three more in the attic—and only one bathroom to serve them. It was a big one, though, easily the size of her and Evan's bedroom in their first small apartment, with plenty of room for cozying up the large space. Fortunately, the plumbing had been updated in recent memory—about forty years ago, as far as the former owner could recall—but it still had no shower, only a pedestal sink and a great old claw-foot tub. Both had been layered with dirt and littered with leaves and trash that had blown in through the broken window, and the toilet had been enough to make a person shudder. Wearing rubber gloves and armed with ammonia, cleanser and bleach, she had spent nearly three hours yesterday scrubbing cast iron, tile and wainscoting to meet her standards of cleanliness. Today she intended to repair the broken window—all the broken windows—and paint the bathroom walls the brightest shade of white she could buy. Then she would tackle the kitchen and her bedroom, the living room, the other five bedrooms and all those rooms downstairs, plus the exterior of the house, the veranda, the fence, the outbuildings and the yard....

Just thinking about all the work that awaited her before Kathy's House could open for business was enough to make her tired.

So she wouldn't think about all of it. She would take it one step at a time, one job at a time. She would get dressed, grab some breakfast out, then head for the nearest building supply center. She had already measured all the windows that needed fixing. She would buy panes of glass and caulk and make herself visible and approachable to any and all neighbors while she worked. Maybe curiosity would accomplish what hot weather hadn't: getting them out of their apartments and out on the street.

She was planning a fast-food breakfast, but, seeing a rare empty parking space across from the Café du Monde, she grabbed it. Why not celebrate her first morning on Serenity with something special?

She was looking for a table when a steady gaze caught her attention. Her neighbor and devil's advocate, Jamey

O'Shea, was sitting at a table next to the iron railing, a cup of coffee and a plate of beignets in front of him, a newspaper opened but going unread while he watched her instead. His gaze wasn't friendly, unfriendly or even the slightest bit personal. For all the expression he showed, he could be looking at a total stranger.

Finding no tables available and unwilling to wait, she made her way along the narrow aisle, stopping at the empty chair across from him. "Mind if I join you?"

He answered with the slightest of shrugs. He did, at least, fold the newspaper and set it aside as she seated herself. After she placed an order with the passing waiter, she covered the sticky rim of the table with napkins, rested her arms there and spoke. "You're up bright and early." She would have assumed that his business required late hours, that he probably slept much of the day away, but obviously she was wrong.

"So are you. I don't imagine it's in preparation for the long drive back to Landry."

Forcing back a smile, she shook her head.

"I didn't think we could be so lucky. How was your first night on Serenity Street?"

"Peaceful."

He snorted. "Serenity Street has been many things over the years, but 'peaceful' has never been one of them."

She acknowledged her lie with a shrug. "So I didn't sleep well. That's to be expected in a new place. I'll get used to it. I'll adjust."

"Or you could go back home where there are no adjustments to make."

That was certainly true. Everything was familiar in Landry. She knew practically everyone in town, and they knew everything about her. Her and Evan's efforts at having a baby, his death, her return, the whole nightmare with Kathy and now this foolish scheme of hers...none of it was secret in Landry. There was a certain comfort in such familiarity—and a certain discomfort, too. Sometimes she had felt as if she were slowly suffocating, strangled by all the sympathy, the concern and the well-meant advice. In the last year she had begun dreaming of a place where she could put Evan's insurance money to good use, where she could help save other women from Kathy's fate, where she could be just plain Karen Montez and not the Taylors' poor daughter or the Montezes' sweet daughter-in-law, not Evan's grieving widow or Kathy's grieving sister. She hoped she'd found that place on Serenity Street.

"How long do I have to stick around before you quit trying to convince me that I should leave?"

Jamey shrugged. "I don't believe any of the others like you have lasted more than six months."

"It's going to be a boring six months if we have to have this conversation every time we meet." She pulled some money from her purse to pay for the breakfast the waiter delivered, uncovered one square pastry from a mountain of powdered sugar and leaned forward to minimize the white fallout as she took a bite. In spite of her precautions, some sugar drifted onto her blue T-shirt anyway. She didn't worry about it. The Café du Monde's beignets were well worth the telltale sprinkling on her clothing. "All right," she said once she was able to speak. "If I'm still here six months from today, you'll give up your efforts to drive me away. Deal?"

"Make it one day less. I'll give you credit for yesterday."

"You're so generous," she said dryly. Turning from him and the subject, she gazed across the street to the Pontalba Apartments, Jackson Square and, rising tall against the summer sky, the St. Louis Cathedral. "I love the French Quarter," she said with a sigh. "Evan and I used to come down here all the time. He and his partner shared an apartment here before we got married, then after we did, Michael moved into that top-floor apartment." She gestured with a beignet across the street to an apartment where the French doors were open and white curtains fluttered in the lazy breeze. "He finally got married himself a few years ago and moved into a house with a yard for the kids. They have two now, both girls."

"Why didn't you and Evan have kids?"

It seemed that the muscles in her face went rigid, freezing her smile in place before slowly letting it slide away. "We tried," she said with a carefully careless shrug. "It just didn't work out." Then, before he could say anything else—a quick glance his way revealed that an uncomfortable apology was surely on its way—she went on. "I bet we have a mutual friend."

The regret was replaced with a now familiar scowl. "I seriously doubt it."

"Why do you find that hard to believe?"

"Let's see…a middle-class social worker from Landry, Louisiana, knowing anyone in common with the owner of a run-down bar in the sleaziest, shabbiest section of the Quarter. Why would I find that hard to believe?"

"You grew up on Serenity. So did my friend. She went away to college, though, and didn't go back."

He settled more comfortably in his chair, leaning back, propping one ankle on the other knee. "So how do you know Jolie?"

"She was a friend of Evan's from work. How did you know I meant her?"

"Not too many people from Serenity Street make it to college. Of my friends, Jolie and Nicky were the only ones."

Nicky. Like Jamey, it was a sweet name for a grown man. Unlike Jamey—who looked every bit a Jamey and not a James, Jim or Jimmy—Nicholas Carlucci hardly deserved a sweet name. Because she'd known so many of the people involved in the Falcone case—Michael, Remy, Smith and Jolie—and because of Evan's interest in the man, Karen had followed the trial with interest. Nicholas Carlucci had been the government's most damning witness against his boss and had drawn the lion's share of the media attention. Dark, as befitted his Italian heritage, handsome as the devil and twice as wicked, he was tough enough, dangerous enough and cold enough to make Ryan Morgan look like a little boy playing little boys' games. And he was a friend of Jamey's.

"What does Jolie think of your plan to save Serenity?" he asked, drawing her attention back to him.

She smiled sunnily. "She doesn't know yet. None of my friends know. But I'm sure she'll think it's a wonderful idea."

His laughter was unexpected and good-natured. "Yeah, right. It's no secret, darlin', that Jolie's idea of what's best for Serenity involves bulldozers, tons of concrete and parking meters."

Karen's smile didn't falter. Neither did her confidence. "But you never know. I might be right. She might be wrong." After wiping her fingers on a napkin, she took a swallow of the now cooled coffee before continuing in a slyly innocent voice. "Just once in his life even Jamey O'Shea might be wrong."

Chapter 2

Jamey O'Shea had often been wrong, he thought with a scowl as he walked the half-dozen blocks back to the bar. He'd been wrong to ever get involved with Meghan, wrong to let her set the terms of the divorce, wrong to have been such a lousy father. Who was he to criticize the bad mothers he'd known—Meghan, his own mother, Nicky's—when he'd been an even worse father? At least his own father had had an excuse for being such a poor role model in the alcoholism that had driven him to an early grave. Jamey had no excuse at all except that it had been easier to sit back and do nothing.

But he wasn't wrong about Karen Montez. Serenity Street was no place for her. It would chew her up and spit her out. She would go crawling back to Landry, wishing she'd never ventured out—or worst case—she would go back in a coffin, like that do-gooder down the block. She was naive, and while ignorance of what she was up against might work in her favor in some instances, on Serenity it was liable to get her hurt or killed.

And the punks most likely to do the hurting or killing were lounging in the early-morning shade provided by O'Shea's. They were all facing the house across the street, smoking, talking quietly among themselves. When they became aware of him, the conversation stopped, and all four turned to face him.

Drawing his keys from his pocket, he stepped over Trevor Morgan's legs where he sprawled across the uneven sidewalk and stopped in front of the French door with the dead bolt lock. Ryan Morgan was right beside the door, Marino behind him. Reid stood a half-dozen feet away, his sullen gaze directed toward the ground. He wasn't as quick to confront anyone as the others were, and he was downright reluctant to ever confront Jamey. A part of Jamey wished he could say it was a matter of respect, but it would be a lie. There was no respect between them, no affection, nothing at all good or honorable. Derision, hatred and disgust seemed to cover Reid's feelings, and disappointment and regret were all Jamey would admit to.

He twisted the key in the lock, then opened both doors. Stale, warm air drifted out to meet him. Breathing deeply, he gave each of the four young men a hard, cold look. "If you're hoping to catch a glimpse of the new neighbor, she's not home. If you were foolish enough to think of speaking to her, forget it. You want any contact with her, you go through me."

"So *you* say," Ryan replied. "But maybe she don't want it that way. Maybe I'll ask her myself."

"Yeah, and maybe I'll break your face."

Morgan moved a step closer. "You talk big, O'Shea."

"Yeah, and I can carry through. You talk a lot, too, Morgan, but when you take action, you show what a coward you are. You shoot old ladies and little girls from the safety of your car. You slap around that little girlfriend of yours. But when it comes to standing up to a man, you have to get your buddies to do it for you because you don't have the courage.'' He closed the distance between them, moving threateningly, intimately close, and stared down into hostile dark eyes. ''If you mess with her, you'll pay. You'll pay dearly. Do you understand?''

For a long moment, Ryan stared back at him, then he backed off and nervously laughed. ''Hey, Donovan, sounds like your old man wants the redhead for himself. Maybe you'll be calling her mama before too long.''

The others took up the teasing, causing Reid to meet Jamey's gaze for the first time. His eyes, the same clear blue, were angry, so damned angry. He'd been filled with anger from the time he was little, fed a steady diet of bitterness and hatred by his mother. Jamey hadn't been around to counteract it then, and now it was too late. The kid was so eaten up with animosity that someday he was going to explode. Jamey's only hope was that they would both survive it.

Turning away from Reid and giving Ryan the same sort of dismissive look he might give a fly, he stepped inside, unlocked and opened the remaining three sets of doors and walked back behind the bar. He was still standing there, drinking a glass of iced tap water, when the punks walked away. When the sounds of their passage had long since faded, he finally let the muscles in his neck and jaw relax, and he muttered a soft, vicious curse.

It didn't matter that, like their own parents, he and Meghan had married far too young and for all the wrong reasons. That didn't excuse the miserable upbringing they'd given their son. Reid hadn't asked to be born to a couple of seventeen-year-olds. He hadn't wanted his mother to disappear with him only five days after his birth, hadn't wanted his father to accept their disappearance as an easy way out of a marriage and responsibilities he hadn't been ready for. He certainly hadn't wanted to live the kind of life Meghan had forced on him for the fifteen years before she'd abandoned him here on Serenity.

Maybe he would have been a bad kid anyway, but under the circumstances, it had been just about guaranteed. No one had ever wanted him—not his mother, not his father, not the grandmother who'd been saddled with him when Meghan had taken off on her own. With no one else to turn to, it was no surprise that he'd become one of Ryan Morgan's boys. It was no surprise that he hated Jamey with a vengeance. What did come as a surprise was the fact that Jamey cared, but it was obviously too little too late.

Picking up the remote, he switched on the television, then turned to a sports channel. The game was golf, not even considered a sport on Serenity. Down here activity was a little more physical, like running for your life or ducking stray bullets. Golf did have one thing going for it, though: the places where the game was played. There wasn't a single blade of green grass down here. The few trees were dried up and unhealthy—like the people—deprived of the nourishment necessary to sustain life. As for the pretty water hazards, the closest these people got to water outside their houses was puddles in the street after a rain or an occasional walk along the banks of the muddy Mississippi.

Taking a broom from the back, he swept around the tables, depositing four small piles of dirt on the sidewalk outside the doors, then sweeping them into the street. Back inside he took the chairs down from the tables, then drew one out onto the sidewalk, where he leaned back against the brick wall and made himself comfortable. Except for movement down where the street dead-ended—Morgan and company—he was the only person out. His television was the only noise.

He remembered when Serenity hadn't been a bad place to live. When he was a kid, all the shops down here had been occupied. They'd had their own grocery store, drugstore and Laundromats. There had been a couple of restaurants, a bank, beauty shops, barbershops and clothing stores. Over on Divinity Street had been the churches—the Baptists, the A.M.E. Zionists and St. Jude's, where all the Catholics had attended, where Nicky, out of necessity, had sometimes lived, where Jamey on occasion had also bunked. Just outside the neighborhood had been three doctors, a dentist and the schools, all within easy walking distance. Now the nearest schools were several miles away, the buses didn't run, and the kids, fearing for their safety, usually didn't go.

Karen Montez thought she could make it safe again.

If he thought she had a chance in hell of succeeding, he would be the first in line to help her. He wouldn't mind if the street got cleaned up, if the empty businesses were suddenly occupied again, if the street started showing some signs of prosperity. He wouldn't mind if the hookers and the dealers went home to someplace else when their night's work was finished, if Ryan Morgan and the others were forced to move on, too. He wouldn't mind at all if Jimmy Falcone found it impossible to conduct his sort of business on Serenity.

But it wasn't going to happen. The decent people in this neighborhood were far outnumbered by the scum. They were scared and hopeless, and they weren't going to trust some outsider do-gooder to make it all better for them.

Speak of the devil... The sound of an engine made him turn to the left. Her car was an older mid-sized sedan, nothing flashy or expensive, perfectly suited to a woman with a social conscience. All of her money was probably tied up in this project of hers. It certainly wasn't being wasted on the car or particularly nice furniture. Her clothes so far were nothing special—jeans and a T-shirt yesterday, shorts and a T-shirt today, all plain, all well worn—and she'd worn no jewelry—no watch, no necklace or earrings, not even her late husband's wedding ring. Of course, maybe that was common sense. Maybe, naive as she was, she was too smart to set foot on Serenity looking as if she had anything worth stealing.

She waved when she slowed to turn into her driveway. He didn't wave back. He didn't rise from his chair when she got out and began unloading panes of glass from the back seat. He didn't offer his help with the gallon cans of paint or the clear plastic bags holding caulk guns, paintbrushes, roller pans and mineral spirits. He simply sat and watched.

And enjoyed doing it. He had to keep reminding himself that redheads weren't his type. In all his life he'd never been attracted to a red-haired woman, had never been the least bit drawn to pale skin or delicate little bodies. He preferred tall women, athletic brunettes with short hair, big boobs and legs a mile long. In a pinch he could settle for average, but he'd never considered a petite, china-doll redhead an option.

But then, he'd never known a short, slender woman quite as perfectly proportioned as Karen, whose skin was quite as creamy, whose hair was quite as wild—or even remotely as red. He'd never known a woman with her determination...or her optimism...or such faith in herself.

She made a dozen trips from the car to the veranda, stacking everything there. In any other neighborhood, the supplies would be safe there, inside her fenced yard, right outside her door. In this neighborhood, she would have to move them inside where they could be locked up. If they were left unattended for long, someone would surely steal them, and they would do it just out of meanness. They wouldn't use the paint to fix up their own place, wouldn't even begin to know how to replace their own broken windows with the glass. No, they would shatter the glass on the sidewalk, leaving her a million fragments to clean up, and they would pour the paint over the porch or her car, or in the middle of the street.

After her last trip, she disappeared inside for a few

minutes, then came out again, all those wild curls pulled back in a clamp. Carrying a glass of cold lemonade, she came through the gate, sat down on the curb across the street from him, and heaved a sigh. "Just unloading the stuff is enough to wear me out. I'm in sorry shape."

His eyes half closed—because of the brightness of the sun, of course—he resisted the obvious comment that, as far as he could see, there was nothing at all sorry about her shape. Other than the fact that, with her redhead's complexion, she looked as if she had never, ever been exposed to the sun, she looked damned fine.

"Is this what you do all day?"

"Depends on the day. O'Shea's doesn't officially open until ten. No one comes around before then unless it's too long to wait." Some days no one came around anyway, not until midafternoon. Some days they would be waiting at nine.

"Have you ever considered..." She broke off, looked down the street as if debating the wisdom of what she was about to ask, then looked at him and asked it anyway. "Have you ever wondered if maybe you're part of the problem here?"

His annoyance with her immediately outstripped his attraction to her. "Because I sell liquor to drunks?" he asked irritably. "Honey, if they didn't drink here, they'd go someplace else. At least here no one takes advantage of them. No one sells them watered-down drinks for prices they can't afford, no one tries to con them out of their money, and they're not going to get rolled by the employees or the other customers. I can keep an eye on them. I know when everything's okay, and I know when it's not." He didn't go on, didn't tell her what he did when everything wasn't okay. He couldn't count the number of times he'd sat up with one or another of his customers, listening while they poured out their souls, commiserating over their losses. He had fed them, taken them to doctors, had even, on occasion, taken them to church when that was what they'd wanted. He was the closest thing to family some of them had, the only friend others had.

"I'm sorry." She rested her arms on her knees, her chin on her arms, so that her next words came out muffled, not meant for his ears. "You don't have to be so touchy."

"Touchy?" he repeated, leaning forward, letting the front legs of the chair hit the ground with a thump. "You come onto my street, intending to force your way into our lives, planning to fix our lives for us because we're too stupid or inferior or childlike to fix them ourselves. With your privileged background and your college degree and your Pollyanna attitude, you're going to make all our problems go away—including even the ones that *I'm* responsible for, in your oh-so-wise judgment—and you don't think I should be *touchy?*"

She scowled. "I didn't mean... I don't think anyone down here is stupid, inferior or childlike. I think they need help—and, yes, I think I can help them, at least, some of them. As far as my 'privileged background,' you had it right earlier. I'm strictly middle-class. That's hardly 'privileged.'"

"Down here it is. You don't know anything about these people. You don't understand their problems. You don't know what it's like to start with nothing and lose even that. You've had everything you ever wanted. You lived in a nice house with grass and trees and air-conditioning. You had new clothes and plenty of food to eat and money to spend. You went to college. When you were a kid, you always said, 'When I grow up...' not '*If* I grow up,' like the kids around here." He shook his head in disgust. "You don't know what it's like to be poor, to be afraid, to never have a chance. You don't know what it's like to lose hope."

She got to her feet and tossed the remaining lemonade into the dirt. "You're wrong," she said quietly. "If I'd gotten everything I ever wanted, I'd be living ten miles away from here in a nice house with grass and trees and air-conditioning. I'd have a husband who'd come home from work every day and children to raise and love and protect from ever losing hope. If I'd gotten everything I'd ever wanted, Evan damn sure wouldn't have been killed by some crazy who liked to do evil things to little girls, and I damn sure wouldn't have had to sit three days later and listen to some doctor explain that it was my fault we'd never had those babies we'd wanted so badly." Her voice thick and choked, she broke off, breathed deeply, then continued in a quieter, shakier voice. "If I'd gotten everything I wanted, I sure as hell wouldn't be here."

Feeling like a bastard, Jamey watched her go. He didn't follow her, didn't shout out an apology, didn't say or do anything at all. Let her walk away angry. Maybe anger could accomplish what reason couldn't. Maybe anger would make her admit the futility of her plans for Serenity. Maybe it would make her admit defeat and get the hell out of there before it was too late. For her, for him, for all of them.

Upstairs in the bathroom, Karen propped her how-to book on the sink, using a towel to hold it open to the pages on removing and installing window panes. She had already read the instructions once, had pulled on leather gloves and removed the glazing putty around the broken pane. She carefully pulled the smaller of the two pieces free and dropped it in a big garbage can behind her, then turned back, clenched her right hand into a fist and deliberately put it through the center of the remaining piece. It shattered, raining shards of glass onto the roof that caught the sun and glittered in a rainbow of colors. Feeling a little better, she began gathering the dozens of small pieces, stopping only when movement on the street caught her attention.

The bathroom was located at the side of the house, with

windows overlooking both the back and side yards. From
the side window, she could see just a little of the street, the
last set of doors at O'Shea's and the abandoned building
next door. The young blond-haired man who had been with
Ryan Morgan yesterday—Reid, the punk, with suitable emphasis, courtesy of Jamey—was standing in the recessed
doorway, hands shoved in his hip pockets, watching her.
She automatically smiled, but the gesture merely served to
deepen his scowl, which chased away her smile.

Her first thought was that he was handsome, with golden
skin, shaggy blond hair and eyes that were sure to be the
bluest blue. Although Evan had been as dark as night, with
black hair and sweet dark eyes, she was discovering that
there was something to be said for the pure appeal of blue-
eyed blonds. First Jamey O'Shea, and now this kid…

Thoughts of Jamey gave her a scowl to match Reid's,
and she forced her attention back to him. He looked too
young to be as dangerous and tough as she'd been
warned—although she knew, of course, that was a naive
presumption. Age had nothing to do with malice or evil.
There were little kids who could plan and execute a murder
with an utter lack of regret and ninety-year-old grandpas
who couldn't kill to save their own lives. Reid, though he
couldn't be older than his early twenties, might very well
be as bad as Jamey described. But he looked to her like
just another unhappy kid whose life had turned out rotten,
who had no one to care about what he did or how he behaved.

Just another unhappy kid who was looking at her as if
he wished she would disappear off the face of the earth.

So he shared something in common with Jamey.

She wondered where Reid's parents were, if he'd ever
had any sort of home to speak of, how far he'd gotten in
school before boredom, circumstances or peer pressure had
led him to drop out. She wondered how much of the crime
on Serenity he was personally responsible for, how he'd

wound up working in a roundabout way for Jimmy Falcone, why he'd never left Serenity looking for something better. He obviously wasn't happy here. Nobody with even an ounce of satisfaction in his life could pull off such a heavy-duty scowl.

As she watched him, she became aware of a blue mood creeping over her, replacing the last of her annoyance with Jamey. She felt sorry for Reid, although he would undoubtedly hate her for it. At some time in this young man's life, he could have been saved. Just a little attention, a little love, the right influence at the right time, and he could be living a fulfilling, productive life instead of terrorizing helpless victims on these streets. Would that have been so much for his parents—or any other adult in the boy's life—to offer? Would it have hurt them to devote just a little time and effort to the child they'd brought into the world? Had they wanted him to turn out like this—uncaring about the law, society, people around him, about anything but his own needs, his own desires and his own fun? Had they wanted him to choose a life that carried with it a major risk of being dead before he was twenty-five?

That was why she was here—to try to save the four- and six- and ten-year-old kids on the street from the same fate. To help their mothers and, eventually, their fathers provide them with a healthy, safe environment to grow up in, free of anger and violence within the home. If she and her staff could help the families, the families could help their neighbors. If they could make their homes safe, then they could extend that safety to their buildings, their blocks, their streets and their entire community. When it was safe, they could bring in the businesses that would make it a community in every sense of the word. That was her long-term goal.

Her short-term goal, though, was to get this place in shape so Kathy's House could eventually open, and she wasn't doing anything to accomplish that standing there and staring out the window at a young man who just might prove to be one of her major adversaries.

With a sigh, she cleaned the rest of the glass from the window frame, scanned the how-to directions once more, then began following them step by step. She'd never been the slightest bit handy, had never done anything more difficult than change a light bulb while balancing on top of a stepladder. When she'd told her parents that she intended to do the bulk of the work on the house herself, they were appalled. Even in the nineties, Robert and Kathryn Taylor still believed in the division of labor practiced by their parents, their grandparents and everyone around them. Kathryn took care of the housework and the flowers, and Robert handled the repairs and the yard work. She never took out the trash. He never washed a dish. She didn't know the working end of a hammer. He was stymied by the operation of the stove. During her own marriage, Karen and Evan had fallen into the same habits. He had handled the man's work, and she had taken care of the woman's.

And here she was, replacing a broken windowpane, she thought, smiling as she slipped the glass into place, and with no help from anyone but her neat little handyman how-to book. Finishing the job, she took a step back to examine it, and her smile grew into a foolishly wide grin. The work might be hard, but it was going to be good for her ego.

Maybe her parents and Evan's believed she was crazy for coming here. Maybe every single friend she'd ever had in the city would share their opinion once they found out. Maybe Jamey O'Shea could think of nothing that would brighten his day more than seeing her drive away never to return. Even young Reid with the world-class scowl seemed to want her gone. No one believed in her, not the people who knew her or the ones who didn't. They all thought she was chasing a foolish dream, but, hey, she could replace a broken window. She could repair damaged walls and brighten them with paint. Over the next few months, she would do a million other things that no one thought she could. By the time Kathy's House opened for business, she would be more than ready to take on the problems of Serenity Street, because she would have proved to herself and everyone else that, with a little persistence and a few good directions, she could learn anything.

After giving herself a pat on the back—mentally, at least—she dragged the trash can from the bathroom, then made a quick trip downstairs for painting supplies. The trim would have to wait for a coat of paint, since her book recommended letting the glazing compound cure for a week, but she could get the walls painted. A couple coats of fresh paint would do wonders in brightening up the room. Then she would add throw rugs in soft pastels, a ladderback chair that had once belonged to her grandmother, a pink wicker table to hold stacks of towels, and a few arrangements of dried flowers on the wall, and it would be as homey as any bathroom she'd ever seen.

Hopefully, it wouldn't be too long before the entire house started feeling equally welcoming.

She painted until her arms were tired and her head ached. She tried opening the windows to help disperse the fumes, but the occasional breeze blew in dust that embedded in the wet paint, so she closed them again. When she finished, she set a small oscillating fan in the open doorway, turned it on high, then headed downstairs once more. She would take a break for lunch, she decided, before starting to work on the remaining dozen or so windows. She'd brought a few groceries with her yesterday—lemonade and coffee, milk and cereal, chips and cookies, the makings for salad and sandwiches. She had figured she wouldn't want to be doing any cooking until she'd spent about a hundred hours scrubbing ten years of filth and grime from the kitchen.

She was just passing through the kitchen door when a shout echoed through the house. If it had been a man's voice, she probably would have panicked. As it was, recognizing the woman's voice, she almost panicked anyway. She considered beating a retreat out the back door and taking refuge in the barren yard until her uninvited guest—uninvited by *her,* at least, though she suspected an invitation had been made by someone down here, damn Jamey O'Shea's scheming heart—gave up and went away. But she knew better. Jolie Wade Kendricks never gave up. That was what made her such a hotshot reporter.

Wiping away the sweat that had collected across her forehead, Karen turned in the doorway and headed back to the front of the house. When she'd brought the paint in, she had left the door open for a little air, with only the unlocked screen door between her and company. A screen door was far too flimsy an obstacle to deter Jolie.

When she came into the foyer, the smile she'd pasted on faltered. It wasn't just Jolie who had invited herself in. Smith was with her, and they were both looking dismayed. "Hey," Karen greeted, tucking a stray curl behind one ear, wishing they didn't both look so cool and perfectly put together while she was so hot, sweaty and paint-spattered. "I was planning to call you guys soon, but I guess my neighbor beat me to it. How are you—"

Jolie gave her a crushing hug. "It's been so long. We haven't seen you since our wedding, and that was four years ago. How *are* you and what the *hell* are you doing here?"

"I'm fine. I take it you guys are fine, too. You've never looked better." A little flattery never hurt, especially when it was true. Jolie's blond hair was short and sleek, her skin was burnished gold, and she still had the lean body of a distance runner. No one would ever guess looking at her that she was past forty and had gone through two pregnancies practically back to back, resulting in one sweet two-and-a-half-year-old son and twin daughters not far behind. Smith was as handsome as always, with the same aura of power and authority. That little bit of gray at his temples only served to emphasize his good looks...and to stir a twinge of longing deep inside Karen. She and Evan had often joked about growing old and gray together, just them, their kids and the guys—Smith, Michael and Remy. But Evan had died far too young, there had been no kids, and the guys all had families of their own now. And she was alone. It just wasn't fair.

But life wasn't fair. That was why Evan had become a cop, why he'd risked his life for strangers, why he had died saving the lives of an innocent little girl and the best partner and friend any cop could ever ask for.

Smith gave her a gentler hug when Jolie stepped back. "It's good to see you, Karen."

"It's good to see you, too. You look more satisfied with life than any man has a right to be."

"I am." Taking a few steps back, he looked around, then fixed his most serious look on her—and, being the U.S. Attorney, that was pretty serious. "What's going on, Karen?"

"What did O'Shea tell you?"

It was Jolie who answered. "Just that you'd bought this place and moved in. I know Evan never brought you down here, Karen, and there was a reason for it. Serenity is a bad place. It's nowhere you want to be."

"No, it's no place that *you* want to be. It's exactly where I want to be." Karen faked more confidence than she actually felt as she opened her arms wide to encompass the entire house. "Welcome to Kathy's House, Serenity Street's first—and hopefully last—women's center. I'd ask you to sit down, but the furniture is all upstairs. Would you like a tour instead?"

Her guests exchanged dubious glances, but Jolie gestured for her to lead the way. "We can talk while we look around," she said determinedly.

Not if she could avoid it, Karen thought. "Do you remember this house from when you were a kid?'' she asked, leading the way into the front parlor.

"Yeah. It looked almost this bad then. You really don't think you can undo eighty years of neglect, do you?''

"Yes, I do, with a lot of work.''

"And a lot of cooperation from the punks on the street. They'll take great pleasure vandalizing every bit of work that you do.''

"Maybe. Maybe not,'' Karen said optimistically.

Wide double doors and hallways led from parlor to study to dining room, from gentleman's parlor to keeping room to kitchen to pantry. Off a hall on one end were the turret room, the door to a glassed-in back porch, and a bathroom, long and narrow and lit with stained-glass windows in bright royal blue. She loved the windows but had every intention of removing them intact and using them for decoration someplace inside, because Jolie was probably right. Until Karen gained acceptance on the street, Ryan Morgan or others like him would delight in destroying every part of her dream that they could reach.

Once they finished the tour of the second floor, she faced them, waiting for judgment. They were standing at the top of the stairs, and the smells of paint and dust were heavy in the air. Jolie started to speak, but closed her mouth, leaving the task to Smith. Instead of criticism, though, or questions about her sanity, he made a friendly suggestion. "Let's get some lunch, okay?''

"Sorry. I've got too much to do.''

"At least come across the street. Let us buy you a beer.''

The best use she could think of for a beer at O'Shea's was throwing it in Jamey's smug face, but she didn't say so. She just shook her head. "I'll go out on the veranda with you. There's a bit of a breeze today. But there's no place to sit out there, either,'' she warned as she made her way down the stairs. That was one of her goals—to fill the length of the veranda with rockers or wicker chairs, to boldly announce her intention to the Ryan Morgans and the Marinos and the Reids—and the Jamey O'Sheas—that she was determined to turn this street, starting with her little piece of it, into a front-porch sort of place.

Outside, she sank down on the porch floor and stretched her legs out into the sun. Her skin was whiter than the paint on the weathered boards, she noticed. Fish-belly white, Evan had often teased her. Unlike some redheads, she could tan, but it was a slow, tedious process, one that she hadn't had much patience for lately. Maybe once she started working on the house's exterior, she could get a little badly needed color.

Across the street, the doors to O'Shea's were open, but the van in the driveway blocked most of the view. Telling herself she didn't want to see Jamey anyway—not yet, at least, not while her friends were still there—she focused instead on the vehicle. "I remember a time when you drove a Lexus, Smith, and Jolie had a fast little red Corvette. Now you're in a minivan."

"I still have that fast little Corvette, and he still has his Blazer," Jolie replied, sitting on the top step. As her husband leaned against the railing beside her, she gave him a chiding look. "And I didn't know about a Lexus. When we began dating, he made me think I was a snob for expecting him to drive a Mercedes or Lexus."

Smith shrugged. "We can't fit three kids and all their gear into anything smaller than a van." After a moment, he said seriously, "You've got a great idea, Karen."

"But?"

"But Jolie's right. This is a bad neighborhood. The cops don't even come down here without backup."

"That's their problem," she said stubbornly. "They've let Ryan Morgan and his—"

"You've met Ryan Morgan?" he interrupted, looking grimmer than before, making her wish she could recall the name. Morgan worked for Jimmy Falcone, according to

Jamey, and Smith had convicted Falcone in federal court, only to see the man walk free. Naturally he would still keep up with Falcone and his dealings. Naturally he would be familiar with anyone who worked for him.

She tried to shrug carelessly. "I've seen him. I've been warned about him."

He crouched in front of her. "Ryan and Trevor Morgan, Vinnie Marino, Reid Donovan, Tommy Murphy—they're all bad news. Vinnie Marino would as soon kill you as look at you—unless he took some perverted liking to you, in which case you'd probably be better off dead. If they're coming around here, you don't stand a chance in hell. They like Serenity the way it is. They won't let you change a thing."

"I'm not stupid," she insisted. "I'm not going out looking for trouble—"

"Honey, just being here is an invitation to trouble to guys like that," Jolie said, her voice soft but tense, verging on pleading. "This is a dangerous place, Karen. You want to help out down here? Help the few decent people relocate, then burn the place down."

Karen refused to give the little shiver of fear deep inside any room to grow. Instead she shook her head and forced a chastening smile. "Serenity can't be so bad. It produced thirteen good, upstanding, law-abiding Wades."

"Yeah, and it also produced the Morgans, the Marinos, the Donovans, the Murphys," Jolie said hotly. "You want to help people, Karen? Try another neighborhood, someplace where you have a chance, someplace where you can truly make a difference. Forget Serenity. Let the punks have it. Let Falcone have it."

Karen shook her head once more, this time with finality. "People have forgotten Serenity for too long. The people who never lived here ignore it. The people who did live here and got out, like you, Jolie, pretend it never existed.

But what about those people who still live here, those few decent people? Do we pretend that they don't exist?''

"No," Smith said, his patience tried but his voice still calm. "But you don't risk your life for them, Karen."

"Michael does. Remy does. Evan did. To some extent, you two do." Jolie never backed away from a story, or Smith from a case, simply because it might endanger their lives. "All my life I've sat back and done nothing, and it's cost me dearly. Now I'm going to do something. I'm going to try. If it doesn't work out, well, at least I've made the effort. And if it does?" She smiled a little cynically. "We just might turn this neighborhood into a community where even Jolie would be happy to raise her kids."

Jamey was in the kitchen, fixing a tray of sandwiches, when an impatient customer called his name from the bar. Karen, he thought, more than a little disgusted with how quickly he'd come to recognize her voice. He had seen the Kendrickses drive away a few minutes ago and had figured that was as good a time to retreat as any. Not that he regretted the call to his old friend Jolie one bit. He would use whatever ammunition he had to get rid of Karen before she got herself hurt—or the people on the street, people who just might come to believe in her. If that included Jolie and her prosecutor husband, no problem.

After putting the last sandwich together, he picked up the tray and a bag of apples from the counter and went around the corner and through the swinging door to the bar. Old Thomas was at his usual table, and Pat, one of his few regulars who held a job, had taken the best table for watching the ball game on television. Karen was seated at the bar, her paint-splattered tennis shoes dangling six inches above the floor, and she was giving him her sternest, most severe look. "I thought bartenders were supposed to be very good at keeping their mouths shut. Now I know not to trust you with any more confidences."

He set the tray down, took two paper plates, each holding a sandwich and a helping of chips, and two apples, and delivered one to each of his customers. O'Shea's was no restaurant—although it had been, in one of its earlier lives, back before he was born—but any of his customers who'd missed a meal could always get something here. Most of them didn't even have to ask. They just got this look about them, one that he'd come to know well, one that he'd worn himself often enough when he was a kid. Old Thomas had that look today. As for Pat, hell, it would be rude to feed one and not the other.

When he returned to the bar, he fixed himself a glass of iced water and wordlessly offered Karen a cold soda. "You weren't trusting me with confidences," he pointed out at last. "You were making conversation."

"Which you immediately tried to use to your advantage and my disadvantage by tattling to Jolie that I was here."

"Not immediately. I waited a couple of hours." He took a sandwich half from the tray, then slid the remaining half toward her. "I didn't want to wake the kids from their morning naps."

"How considerate of you." She picked up the sandwich and peeled back one slice of bread to look inside. They were nothing fancy—a couple slices of salami and cheese with spicy mustard on rye—but they suited him. If she didn't like them, she could go back to her house and find something there. Better yet, she could go all the way home to Landry for lunch, and stay there.

She took a bite, chewed and swallowed. "You know, all you succeeded in doing was making two nice people who have plenty going on in their own lives think that now they need to worry about me, too."

"They do need to worry about you. You don't belong down here."

"It's not your place to make that determination." She

took another bite, then glanced around behind her. "Do you always feed your customers?"

"When they're hungry."

"Why?"

He leaned back against the counter. "Because the people in this neighborhood used to feed me when I was hungry."

Leaning forward, she infringed on the space he'd just put between them. "So you're giving something back. See, you do have a social conscience."

Jamey scowled at her. "I never said I don't. We don't need *your* conscience trying to run our lives. If you want to give something back—" he gave her words a mocking twist "—do it in your own town, not here."

She refused to take up the argument with him. Instead, she settled comfortably on the stool again and concentrated on the meager lunch he'd offered. After washing down the last bite, she asked, "Was your family poor?" At his blank look, she started to explain. "You said the people used to feed you—"

"We lived on Serenity Street. Of course we were poor." Even when it was a decent neighborhood, it had still been a low-rent one. Everyone lived there because they didn't have anyplace else to go, because their income or their health or the size of their families kept them in these fourteen blocks.

"Did your father work?"

"When he could." At the curiosity that tidbit created in her blue eyes, he scowled and answered before she could ask. "He was a drunk. When he was sober, he worked. When payday came around, he'd go off on a binge, drink away his check and, more times than I could count, lose his job."

"And your mother?"

He smiled tightly. Forty years ago his mother would have been one of the women Karen was so sure she could help. Who knew? Maybe she—or someone like her, someone with her education—*could* have helped Margie. "My mother was sick," he said at last, meeting her gaze head-on. "She drank, too, but that wasn't her problem. She used to lock me out of the apartment from the time my dad left for work until he came staggering home fifteen or eighteen hours later. She refused to eat until she got weak. She cried for hours at a time for no reason. She went weeks without leaving her bed."

"She suffered from depression."

"That would be my best guess." But there had been no money for doctors, and so Margie had remained depressed and James had continued to drink, right up until their deaths within one sad three-month period. Jamey had been in his mid-twenties, about the same age Reid was now. He hadn't been close to either parent, but for a time he had felt lost without them. They had been his only family, except for a young son living someplace unknown, who would have preferred no father at all over the one fate had stuck him with.

"I'm sorry," Karen said quietly.

He shrugged. "Everyone's sorry for something." *He* was sorry for the conversation they'd had earlier, for bringing her closer to tears than he was comfortable with. He was sorry he'd forgotten that she'd lost her husband, sorry that he'd provoked her into admitting the painful fact that she was the reason they'd had no children. For someone who wanted babies, who would be a good parent, that had to be a bitter sorrow.

And people like him and Meghan, who never should have been parents, managed it when they weren't even trying. Hell, they'd been trying not to, and she'd gotten pregnant anyway.

"How's the work going?" he asked, changing the subject before he felt compelled to offer an apology that would make them both uncomfortable.

"Fine. I've replaced one window and painted the upstairs bathroom."

"You're not going to paint everything white, are you?"

"Of course not." Then she frowned. "How did you know I painted it white? I washed up before I came over."

"It's in your hair." He reached out and caught a handful of coppery curls that had been liberally coated with white and immediately wished he hadn't. He wasn't an impressionable kid. He was forty-three years old—too damned old to find the simple touch of a woman's hair erotic. Too damned old to think that, true to its red-hot color, it just might burn him. Way too damned old to want to wrap both hands in her hair, to use it to pull her close, to use it to trap himself alongside her.

She pulled the curls from his hand, picked at the blob of paint, then shrugged and tossed her hair over her shoulder. "It's latex. It'll wash out." With a sigh, she slid to the floor. She wasn't so short, he realized—maybe five five to his six feet. She just seemed shorter because she looked so damned fragile. "I'd better get back to work. Thanks for the lunch."

"Let me know when you're ready to leave, and I'll fix you a real meal."

The look she gave him was dry. "All right. Saturday, August 10th—"

He waited for her to go on. August 10th was this Saturday. He couldn't possibly be lucky enough to get rid of her that soon.

"—Of the year 2025. I just might be ready to go by then." She gave him a smart-ass smile. "See you later."

After she left and crossed the street, he slowly approached the French doors. Leaning his shoulder against one wall, he watched as she climbed the steps to the porch, picked up a pane of glass and went in through the unlocked door. Her willingness to trust people who deserved no trust at all amazed him. It was just further proof that she was in way over her head here.

He was about to go back inside when a familiar figure down the block caught his attention and made him frown. Reid was on the stoop of the apartment house where he had once lived with his grandmother, sitting motionless and in the shade, maybe because it was too hot a day to be out and about in the sun, maybe because he didn't want anyone noticing him. Considering that his gaze appeared to be locked on the old Victorian, it was a fair bet it was the latter.

Jamey hesitated, knowing he should go back inside the bar and forget Karen and Reid and anyone else who might be out, but when he moved, it wasn't inside. He was halfway to the house before Reid noticed him. He stiffened, and his features formed that sullen look that was just about the only expression Jamey had ever seen on him.

The porch was small, with a two-foot-wide stoop and four steps centered between low brick walls. Reid was at the top, his back against the wall, one leg stretched out along the lower wall. Jamey sat on the opposite wall, his ankles crossed, his hands resting on the sun-warmed bricks. "You waiting for someone?"

The kid grew even more sullen, and the beginnings of a flush turned his face faint red. "It's not against the law to sit on the steps."

"I imagine if the people who live here had anything to say about it, it would be, at least for you and your friends."

"Hey, I don't care if they don't want me around. I'm used to that."

No doubt he was, and Jamey regretted it more than words could ever express—far more than Reid would ever believe. For a time, years ago when Meghan had brought the kid here to visit her mother and had never come back for him, Jamey had tried to tell him so. He had offered a thousand apologies and had gotten every one thrown back in his face.

He had offered advice and gotten that thrown back, too. He had foolishly offered discipline, and Reid's temper had exploded. With an ache in his jaw from the punch the kid had landed and nothing but anger in his heart, Jamey had washed his hands of the boy who would never be his son, who had grown up to become nothing but a punk, who would die nothing but a punk, and he had walked away.

Eleven years later, he still felt guilty. He still wondered if he hadn't lost something he couldn't afford to lose. He still wondered if he should have offered a thousand and one apologies, two thousand and one or however the hell many it took.

"Where are your buddies?"

"Taking care of business."

"Why aren't you with them?"

Reid gave him a look of pure insolence. "Because it's not *my* business."

"So what are you doing here?" Jamey waited a beat before adding, "Watching Karen Montez?"

The flush that had so recently faded came back to a fast burn, reminding Jamey of nothing so much as a kid with an innocent crush on an older girl. But Reid was no kid—he'd never had the chance to be one; his parents had seen to that—and there was nothing innocent about him.

"Leave her alone," Jamey warned, his tone friendly, his meaning not. "She's practically old enough to be your mother, and she's sure as hell not your type." In truth, he had no idea how old Karen was—early thirties, if he had to guess. For all he knew, she could be closer to Reid's age than his own.

"She's not your type, either, but that doesn't keep *you* from watching her."

He hadn't been watching her, Jamey silently defended. He'd been watching out for her. There was a difference. Without pointing that out, he coolly asked, "And what is my type?"

"Long legs, chesty, brown hair," Reid replied sarcastically. "Elizabeth, Janis, Rita, Donna, Meghan."

The most recent women in his life and the first. He had
never thought that Reid might have noticed. Then he focused on the last name. The kid called his mother by her
first name, and the only thing he'd ever called his father—
to his face, at least—was bastard. What a fine family they
were.

Getting to his feet, Jamey started to walk away. After
only a few steps, though, he turned back. "Stay away from
her, and keep your friends away from her. I don't want
anything happening to her before I convince her to leave.
Understand?" He waited a moment for a response. When
none came, he turned and left, and for some odd reason,
every step he took away from his son felt like a mistake,
just as it had that night eleven years ago.

It was stupid. He didn't want a son, and Reid had made
it abundantly clear that he had no need of a father. He was
a grown man, for God's sake. Jamey had had little to offer
him when he was a boy and even less now.

Somehow this was Karen Montez's fault. If she hadn't
come here, he wouldn't have to be concerned with her
safety. Reid wouldn't be interested in her, and Jamey
wouldn't have to be dealing with that. And if she hadn't
come talking about saving the women and the children, he
wouldn't be thinking about one kid who—thanks to him
and Meghan—was beyond saving.

It was all Karen's fault, and just one more reason why
she had to go.

Chapter 3

Gunshots awakened Karen in the middle of the night. For a moment she lay in bed, her heart thudding, wondering where they'd come from. Not Serenity. They'd sounded more distant than that. Maybe a block over, on Trinity, or even someplace further. She said a silent prayer that it'd just been aimless shooting, that no one had been hurt, that no one lay dying in a dark, lonely street somewhere, then settled more comfortably in the bed.

The night would come when she would awaken to such a disturbance, yawn and go back to sleep, but tonight wasn't it. After five minutes passed into ten, she left the bed, pulling a robe on over the raggedy NOPD T-shirt she slept in. A night-light in the bathroom cast a soft pink glow through the open door and a dozen feet down the hall, enough to show her the way into the living room and to the windows. Staying in the shadows, she looked out, first across the street, then down in each direction.

O'Shea's was still open, the doors propped wide, light spilling out. She could see a few customers nursing what she hoped would be their last drinks of the night, but there was no sign of Jamey. He was probably behind the bar, a towel over his shoulder, a toothpick in his mouth, a glass of water on the counter in front of him. She hadn't seen him drink anything stronger and wondered why. Was it because his father had been an alcoholic, because alcohol had surely added to his mother's problems? Maybe because he'd seen the effects alcohol had on already sad lives? Maybe it was a business decision, like the drug dealer who used no drugs himself, or maybe he just didn't like the taste.

To the right the street was quiet. That was the escape from the neighborhood, the only way in and out of the fourteen-block district. A couple of blocks to the end of Serenity, a right turn and only a half dozen blocks to the bustle of Jackson Square. A half-dozen blocks to a whole other world, one that these people could visit but couldn't—unless they worked hard, unless they scrimped and saved and paid their dues—live in.

Three and a half of Serenity's six blocks stretched to the left. Once it had gone further, but the road had been bull-dozed away, a guardrail and a fence put up to mark the new end. If people like Jolie had their way, the same thing would be done at the opposite end, creating a little island with the dregs of society stranded inside. There were bars in those three and a half blocks, a couple of warehouses, an occasional single-family home, more that had been con-verted to small, overpriced apartments, a dozen or more abandoned storefronts and a park.

She had driven by the park when she'd come to look at the house weeks ago. At one time it might have been a lovely little place, but now it was just depressing. The play-ground equipment had been trashed, the grass was gone, the benches had been torched where they stood in concrete, and obscenities had been sprayed on every surface. It was empty during the day, but around sunset she had seen kids wandering in—aimless teenagers, young men and women, the punks and troublemakers, gathered to smoke, drink and party. They had stolen the park from the kids and claimed it—ruined it—for their own. If she listened now, even from this distance, even through closed windows, she could hear their music, loud enough, inharmonious enough, to jangle a person's nerves. It must be hell for the poor people who lived on either side down there.

With a heavy sigh, she moved from the shadows to the long seat underneath the bay window and stretched out, plumping a pillow underneath her head. They were right— her parents, Evan's, Jolie, Smith and Jamey. Serenity was a bad place...but it was also a sad place, and it could be fixed. Anything could be fixed with the right tools, with cooperation from the right people. Look at her. When Evan had died, she had wanted nothing more than to crawl into the casket with him and die, too. She had been convinced that her life was over, that she had nothing to live for, no reason to go on. She had been about as low as a person could go...but she had survived. She had grieved for years—she still grieved—but she had put her life back together. She had found a new reason for living. She had been *fixed*.

If Ryan Morgan and his gang didn't want her there, if they were going to be her biggest problem, fine. She would fix them. She would see about getting rid of them. If they were as bad as Smith and Jamey said, then surely the police or the feds were interested in them. Surely, with a little prompting, a little encouragement, they could make some sort of case against the whole bunch of them and get them off the streets. Since she just happened to be friends with both a cop *and* a fed, she would see what they could do. And once those troublemakers were gone, she would focus on the other, lesser troublemakers, and sooner or later the good people of Serenity would have to see that she was making a difference. They would have to trust her.

Across the street, a couple of elderly men shuffled out of O'Shea's, walking to the end of the block together, then turning in opposite directions. A pair of broken-down tennis shoes and faded jeans came into view through the open doors as Jamey turned the chairs upside down on the tables. Most of the lights went off, just one at the back burning, then he appeared outside, carrying a chair, setting it between doors and leaning back against the brick. The nearest streetlight wasn't burning—like about half the lights on the street; she intended to call the city about it tomorrow—but she could see clearly enough to know that he was tired. He deserved to be. It was a little after 2:00 a.m.; he had opened the bar at ten yesterday morning. Even if you weren't particularly busy, that was a long workday.

She wondered why he lived here. Why he kept such long hours at that shabby little bar when he could earn a decent living with a lot less effort elsewhere in town. What attachment kept him on Serenity when everyone else who could leave had. Why he wasn't married. Whether he ever had been. Mostly she wondered why he refused to support her efforts. He knew the people needed help. Why wouldn't he give her a chance to provide it? Why wouldn't he help her? If she was right and she could help them, it would improve life on the street. If he was right and she couldn't, well, the sooner she failed, the sooner she would leave. Surely that would make him happy.

Somehow, she didn't think being happy ranked very high on Jamey O'Shea's list of priorities.

With a big yawn, she considered going back to bed, but she was comfortable where she was. She could keep an eye on the street—and on her neighbor—and no one could see that she was there.

The sound of an engine in need of tuning drew her attention to the street. It was that old Impala—the only car besides her own that she'd seen regularly in the last two days—and its driver was once again taking his half of the street right out of the middle. At the grand speed of maybe five miles an hour they approached the street, then slowed to a stop as they drew even with O'Shea's. The right rear door opened, and Reid Donovan climbed out. A young woman followed, clinging to his hand with both of hers. She was dressed in a skirt short enough to be illegal, a vest skimpy enough to be indecent and heels of the sort Karen dreamed of being able to wear. She looked cheap, trashy, like someone a man might pick up for twenty bucks or so a few blocks away. It was the way of the kids down here. Most of the boys and young men were cocky, blustering, arrogant or sullen, and most of the girls were flashy, brash, arrogant or sullen.

But as soon as Karen completed the thought, another girl climbed from the car to prove her wrong. She came from the front seat with Ryan Morgan, and she was absolutely beautiful—slender, dark, wearing a simple white dress that could easily be hanging in Karen's closet. This was a young woman with class, even if she was on Serenity Street, even if she was with Ryan Morgan. A dark-haired angel...who looked about seven months pregnant.

The sudden ache around her heart was physical, causing Karen to hug herself tightly to keep it in. Sometimes she thought she had come to terms with the fact that her body had betrayed her, that she could never have a baby of her own, could never know the awe-inspiring experience of feeling a child grow within her, of giving birth, of bringing an innocent new life into the world. Sometimes she thought she had accepted that there must be some other purpose for her—perhaps helping the children on Serenity, since she couldn't have any of her own.

Other times—when she'd shopped for gifts for each of Michael and Valery's two babies, for Smith and Jolie's three and for Remy and Susannah's son, or when she unexpectedly came in contact with someone obviously pregnant...and probably as ill-suited to be a mother as anyone could be, and whose child would have a father who should never be allowed in the same universe with an innocent baby... Those times, she was sure she would die before she accepted it.

Morgan hung his arm around the girl's shoulder, called to his brother, Trevor, to find someplace else to spend the night, then started down the street. Seeming reluctant, almost embarrassed, Reid followed them, practically dragged along by the girl, who held on tightly as if he might try to escape. He made a point of not looking at Jamey, sitting only a half-dozen feet from where he'd left the car, or anything else. For a young man who was about to get lucky, he certainly didn't look as if he felt lucky.

Karen slid further down on the cushion and turned her head so that her face was half buried in the pillow. She hadn't gotten lucky, in any sense of the word, in too long to recall, but maybe coming to Serenity Street, contrary to everyone else's opinion, would prove to be lucky for her. Maybe the changes she could make for the people here and the changes they would make in her would be a good thing.

Maybe her luck was about to change.

She wasn't sure when she dozed off—after the Impala had driven away, after the voices had faded from the street, long after Jamey had gone inside, closed the doors and locked up O'Shea's—but the next thing she knew her neck was stiff, her robe was tangled underneath her, dawn was breaking...and someone was in her yard. Not in her yard, exactly, but rather on the sidewalk where the gate stood open—the same gate that she had tried without success to open her first afternoon there.

Rising onto one elbow, she looked out. Except for a bone-thin puppy sniffing around the garbage cans next door to O'Shea's, her uninvited visitor was the only one out. The street was quiet, the apartments dark, the only sounds the mournful whistle of a ship on the not-too-distant river and the creak of rusty metal grating against metal. She didn't need the thin light from the closest working street-lamp or the ray or two of sunlight that had cleared the buildings to the east to recognize the man. It was Reid, and he was fixing that stubborn gate.

Filled with a silly sense of wonder, she watched until he was almost finished. Rising quickly from the window seat, she hurried into the bedroom, threw off her robe, pulled on a pair of shorts and shoved her feet into a pair of rubber thongs. Downstairs in the kitchen, she tossed a couple of pieces of bread in a bowl, covered them with milk; then, refusing to consider the wisdom of what she was about to do, she let herself out the front door.

He was finished with the gate, but he hadn't left yet. She wondered as she made her way down the sidewalk if he had a place to go. Did he live by himself or with family, or did he bunk with whichever friend had room for him?

He was crouched on the sidewalk outside the fence, petting the dog. When the gate squeaked as she opened it, he jerked his hand back and got quickly to his feet, edgy as if he might run at any second. She had never met such a skittish young man. She was supposed to worry about her safety with him, but he looked far more afraid of her than she might ever be of him. She approached him as if it were the most normal thing in the world at dawn, still in her nightshirt, on a street like Serenity. "Is that your puppy?"

He shook his head.

"I thought he looked hungry. Do you think anyone would mind if I fed him?"

Another shake of his head.

She knelt down, the sidewalk gritty under her bare legs, and set the bowl down. The puppy fell over himself to reach it and almost literally dove in. "Does he have a name?"

"No. He's just a stray. Nobody wants him."

"Then I'll take him." Not that *she* wanted him. Dogs were messy and required food and attention and visits to the vet. She didn't have time to devote to housebreaking, and no animal should live in the dirt of her yard. Still, he would be company when she was alone, and he might prove useful with the kids in the neighborhood. All kids loved puppies. If she could ever catch any of the children outside, maybe this scrawny little creature could provide an introduction, and if she met the kids, she could meet their parents, and if she met their parents...

Smiling at the great expectations she had suddenly developed for a half-starved little ball of fur, she looked up at Reid and stuck her hand out. "I'm Karen Montez, and you're Reid Donovan."

He ignored her hand and instead directed that consummate scowl across the street. "Did *he* tell you that?"

"I'm sorry," she said very seriously, hoping he didn't mind a little gentle teasing. "I didn't realize your name was a secret."

He looked back at her, but still didn't accept her handshake. He really was a good-looking kid—and she'd been right yesterday. His eyes were the bluest blue she'd ever seen. If he were twenty years older or she were twenty years younger, her heart would be fluttering.

She dropped her hand back to her side. "Thank you for fixing the gate."

Color flushed his cheeks a dark bronze. He was at least twenty-two, rumored to be dangerous, bad news, trouble on two feet, and he could still blush over a simple thank-you. She was beginning to believe that there was a whole lot more to Reid Donovan than met the eye.

"If you oil the hinges, it should stop that squeaking," he said, sullen now. "Don't tell anyone..."

Once again she smiled gently. "You have a reputation to protect?"

He shrugged impatiently, as if his reputation was the last thing on his mind. "O'Shea said..." Another look across the street before he went on, grudgingly. "O'Shea said to stay away from you."

"And do you always do what Jamey O'Shea says?"

"When it makes sense."

Interesting answer. But why did it make sense to him to stay away from her? And if Jamey was so determined to get rid of her, why was he warning the troublemakers away from her? The answer came easily enough: because that was what Jamey did. He looked after people. He watched out for those too weak, too vulnerable—or, in her case, too foolish—to watch out for themselves.

Down the block a screen door slammed. Karen looked past Reid to see the girl from last night, the pregnant one, come out of one of the converted houses and start down the sidewalk toward them. She was dressed in yellow this morning, a bright, sunny color, and looked amazingly well rested to be heavily pregnant and to have just spent the night with Ryan Morgan. "Who is she?"

Reid glanced around. "That's Alicia." He gave her name the ethnic pronunciation of four syllables, making it sound foreign and exotic. "She's Ryan's woman."

"Woman?" she echoed with a grin. "She can't be more than twenty."

"Last week."

"When is her baby due?"

"I don't know. Two months, maybe three."

"Will you introduce me to her?"

He gave her a wary look. "Don't mess with her, lady. Don't give Ryan a reason to mess with you."

Feeling as if her life had taken a turn into permanent stubbornness, Karen got to her feet, taking the puppy with her. "Good morning," she greeted when the girl had come close enough.

Alicia's look was suspicious until it shifted to Reid. "So this is where you disappeared to. Tanya kept me up half the night, whining that you weren't any fun anymore, be-

fore she finally went off someplace.'' She gave Karen another long, judging look. ''She's a little old, isn't she?''

Reid blushed again, but Karen smiled. ''A little? Honey,
I'm old enough to be mother to you both.'' Offering her
hand once again, she introduced herself. ''I'm Karen Montez.''

''Alicia Gutierrez.'' The girl gave her a quick, firm handshake, then gestured toward the sign. ''If you're Karen,
who's Kathy?''

''She was my sister.''

''Was?''

''She's dead. Her husband beat her to death.'' She said
it matter-of-factly, as if it didn't damn near break her heart.

Alicia accepted it matter-of-factly, as if she'd heard it
too many times before. ''Too bad. You taking in the
mutt?''

''If nobody objects.''

''Nah, nobody around here'll care. Nobody feeds him or
nothin', except Reid. He's got a soft spot for strays, being
that he was one himself.'' Her smile for him was meant to
soften the sting of her words. Karen wasn't sure it worked.
''I've got to get going or I'm gonna be late for work. I
work mornings at a coffee shop in the Quarter.''

''If you're free in the afternoons, why don't you come
by sometime?'' Karen invited.

The girl looked skeptically at the house, then her, then
nodded. ''Yeah, maybe. See you, Reid.''

Karen watched her walk away. After she crossed into the
next block, Karen looked back at Reid. He didn't look skittish or embarrassed or sullen anymore. He looked angry.
''I told you to leave her alone. Ryan might put up with you
as long as you don't mess with him, but Alicia and that
kid are *his*. If she starts coming around here, you're in
trouble.'' He muttered a curse. ''Don't you ever listen to
anyone?''

''Not very well,'' she said, her tone mild.

"You'll be lucky if he doesn't kill you. He's done it before."

"Have *you* ever killed anyone?"

For a moment he seemed so full of nervous energy that she thought he just might erupt. Then he drew a deep breath and unwillingly, grudgingly, answered, "No."

"Then what are you doing hanging around with someone who has?"

She suspected that she already knew the answer, hinted at in Alicia's comment about strays. He didn't seem to have any family, certainly not any who cared about the direction he was headed. He'd probably never had the love and guidance every child deserved, had probably been on his own since he was young. Kids like that made a place for themselves wherever they could, usually with other kids whom no one loved or wanted. Ryan and Trevor Morgan and Vinnie Marino were probably the closest thing to family Reid had. Maybe no one else wanted him, maybe no one else had any use for him, but they did. He had a place with them…even if every instinct she possessed told her that he didn't belong with them.

In the end he didn't answer. He just gave her another angry look, muttered, "I've got to go," and took off.

With a sigh, Karen looked down at the puppy in her arms. He was snuggled close, his eyes were closed, and he was starting to snore. She hadn't particularly impressed Alicia, and she had only angered Reid, but the morning hadn't been a total loss. At least this little guy had been won over.

"Now there's a sight you don't see every day."

Jamey looked up from the newspaper he'd spread over the bar and saw his Friday afternoon customers, all five of them, looking out the door. He didn't need to see the direction they were turned to know they were watching their new neighbor. It seemed to be all anyone on Serenity wanted to do lately. He couldn't fault them, though. If he was honest about it, he'd probably spent more time focused on the house across the street than everyone else combined. The first thing he did when he got up in the morning was look that way. Every time he went out the door, every time he went near it—hell, even when he couldn't see anything at all, he was still looking that way. It was getting pathetic.

Especially since looking was all he'd been doing. Karen hadn't come to the bar since Tuesday afternoon, when she'd shared his sandwich and taken him to task for alerting Jolie to her presence in the neighborhood. She hadn't wandered over the times he'd taken a chair outside to take advantage of the minimally cooler temperatures, and he hadn't found a valid reason for heading over her way.

He didn't try to resist the curiosity that had drawn his customers to the doors. Pushing the paper aside, he moved that way himself, taking a position in the one unoccupied doorway. Karen was outside for the first time in several days, wearing bright red shorts and a lemon yellow tank top, her hair somehow confined underneath an Atlanta Braves baseball cap. She looked about half the age he thought she was, about a tenth the age he wished she was.

It wasn't just the sight of her that attracted so much attention; it was what she was doing. She had raised one of those upstairs windows without screens, climbed out onto the roof and was cleaning the gutters that ran above the veranda of probably forty years' debris. Virgil was right: it was a sight a person didn't see every day.

"What's she doing over there?" old Thomas asked.

"Fixing up the house," Virgil replied.

"Why?"

"Because it needs fixing."

Amen to that, Jamey thought skeptically. It needed more fixing than any five-foot-five hundred-and-ten-pound redhead could ever manage. Not that she wasn't making headway, if the trash pile growing next to the driveway was any indication. She had replaced all the broken windows and had added two empty gallon paint cans to the garbage. She'd done some heavy-duty cleaning, and the front gate was still rusty, but at least it was back on its hinges. Idly he wondered how she had accomplished that without his noticing.

"She sure is a pretty little thing," one of the men remarked.

"She obviously ain't married."

"How do you know that?"

"If she had a husband, he wouldn't be letting her waste her time on a place like this."

"No, he'd be keeping her busy wasting her time on him."

"She's got to be crazy to move down here."

"Plumb out of her mind."

"Yeah, but she sure is pretty."

Karen picked that moment to notice her audience and raised one hand in a wave. "Good afternoon, gentlemen."

Jamey watched their responses with a grin. Every one of them looked like a lovesick adolescent—shuffling their feet, avoiding her gaze, one or two of them shyly returning her greeting. After a moment, he touched old Thomas on the shoulder. "Watch things here, will you? I'll be back in a minute."

Without considering the folly in his decision—after all, he *had* stayed away more than seventy-two hours; why break his record now?—he crossed the street and let himself into the yard through the squeaky gate. From a position solidly on the ground, he tilted his head back and looked up at her. "You have an interesting effect on people. You've got men over there old enough to be your grandfather acting like lovestruck kids." And one kid around here somewhere acting too much like a lovestruck man.

"That's sweet." She dropped a handful of slimy black muck to the ground less than five feet from him, then turned to sit on her bottom and gaze down at him. "Are you busy tomorrow?"

"The bar is open six days a week." Then, wishing he wouldn't, he asked, "Why?"

"I'd like to introduce myself to some of the people in the neighborhood. I thought it might go a little easier if I was accompanied by someone they know. But never mind. I'll ask Alicia to go with me."

His gaze narrowed, and it had nothing to do with the sun behind her house. "How did you happen to meet Alicia Gutierrez?"

"I met her the same morning I met Jethro."

"Jethro?"

"Yeah." She gestured behind her, and for the first time he noticed the dog in the window. Standing on its hind legs, its forepaws balanced on the windowsill, it was just barely tall enough to see and be seen. "Doesn't he look like a Jethro?"

The mutt was a mix of many breeds, most indistinct, but even from the ground, Jamey could identify the hound in him. It accounted for the longest ears and droopiest face he'd ever seen on an animal. "So you have a guard dog," he said, half surprised to find there was little sarcasm behind the teasing.

"Heavens, no. He's the biggest baby in the world. He snores like a freight train and pees every time something startles him—and *everything* startles him. It's a good thing I don't have any carpeting inside, or I'd be spending all my time cleaning up after him instead of getting ready to open."

Mention of the opening of Kathy's House added a layer of tension just when he'd been starting to relax. He ignored it, though, and returned to the original topic. "You know Alicia is Morgan's girlfriend."

"Uh-huh."

"Don't try to come between them."

She gave him an angelically innocent look. "I wouldn't dream of it." Then... "Of course, if a stranger could affect their relationship, that would mean there wasn't much of a relationship to start with, wouldn't it?"

He should return to the bar and wash his hands of her. She wasn't his responsibility. Just because he looked out for the customers in his bar didn't mean he also had to look out for anyone else who wandered into the neighborhood. He owed her nothing, not even a few carefully emphasized warnings to the people most likely to cause her trouble. But he didn't walk away. He'd done that once—with Reid— and had regretted it ever since.

"Wait until Sunday," he said, glaring up at her.

"What?"

"Wait until Sunday, and I'll introduce you to some of the families on the street."

She rewarded him with a bright, warm smile. "Thank you, Jamey. Why, you're not so bad, after all."

"Of course I'm not. I'm not the one you have to worry about around here," he said sourly.

Her smile turned a little secretive and she murmured something as she turned away. He wouldn't swear to what he thought he'd heard, but it had sounded vaguely like, "I'm not so sure about that." It would be only fair if he'd given her a few moments of serious thought, since she'd kept him preoccupied pretty much since the first moment he'd seen her.

She made her way carefully back up the slope of the roof, swung one leg inside the window, then looked back down. "To show my appreciation, how about if I fix you dinner tonight? I'll bring it over to the bar around seven."

He considered it a moment, then shrugged. "All right."

She smiled again, an unrestrained, whole-body sort of smile, and climbed inside. "Good. I want to ask you about Reid."

Before he could protest, before he could even summon

up a frown, she had slammed the window shut, waved, then disappeared from sight, no doubt with that floppy mutt on her heels.

Yeah, hell, he groused as he returned to the bar. Talking about Reid was his idea of a fun evening. What had the kid done to catch her attention? He'd been making himself scarce in the last few days. Jamey had seen Ryan and the others any number of times, but there'd been no sign of Reid.

There had been a time—eleven years ago—when that had worried him. Jamey had known that he couldn't count on Mrs. Donovan to let him know if the kid quit coming home sometime and so he had watched the streets for him. If even a day had gone by with no sign of him, he had begun to wonder if something had happened. In a place like Serenity, sometimes people just disappeared. They angered the wrong people, fell in with the wrong crowd, were in the wrong place at the wrong time. Some of the people who had gone missing over the last twenty years had probably moved on to someplace better, but some were undoubtedly dead. With no identification like a driver's license—hardly anyone on the street had a car—or with a body too badly decomposed to identify and no concerned family members out looking for them, they wound up unclaimed in the morgue and eventually buried in a pauper's grave.

Jamey had once made a visit to the morgue. It had been only a month after Meghan had dropped Reid off on Serenity for a ten-day visit with the grandmother he'd never met, then disappeared. Three weeks later he had disappeared, too. The old lady hadn't been concerned. He could take care of himself, she had insisted. Yeah, right. He'd been all of fifteen and recently abandoned by his mother. When the body of an unidentified teenage boy had been discovered on the banks of the river—five foot ten, blond hair and blue eyes, wearing torn jeans and a Hard Rock

Café T-shirt—Jamey had expected the worst, had feared the worst, and he'd gone to the morgue for proof. He had been so relieved to discover that it wasn't his kid lying there dead, so relieved that some other father's son had died instead.

And so angry to discover a few days later that Reid wasn't dead or missing or in trouble but was simply stupid. He'd decided to return home to Atlanta, to hitch a ride with strangers, and he'd left without a word to anyone. There he'd found that his mother hadn't simply forgotten about him down in New Orleans; she had skipped out on him. Their apartment was empty. Everything they'd owned, including his own things, was gone. Having nowhere else to turn, he had hitched his way back, no big deal.

No big deal. In those few moments before Jamey had looked into the face of that dead blue-eyed, blond-haired teenage boy, it had seemed a *very* big deal to him.

That had been the way of their relationship. Reid did stupid things, Jamey got angry, and Reid got angrier. He couldn't recall ever having a single civil conversation with the kid. He couldn't remember a time, from the day Meghan had dragged him into the bar for a quick introduction between father and son, that Reid hadn't been hostile and determined to get under Jamey's skin. To be honest, though, he also couldn't remember a time when he hadn't expected the worst of the kid. Had he been taking a genuinely realistic view—the kid was a punk before he came to New Orleans and would always be a punk—or had Reid simply sunk to the level of Jamey's expectations?

Back in the bar he settled in with the newspaper, refilled glasses, made small talk with the occasional gabby customer and surreptitiously watched the clock. Seven o'clock was a long time coming, but at last it arrived, and so did Karen. She had showered—her hair was still damp—and changed into a denim skirt and a plain green top, and she was carrying a box. With a smile friendlier than most people in the bar ever saw, she greeted several of his customers as she made her way to the back.

Without removing the toothpick from his mouth, he gestured for her to come around behind the bar. There was a table back there, situated where he could see the room but still have some small measure of privacy. He'd shared it with many people in the years he'd had the bar—women and men alike, friends and enemies, partners and rivals, an ex-wife and a few women who'd been angling to become a new wife—but never anyone quite like Karen Montez. Hell, he had never *known* anyone quite like Karen.

"I decided it was too hot to really cook, and I made olive salad yesterday, so..." She uncovered a platter with a homemade muffaletta—a round Italian loaf layered with thinly sliced meats and cheeses and topped with chopped olives marinated in olive oil. It was a specialty at a number of French Quarter restaurants and a favorite of just about everyone who'd ever tried one. One sandwich was big enough for two, maybe even three, depending on their appetites. Tonight Jamey had quite an appetite.

She had fixed potato salad to go with it and had brought plates, forks, napkins, everything but their drinks. He provided those while she dished up the food.

"Are Friday nights busy for you?" she asked, gazing across the room at the dozen or so people.

"Depends. Any night can be busy if enough people feel the need to forget."

"Do you ever feel that need?"

The potato salad was the way he liked it—creamy and just a little sweet—but it needed seasoning. He added salt and pepper before answering her question. "Everyone does from time to time."

"But you don't forget in a bottle."

He laughed. "Do you think I'd be in this business if I had a drinking problem?"

"So what are your sorrows, Jamey?"

After a long, uncomfortable moment, he shook his head. "They're none of your business."

He'd thought she might take offense—after all, he knew what surely must be her two greatest sorrows: her husband's death and her inability to have children. But she didn't seem at all offended by his blunt response. Maybe, when you spent your working hours probing into people's private problems the way social workers did, you got used to such responses. She simply nodded once, then asked another question. "What about Reid?"

For a time he simply stared at her. How did she know that, if he were going to classify *anything* in his life as a sorrow, it would be Reid? For that matter, how did she know about them, anyway? He'd never said anything that might make her suspect they were related, and it was a sure bet Reid hadn't, either. Granted, they had the same coloring, but if there was any real resemblance, he couldn't see it. Their relationship wasn't a secret in the neighborhood, though. Someone—Alicia—could have told her, or maybe she had simply guessed—

"What are Reid's problems?" she went on. "What made him the way he is today?"

He felt a little rush of relief. She didn't have any idea that Reid was his son. She was just being nosy, the way she was nosy about everyone down here. But there was no way he could answer her questions without telling the truth, and what would she think of him then?

He didn't care what she thought. He just cared that she stayed in one piece long enough to give up and get out of there.

"If you want to ask specific questions, I'll answer them, but I'm not going to analyze the kid for you."

"All right." She finished her quarter of the sandwich, fastidiously wiped her fingers on a napkin, then rested both arms on the edge of the table. "Has he always lived here?"

"No. His mother brought him here when he was fifteen and left him."

"Left him?"

"She told him she would pick him up in a week and a half. She didn't. He hasn't seen her since."

"Why here?"

"She was from here. Her mother lived a couple buildings down. He lived with the old woman until she died about seven years ago."

"What about his father?"

Jamey moved the last fourth of the sandwich to his plate and took a bite before answering. "His parents split up when he was a baby. His mother took him to Atlanta, and his father never saw him. He didn't know where they'd gone, and he didn't care enough to find out."

"Does he live around here?"

His expression settling into grimness, he nodded.

"Does Reid live with him?"

"The kid hates him. He avoids him as much as possible, and you can't blame him. His father was never around when he needed him. Life with Meghan was rough. He could have used a male influence. Hell, he could have used an *adult* influence. God knows, Meghan never behaved like an adult a day in her life."

"So where does Reid live?"

"He shares an apartment with the Morgans. Why all the interest?"

"He's an interesting young man."

"He's a punk. He had an arrest record in Atlanta before he came here. He spent time in juvenile detention here. It's only pure luck that he's not in prison now. It's only by the grace of God that he's not dead."

"He fixed my gate."

Jamey stared at her. "I warned you about him."

"And you warned him about me." Her voice took on a faintly defensive tone. "I didn't ask him to do it. If I hadn't awakened early that morning, I never would have known it was him. He didn't want me to know."

"Yeah, right. Reid and his pals never do anything without a reason. He'll come around sometime, wanting something from you, and if you don't give it to him, he'll just take it."

"I think you're wrong. He's not like his 'pals.'"

He leaned forward, his voice every bit as heated as hers was stubborn. "He's *exactly* like them, Karen. He's no good. Maybe if he'd had a mother who'd loved him or a father who'd been around for him, maybe if he'd gotten the sort of parents he'd deserved, he could have been different. But his parents weren't worth a damn, and he turned out no better than they had a right to expect. *Stay away from him.* He'll hurt you."

Unexpectedly, she smiled. "Oh, he might break my heart, but he would no more physically hurt me than you would."

"Oh, you know that, do you? You've talked to him—what? Once? And you know all about him." His sarcasm erased her smile, but it didn't diminish her confidence one bit. It made him angry, made him want to grab her shoulders and shake some sense into her. It made him want to load her into her car and drive her back to Landry himself.

And, someplace deep down inside, someplace he couldn't even acknowledge, it made him admire her. She had more courage than he did.

"And what makes you such an authority on him?" she challenged.

He looked away, wishing for a distraction, for anything that could halt the conversation right there. But there was nothing going on—no customers needing service, no major news stories interrupting the ball game, no meteors crashing through the roof. Finally he looked at her again and grimly, bleakly, disgustedly answered. "He's my son."

* * *

Sunday morning was a typical New Orleans summer day. The temperature was too high to measure, and the humidity drained the energy right out of a person. Even Jethro found the conditions unfavorable. He'd found a shady spot on the veranda next to Karen, sitting in the old rocker she'd hauled down from the second floor, and stretched out with his tongue hanging out.

She had cleaned and painted all day Saturday, working herself into a headache. It had all been pretty mindless, fortunately, because her thoughts had been otherwise occupied with thoughts of Jamey and his bombshell. His son.

A moment before he told her, she hadn't had a clue. They both had blond hair, gorgeous blue eyes and naturally golden skin that looked like the healthiest of tans, and they were both handsome, about six feet tall, lean and strong. But so what? There were probably a few thousand other men in the city with the same blond hair, blue eyes and golden skin, who were also tall, lean and strong—though she doubted many could compare in the looks department. But as soon as Jamey had admitted it—*He's my son*—she had immediately seen the resemblance: the nose, the jaw, not just the color but even the shape of the eyes. It had seemed so obvious that she couldn't believe she had missed it.

Truth was, with thirty-six hours to get used to the idea, she knew it really wasn't so obvious. It was more a matter of possibilities. A person who didn't know could look at the two of them and say they might be related. They could be father and son.

Jamey had a son. A grown-up, twenty-some-year-old son. That was one she hadn't been prepared for. Oh, she had known he might once have been married—at his age probably had—but to have a son, and one who hated him, one he had miserably failed as a father... Who would ever have thought that she would be attracted to a man whose parenting skills put him in the same group as the people she'd come here wanting to help?

Wiggling in her chair to blot the sweat that was running down her back, she scowled. She liked Jamey, no denying that, but she wasn't looking for anything beyond friendship and assistance. Her mother had pointed out to her a while back that Evan hadn't been the only man in the world, that there would be someone else someday, and Mrs. Montez had gently told her that she didn't have to spend the rest of her life alone to honor Evan's memory, that it was all right to date, that it was even all right to fall in love and get married again, but she had thought they were both crazy. Evan had been the only man in her world. She didn't want to date, didn't even care if she never had sex again.

But if she ever changed her mind, she imagined Jamey could certainly make a woman think about sex—with a great big steamy capital S.

Unfolding the paper fan she held in one hand, she gave herself a few cooling waves, then tilted her head so her hair fell over the back of the chair. Once all the repairs were finished and all the supplies and furniture for the offices had been bought, if there was money to spare, she was going to buy a window air conditioner for the parlor that would become a waiting room. Maybe offering a respite from the deadly heat was the way to bring people in for help. They could print up flyers for the parenting classes an old friend with a master's in psychology was planning to teach: *Stay cool while you learn to keep your cool.* Maybe, like the movie theaters in the early part of the century, they could lure clients in with a big banner advertising Air-Conditioned Inside.

Out front the gate squeaked, and she raised her head in time to watch Jamey walk through. He was dressed in faded blue jeans and a plain white T-shirt and couldn't have looked better if he'd tried. Evan had been a jeans sort of guy. So was Michael. Remy might have owned a few pairs of Levi's, but he'd always preferred something a little less casual, and Smith... She smiled at the memory of him here in her hot, hot house in his immaculate summer suit. Smith didn't know the meaning of the word *casual*. That was okay. It worked fine for him...and jeans worked even better for Jamey.

He was holding a small can in one hand. Before approaching the house, before even greeting her, he stopped inside the gate and oiled the hinges. After a couple of creaky tries and another couple of squirts, the gate operated smoothly and silently. Satisfied, he recapped the can, crossed the yard and climbed the steps two at a time.

"I would've gotten around to it eventually," she said lazily, "but thanks."

"It would've driven me crazy in the meantime." He set the can on the railing, then crouched beside the dog. A sucker for any and all attention, Jethro rolled onto his back, exposing his round little belly. "This weather's not fit for a dog."

"I was thinking I might buy him a little wading pool."

"And climb right in beside him?"

"That's an idea. Too bad Serenity doesn't have a community pool."

"There was one over on Divinity. It closed down years ago and became the community garbage dump. You can find trash, furniture, a rusted-out old car and probably a body or two down in there."

"Is it salvageable?"

He skipped the expected response—the we-don't-need whatever-you're-offering, you-can't-help-us line—and shrugged. "I doubt it. It's been a long, hard time since it last held water."

She couldn't help a wistful sigh. "It would be nice though, wouldn't it?"

"It wouldn't be any different than anything else. The little kids and the decent kids would be afraid to swim there. The toughs like Morgan would take it over. They would use it up, and when they were done, they would tear it up.''

She noticed he didn't automatically mention Reid, as he usually did when Ryan Morgan's name came up, and wondered if he didn't want to remind her that he was Reid's father, and not a very good one at that. Maybe her disapproval had shown in the few minutes of stunned, stilted conversation that had followed his announcement Friday night. Or maybe he was just hoping to avoid an argument. Maybe he was afraid that, if he mentioned Reid's name, she would stick up for him. He was so sure he was right about the kid, and he didn't want to hear anything that might prove him wrong. Just as he was so sure he was right about her future here on Serenity. He was so pigheaded...and so wrong.

"Like the park," she remarked, raising the paper fan once again to cool herself.

"You've seen it?" He sighed. "I helped build that park—me and Nicky, some of the other kids, most of the parents on the street. The house there had burned down, and the owner just walked away. We cleaned up the lot, put in the benches and the playground equipment, planted flowers and bushes and trees. I think half the teenagers in the neighborhood lost their virginity in that park.''

"Including you?"

His smile was faint and, around the edges, derisive. "Yeah, including me.''

With Meghan Donovan? she wanted to ask. Was that where young Reid had gotten his start on what even his hard-hearted father admitted had been a rough life?

"Didn't you ever want him?" she asked softly, only vaguely aware of the longing in her voice.

Jamey looked annoyed, as if he would like nothing more than to ignore her and walk away. She wouldn't be surprised if he did. It seemed he had a little experience at just such behavior. Then, with a loud, heavy sigh, he answered. "I was seventeen, Karen. I'd been looking after my parents for as long as I could remember. I was about to finish school and get out on my own. I planned to enlist in the Army and see someplace other than Serenity Street for a change. The last thing I wanted was the responsibilities of a family."

"But you had those responsibilities, whether you wanted them or not." It was an unnecessary reminder, but she'd needed to make it anyway. She'd wanted to be a parent all her life. Since junior high her only goals had been to marry Evan and raise a family with him, and all Jamey had wanted was to be free of responsibility. She would have given everything to have a baby, and he would have given everything to not have one. "What did you do?"

"We got married. Five days after Reid was born, she took off with him. No one knew where they'd gone."

And no one had cared. Not Meghan's parents and certainly not her husband, Reid's father. "You must have been relieved."

He finally sat down, the house paint flaking off on his shirt where they touched. "Yes, I was relieved. I went ahead and signed up, and for years at a time I didn't even think about them. I'm not proud of that, Karen. If I could go back and do things differently, believe me, I would."

Starting with a foolproof method of birth control, she thought, thereby ensuring that neither he nor Meghan got saddled with unwanted responsibilities, ensuring that Reid never had a chance to screw up his life or live it right because he would never have a life to start with.

"You could do things differently now."

Jamey scowled at her. "Be a father to him now? Yeah, right. He hates me."

"You disappeared from his life before he even knew who you were, and now that you are here, you make it so damned clear that you disapprove of him. You tell people that he's a punk, that he's dangerous, that they should stay away from him for their own safety. You expect the worst of him. You refuse to believe that there might be anything good or decent in him. Of course he hates you.''

"He is a punk," he said defensively.

"Because he's never had a chance to be anything else. Because the only people in his life are punks. That's the only example that's ever been set for him. But you could change that. You could quit being so damned judgmental. You could start looking for the good in him—the part that prompted him to fix my gate when no one was around to see him do it, the part that led him to feed this puppy when everyone else was letting it starve to death.''

For a long while they stared at each other. He was wavering, she thought for an instant; then he disgustedly shook his head. "Whatever he did, he did for his own reasons. He expects to get something out of it. You'll see.''

"Maybe...but you never will. You're too narrow-minded. You treat a bunch of drunks in your bar with more compassion and understanding than you do your own son.''

He got to his feet and paced to the top of the steps. When he turned back, he was still looking annoyed. "If you want to meet some of the people, come on. Otherwise, I'm going to find better things to do with my day off.''

She rocked a couple of times, considering the consequences of letting her temper tell him to go on, that she neither needed nor wanted his help with meeting the neighbors. She could ask Alicia, she had told him Friday, but she had no idea whether the girl would be willing to help her. She could ask Reid when she saw him again, but that might not be a bright idea. If he was even a little as bad as his father insisted, then the people she wanted to meet would be even less receptive to *his* presence in their homes than to hers. Her only real options were to go it alone or with Jamey now.

With a regal nod, she got to her feet, picked up the bright

new leash she'd bought yesterday, snapped it to the matching collar around the puppy's neck and started toward the
steps. "Come on, Jethro, we're going for a walk."

Chapter 4

The visits took more than three hours, though each one passed quickly enough. Jamey avoided the building where Reid and the Morgans lived, as well as those their friends called home. In the buildings he did take Karen to, a number of people wouldn't answer their doors. Plenty of others chose not to invite them inside. As he had expected, they were wary, suspicious and less than welcoming. A couple of kids were happy to see Jethro, but no one was happy to see Karen. He had warned her. It wasn't his fault she hadn't listened.

But she didn't seem the least bit disappointed. She wasn't expecting instant results. She was pleased enough with simply meeting a few people. She'd lived on Serenity a week, and other than the troublemakers and the regulars at O'Shea's, today was probably the first time she'd laid eyes on anyone.

They came out of the last apartment house before the street ended and turned back toward home. They had to pass the park on the way. "Maybe this will be my first project," she mused as she drew one hand along the iron fence. "Maybe the kids would come out if they had a place to play."

"Not when there's a chance they'll get shot while playing."

She pretended not to have heard him. "We could set up some sort of program—have a play period for a couple of hours every morning and every evening when all the mothers and whatever fathers are available could bring their kids to the park. Even Ryan Morgan won't harass one mother when there are ten or twenty others to back her up. We could do the first one early—maybe eight to ten, before it gets too hot." She gave him a sidelong glance. "Before you open O'Shea's."

"Hey, I don't have any kids to take to the park," he warned.

"But you are a father, like it or not. It wouldn't hurt you to act like one."

Reaching out, he caught hold of her hand and turned her to face him. "Acting like a father to other people's children won't fix anything for Reid or me. Mothering other people's children isn't going to fix your problems, either."

Her gaze was steady and even. "Is that what you think I'm doing? Trying to forget my infertility by taking care of other mothers' kids?" When he didn't say anything, she went on. "Or is that what you're doing? Trying to forget your failure to be a father to Reid by taking care of all those vulnerable people at the bar?"

When he still remained silent, she pulled her hand free and turned into the park. Once it had been lush grass with stepping stones making a winding path around the perimeter and to each bench. Now the grass was gone, the stones were cracked, and the benches had been destroyed. All but a few of the trees were dead; three had been set on fire where they'd stood. The dirt was littered with cigarette butts, empty beer cans and liquor bottles, fast-food wrappers and refuse of a more intimate nature. Even without the soft cushion of healthy grass and the cover of trees and shrubs in nighttime shade, kids were still using the park for sex. At least some of them were being careful about it. That should count for something.

He wondered how careful Reid was. The girl he'd been with Tuesday night, Tanya Stanford, had a reputation for being available to just about anyone with the right lines and the right moves. The way she'd been hanging on to Reid had made Jamey uncomfortable—as had no doubt been intended. It had reminded him too much of the way Meghan had clung to *him* twenty-six long years ago. But at least if Tanya or one of his other girlfriends got pregnant and decided to have the baby, Reid would be there. He would know from the example Jamey had set for him everything *not* to do. He would be a better father, with all his disadvantages, than Jamey ever was.

Then Jamey scowled. There was far more risk to casual sex today than he and Meghan had ever faced. Accepting responsibility for an unplanned child paled in comparison to a slow, torturous death from AIDS. Given a choice, he would wish abstinence for Reid. Without a choice, caution was the best he could hope for.

He stopped in the gateway and watched Karen. She was carrying Jethro now to protect his feet from the broken glass that covered the ground and moving in a slow circle around the lot. She paused to glance at the graffiti that covered the walls, neon profanities that were once used for shock, that were now an everyday, every-sentence part of these kids' vocabularies.

When she came full circle, she was smiling just a little. "This will be nice. We can replace the swings and the jungle gym, maybe put in some picnic tables and a grill, plant flowers and some more trees, add a sandbox for the little ones and—"

"Karen, you're wasting your time. The Morgans won't

let you replace the swings, plant some flowers and add a sandbox.''

She faced him stubbornly. "You know what this street really needs? A few residents with backbone. Ryan Morgan is one snotty little kid. Yes, he's a thief and a thug and a murderer, but he's just one guy. How can an entire neighborhood be held hostage by one little bastard?''

"He's one little bastard who would cut your throat in a heartbeat if he heard you talk like that about him. No, wait," he said sarcastically. "Knives are Trevor's weapon of choice. Marino likes fists, shotguns and gasoline. Tommy Murphy prefers baseball bats, and Ryan likes handguns. He would put a bullet right between your eyes if he decided he didn't like the way you look or the way you walk or the way you talk.''

She ignored the important part of his statement and focused instead on something he hadn't said. "What is Reid's weapon of choice?''

He looked at her blankly. "Reid's…'' He'd never given it much thought before. Everyone on the street knew the preferences of every punk—it was almost like a signature with which they claimed credit for their deeds—but he'd never heard anything about Reid. The kid had never admitted to any assault, had never been accused of actually physically hurting anyone. "I don't know.''

Her smile was smugly scornful. "And you say he's *exactly* like the others. I don't think so.'' Bending, she set Jethro on the ground, then started walking. She was halfway to the corner when he caught up with her.

"Let's get some lunch," he suggested.

"Your place or mine?''

"Neither. Someplace away from Serenity.''

"Let's get a Lucky Dog and a Snoball and sit by the river.''

"A hot dog and shaved ice? You're a cheap date.''

"Yeah, but I'm worth every penny. Besides, you'll have

to buy Jethro a hot dog, too, 'cause I don't plan on sharing mine.''

They strolled down Serenity to the end, the only people out in the middle of a hot August day. Once they turned toward the more respectable part of the Quarter, though, they came across other signs of life—kids splashing in plastic wading pools, dogs behind fences barking at Jethro as he trotted past, people sitting on porches. Then houses gave way to businesses and locals gave way to tourists.

They bought hot dogs and sodas near Jax Brewery and crossed a parking lot and the trolley track to reach the levee. They found a bench in the shade and ate their lunch, then Karen broke off bits of the third hot dog to feed to the mutt. Once he'd had his fill of food and sniffing all the new scents, he curled up under the bench and went to sleep.

''That's the laziest dog I've ever seen.''

''He's just a puppy, and he just walked miles,'' she said in his defense. ''Besides, he has to regain the strength he lost when he wasn't eating regularly.''

''Is that why you chose such a big house? So you'd have plenty of rooms to fill with strays?''

She gazed out at the river traffic. ''Alicia says Reid was a stray.''

Jamey didn't say anything. It was understandable that someone who wanted children as much as she did couldn't comprehend someone who had a child giving him up so easily, and all the talk in the world wouldn't make it any clearer for her. Hell, he had trouble with it himself. His only excuse was that he'd been a selfish bastard. The knowledge was little comfort to himself and none at all to Reid, but it was all Jamey could offer.

''Actually,'' she went on, ''I chose such a big house because it fit my budget. All that room will come in handy, though. Once we get to work, we'll be able to use every bit of space.''

"If you actually get this place going, how do you plan to pay your staff?"

"They'll be donating their services to start. Once we've proved that we're there to stay, there are grants and corporate donations for the asking."

He knew getting money wasn't that simple, and knew that she knew it, too. "You know that many do-gooders?"

She gave him a chastising look for both his choice of words and his sardonic tone. "I know enough. People are basically good. They want to help. They just don't know how."

"You can help best by getting your stuff out of that house and setting it on fire. With any luck, the whole block will burn down."

"Jolie made a similar suggestion," she said drily, "but last I heard, arson was still a crime."

"Yeah, but burning the trash isn't, and that's what you would really be doing."

She gave him another of those chastening looks. "Let's make a deal for the rest of the day: you don't bother me about leaving, and I won't say anything else about Reid. Okay?"

Jamey directed his gaze to the ferry crossing the river from Canal Street to Algiers. "The ferry used to be free to pedestrians—may still be, I don't know. When we were kids, we used to ride it back and forth over and over— Jolie, Nicky and me. It wasn't exciting, but it was a nice change from Serenity, and it was the closest we ever got to the water other than sitting on the bank down there—" he nodded toward the warehouses closer to his little corner of the Quarter "—and throwing rocks at the rats."

"I've sat right here and thrown rocks at the rats," Karen said with a laugh. "Evan and I used to come to the Quarter every weekend that he wasn't working. We'd have beignets at the Café du Monde, walk around the square and down Bourbon Street, wander through the shops, then wind up over here with a muffaletta from Central Grocery. We loved this place. It was so different from Landry.''

It was different from the very city that surrounded it, Jamey acknowledged as the ferry docked. It was unique in all of America—at least, on the surface. Historic, exotic, romantic. Also poor, crime-ridden and depressed. But the tourists—and even though she'd lived in the city, that was what Karen had been on those weekend visits—rarely saw those parts. Tourists who wandered into those parts generally got the scare of their lives before they found their way out again. More than a few over the years *hadn't* gotten out again.

''What is Landry like?'' He already had a vision of the town that could produce a bright-eyed optimist like her: Norman Rockwell, Southern style. Mayberry moved down from North Carolina. All-America, Small-town USA. Her reply confirmed it.

''It's a small town—about twelve thousand people. Not very many people there are rich, but not many are poor, either. It's a pretty place, on the older side but well maintained. There's not much crime, all the bars are outside the town limits, the kids do well in school and almost everyone goes to church. It's safe to be out alone at night, and some people still don't lock their doors when they go out.''

''And all the politicians are honest, there's no racial tension, and the sun shines every day.''

She laughed. ''I know. I sound like a Pollyanna, but it's true. Landry is the sweetest, nicest little place to settle and raise a family. They've managed to hold on to the best of the 'good old days' while incorporating the best of the nineties. It's a lovely place.''

So why did you leave it for Serenity? That was the obvious next question, but he didn't ask it. He suspected one small part of her answer—*to settle and raise a family*—played a role in her decision. ''So nothing bad ever happens in Landry.''

He wasn't prepared for the turn her expression took, into sorrow. "Oh, bad things happen, and because they happen so rarely, they seem even worse. People in Landry aren't accustomed to things like rape, assault and murder—the town's had only one murder in seven years—so when they happen, it's so shocking, so far outside their experience, so out of place."

Bad things just didn't happen in All-America, Smalltown USA. How fortunate for them. Murders were so commonplace in New Orleans that people hardly noticed anymore. There had been a time in Jamey's memory when voices raised in anger followed by gunshots would have sent half the residents of Serenity scrambling for a phone to call the police. Now, if they noticed at all, they did nothing. They didn't want to get involved. They were afraid. They just didn't care anymore. Even he felt little or nothing when news of another death filtered its way into the bar. If the victim was remotely innocent, there might be a moment's regret that another soul had lost his chance to escape Serenity. If the victim was scum like the Morgans, there would be a moment's relief that there was one less bastard to fear on the street. Then it was back to life as usual.

He had become almost as unfeeling as the people he despised, he realized. Maybe it had been necessary for his own survival. Maybe the only way to cope with so many people leaving his life—either for a better life, like Jolie; for prison, like Nicky; or for a cheap casket in an aboveground grave like countless others—was to stop being touched by it. To stop caring on any but the most surface levels.

For years Reid had been the only threat to that no-deeper-than-the-surface emotion.

Karen threatened to become another.

He forced his attention back to her, to something she'd said about Landry having only one murder in seven years.

She had looked—still looked—so sad that he wondered if that one murder had been her husband's. He had assumed that Evan Montez had been killed on the job—by a pervert, she'd said, who liked little girls—but maybe that wasn't the case. "Was Evan from Landry?"

She nodded. "His family lived two blocks over from mine. We'd known each other all our lives."

"Did he die there?"

She hadn't expected the question, and for a time it hung between them as stiffness spread through her. Then, abruptly, she gestured toward the west side of the river. "No. Over there. A little girl had been kidnapped by a man with a penchant for kids. Evan's partner Michael found them and, in the process of saving her, got shot. The guy was going to kill him and probably kill the girl. Evan drew his fire so Michael could get the girl out, and both he and the kidnapper died."

Jamey countered the emotion heavy in her voice with silent cynicism. Great. Her husband had died a genuine, bona fide hero. That was a lot to live up to, a lot to compete against. *Not* that he was interested in competing. Once he convinced her to leave Serenity, he would never see her again, would never think of her again. Out of sight, out of mind. He was good at that. He'd managed with Meghan. For a long time, he had managed it with Reid. It would be no problem with Karen.

She continued, her voice growing flatter, less emotional. "You hear how military wives panic at the sight of the chaplain at their door or how cops' wives dread that official visit when their husbands are on duty. For me it was Smith Kendricks and Remy Sinclair. Everyone in the department knew how close they were to Michael and Evan, so they were allowed to break the news. It was a long time before I could look at either of them without feeling that awful grief all over again."

"So he died, and you went home." Whose death would

it take to make her leave this time? If God cared at all about her, if He hadn't already washed His hands clean of Serenity and everyone who lived there, maybe it wouldn't be her own.

"Not right away. I liked it here. We'd made a home for ourselves. I stuck it out for a while, but things didn't get any easier, so finally I left. I sold the house, moved back into my folks' house, right back into my old room, and became their little girl again. I let them and Evan's family take care of me, coddle and baby me until I couldn't stand it anymore. Then I came here."

He shook his head, half dismayed and half amused. From All-America, Small-town USA, surrounded by loving and supportive family, to all alone in hell. She should have her head examined. Come to think of it, for spending all this time with her, for caring whether she stayed or left, for getting involved with her crazy schemes by taking her around this morning...

So should he.

Monday Karen did more cleaning and more painting and, armed with a saw, a hammer and some wood, she repaired a couple of rotted boards on the veranda. She didn't work in any particular order. When she got tired of breathing paint fumes, she tackled the basic cleaning in another of the many rooms. When she tired of dust, she turned to a little small-scale woodworking. When that was done, she raked the yard clean of trash, pine straw and about five years' worth of leaves. She was in bed by ten o'clock and hadn't seen anyone all day—not Jamey or Reid, not Alicia or any of the people Jamey had introduced her to Sunday. In the muggy warmth of her bedroom, tired from the day's labor, she slept like a log. If there were any disturbances on the street, she didn't hear them. Maybe, she thought with a grin the next morning, she was getting used to this place.

After twisting her hair into a knot, she tugged the baseball cap into place to hold it, then left the bathroom for the first floor. She was dressed in shorts and a tank top to take advantage of whatever sun might break through the clouds that still darkened the sky this morning, but it seemed more likely that rain would come first. That was okay. A little rain never hurt anyone, and it just might make the heat and humidity more bearable, at least temporarily.

She'd already been downstairs once this morning, for a breakfast of a muffin, fruit and coffee. She had gathered her equipment then—a rake, broom and shovel, big plastic garbage bags, leather work gloves for handling nasty stuff and softer cotton ones for simply protecting her hands—and loaded it all into the plastic utility cart on the porch, along with a Thermos filled with lemonade, a bottle of cold tap water and Jethro's water dish. She added Jethro to the cart, locked up and bumped her way down the steps. The cart wouldn't fit through the gate at the end of the sidewalk, so she turned at an angle across the yard, pulling it instead through the second broad gate, where years ago the driveway had completed its semicircle around the house and exited back onto the street.

She hadn't been kidding when she'd suggested that cleaning up the park should be her first project. Granted, in its sorry shape, it wasn't the most appealing place for kids, but it beat the streets for a playground. It beat by a long shot spending your entire life behind locked doors. She planned to clean up, paint the rusted fence, cover the graffiti with spray paint now, maybe with a mural later, and make a few minor repairs on the equipment; then she intended to beg, plead and somehow convince the mothers to take back at least that one small plot of ground for their children.

The morning was misty, as if the fog hadn't quite managed to form but drifted instead in small, wispy patches above the ground. It made everything look a little softer, a little blurrier, but no less shabby. Nothing less than the removal of people like Ryan Morgan and his friends and a massive dose of civic pride could combat the shabbiness of Serenity. She intended to talk to *her* friends about getting rid of him and *his* friends, and then she would work on the pride.

She pulled the cart down the empty sidewalk, across the street and to the gate of the park. There she secured Jethro's leash to the fence, took the leather gloves and a garbage bag and went inside to start picking up trash. According to Jamey, there had once been enough privacy in the park for teenagers to indulge in the experimentation that came so naturally to kids, but there was no privacy now. There was no place at all where a person could hide. That was why she saw Reid the instant she stepped through the gate.

He was sitting on the back of the sole bench that hadn't been destroyed, his feet on the slats that made up the seat, and watching her with a definitely unwelcoming look. Now that she knew more about him, she understood his perpetual scowl, but she was no closer to understanding his parents' treatment of him. No matter how many years she lived, no matter how many dysfunctional families she dealt with, she would never understand turning your back on your own child.

"Good morning," she greeted as she began filling the bag. Picking up trash was never fun, but this... She wrinkled her nose with distaste. This went way beyond being *not fun*. This was just about as gross as any job she'd ever done and left her wishing she'd brought a pair of tongs so that not even her gloves would have to come in contact with this stuff.

Reid didn't return her greeting. He didn't speak at all until she'd worked her way to within a few feet of his bench. Even then there was no friendliness in his voice. "What are you doing?"

"Cleaning this place up. Why are you here so early? It's not even seven o'clock."

Ignoring her question, he asked another of his own. "Why? They'll just trash it again."

She noticed he said *they* would, not *we*. Did that mean he didn't hang out in the park at night or simply that he wasn't one of those who dumped his garbage there, smashed his empties against the bricks, set whatever would burn on fire or defaced the walls with obscenities? "Why do they do that?"

"Why not?"

"Wouldn't they like to have a decent place to hang out in? Doesn't anyone on this street besides me miss the sight of grass, flowers and healthy trees?"

His scowl deepened. "Probably no one on this street has ever seen them—at least, not on a regular basis. Not around here."

"Jamey tells me that your friend Ryan more or less runs this neighborhood. Would you introduce me to him?"

"No," he said flatly, vehemently, with no room for backing down. "You'd better stay away from him and hope to God he stays away from you."

She allowed a slight smile. "You sound like Jamey," she said quietly, fully expecting a show of anger, of insult. Instead, his expression turned unexpectedly sad.

"Thanks for the compliment," he said, trying for sarcasm but not quite succeeding. "I always wanted to be like good ol' Jamey, who doesn't give a damn about anybody."

She scooped up the remains of a hamburger, still in its wrapper and complete with ants, and dropped it in the bag before looking his way again. "That's not true, though no one could blame you for thinking it."

For a long moment, he simply looked at her; then he grimly asked, "Who told you?"

"He did."

"I didn't think he'd ever admitted it to anybody." He turned sarcastic, more successfully this time. "Let's face it—I'm hardly the son to make a parent proud."

"He's hardly the father to make a son proud." Finished with the little corner where he sat, she began moving away, picking up everything in her path. When she stopped at a bench to pick up the burnt remains of broken slats, Reid circled around to lean against the wall. "Any chance your friend would make a deal with me?" she asked.

"Nope."

"You haven't heard the deal yet."

"Give him everything you have of value, throw in your body for good measure, get the hell out of here and don't expect anything from him in return. He'd be willing to go for that, but nothing less."

"Ask him if he'll leave the park alone."

"He won't."

"He's got the rest of the neighborhood. It wouldn't hurt him to give the kids this one part."

"No."

"Then I'll ask him."

He moved to block her path. "Are you stupid? He's leaving you alone right now because he figures you're not worth the effort it would take to harass you. You get his attention by going around asking for favors, and he'll make you sorry. He'll make you damned sorry."

She crouched to pick up a cache of broken bottles, then tilted her head back to lock gazes with him. "Why are you friends with a man like that? You're not like him, Reid. You're not that mean. You're not that sick. You're not that worthless."

"Of course I am. Just ask my father. He'll tell you. He'll tell anyone. Hell, he's told me face-to-face what a worthless bastard I am." His smile was thin, mocking. "And he's right. Jamey O'Shea is *always* right."

Before she could respond to that, a sliding noise came from behind her, then a soft little voice called, "Hey, Reid, whatcha doin'?"

For a long time he continued to look at her; finally he forced his gaze away and above her head. "Hey, J.T."

She turned to see a young black boy, barely visible in the shadows of a second-floor window.

"This crazy lady's cleaning up the park for you kids to come and play in," Reid went on, the subtle ridicule in his voice encouraging the same response in the boy.

"Yeah, right," J.T. scoffed. "My mom don't let us play outside. 'Sides, there's nothin' to play with down there. Everything is all broken and burned."

"The broken stuff can be fixed," Karen said, rising to her feet and facing the boy.

"Yeah, but it'll just get broken again. Why bother?"

Why bother? That seemed to be the motto of Serenity Street. Jamey had made a mistake twenty-some years ago and failed his son, but he wasn't trying to make it up to him. Reid was grown, angry and hated his father. Why bother trying to change that? Reid had lived his entire life feeling like an outcast, but instead of trying to fit in, to build a relationship with someone who wouldn't bring him down, he spent his life with people who would destroy him. Earning respect was a difficult thing; why bother? The people in this neighborhood had been run over and beaten down by life, by the system, by people like Ryan Morgan and Jimmy Falcone, but they didn't fight back. They caved in. They gave up. Why bother?

So why the hell was she bothering? She couldn't help anyone who refused to help himself. Why was she wasting her time?

Then J.T. leaned out the window and fixed his gaze on her. "You gonna fix the swings?"

She glanced at the swing set. The metal poles were in place, sunk deep in concrete, but the chains were wrapped around the top crossbar, and the seats they were supposed to connect to were nowhere to be seen. They had probably been burned, hacked to pieces or carried off somewhere and dumped, just for the fun of it. "Yeah, I'm gonna fix the swings," she replied. "I'm gonna fix everything."

"I like to swing," he said wistfully. "When we go to my aunt's, there's a real park by her house, and she takes us there to play. It's got grass and everything."

"This one will have grass, too."

"Real grass and swings?" For a moment the little face looked hopeful; then he shook his head. "It'll all just get torn up again." He looked away, as if listening to something inside, then hastily called, "See ya later, Reid," as he slammed the window shut.

"J.T.'s not allowed to open his bedroom window," Reid said as Karen continued to look up. "He's also not allowed to play outside or talk to strangers or to me."

"Why not? He seems to like you."

"Yeah, well, his mother doesn't."

"Maybe it's the company you keep."

He glowered at her, clearly annoyed. "You talk like it's a matter of choice."

"Isn't it?"

"If I quit hanging out with Ryan and the others, what am I supposed to do?"

"Make new friends."

He laughed scornfully. "Half the people on this street are scared to death of me. None of them want to be friends with me."

"Get rid of Ryan and the others—and that chip on your shoulder," she suggested. "Show them that you're really a decent person. Give them a reason to like you, a reason to trust you."

"Hasn't O'Shea warned you that I *can't* be trusted?"

"Yeah, well, contrary to his opinion, Jamey isn't always right."

His bitter amusement faded, leaving his eyes empty and bleak. "Maybe not...but this time he is." He turned and walked away, stopping only briefly to scratch the puppy, still sitting in the cart and chewing happily on her cotton gloves. Then, realizing that she was still watching him, he shoved his hands in his pockets, ducked his head and took off across the street.

She never had learned why he was alone in the park before seven o'clock in the morning.

She continued to work, circling the lot methodically, filling one bag and making a good start on a second before she reached the gate again. There she traded leather gloves for cotton, trash bags for a broom and dust pan and began sweeping up the broken glass.

"You really are crazy, ain't you, lady?"

Looking up, she saw that the second-floor window was open again, a face pressed up close. "Crazy? Doesn't everyone sweep the dirt around here?"

"People don't even sweep the floors around here. Why're you doing that?"

"It's the easiest way to get up the broken glass, short of bringing in a bulldozer to haul off the dirt. Where did you disappear to?"

"My mom was calling. I'm not allowed to talk to strangers."

"That's a good rule."

"I'm also not allowed to open the window."

That wasn't such a good rule. If these people were worried about someone trying to break in, a pane of glass wasn't going to stop them any more than it would stop a bullet, a brick or a bomb. As a safety feature, keeping a window closed up tight was definitely a failure, and it only served to make the innocent people inside suffer more, especially in this heat.

"My grandma says it's gonna rain."

"I hope it does. I couldn't get much wetter." Her shirt was plastered to her back, and sweat stains were spreading across the front. Her shorts felt pretty damp, too, wherever they came in contact with her body. "Does your grand-mother live with you?"

"Yeah. Her and my mom and me."

"Do you think I could come upstairs and meet them?"

There was a rustle of noise, then J.T. disappeared. The window didn't close, though. Instead a woman came into view. Karen could make out nothing of her features in the shadows, but she could feel her suspicion as if it were a physical thing. Summoning her best smile, she said, "Hello. I'm Karen Montez. I moved into the old Victorian down the street."

There was no matching friendliness in the woman's voice. "What are you doing?"

"Cleaning up the park."

"Why?"

"For the kids."

"To give that worthless bunch that hangs out here every night something new to trash?"

"No. To give the kids like J.T. a place to play, so they can get some sun and fresh air and have a little fun." She hesitated only a second before repeating her earlier request. "Can I come up and talk to you?"

"I don't open the door to strangers."

"All right. Would you come down here and talk to me?"

"I don't go outside with strangers, either."

"It's a public park in broad daylight," Karen coaxed, although that wasn't quite true. The sky was darker than when she'd arrived an hour ago, and the smell of distant rain was sweetening the air.

The woman laughed scornfully. "You say that as if it means something. Do you know how many people have died on our public streets and sidewalks in the middle of the day?"

"Too many. But you won't be in any danger from me, and I'm the only one out this morning. It's just me and my dog.'' She gestured toward the cart, where Jethro was curled up asleep on the blade of the shovel.

After a long hesitation, the woman nodded once, drew back and closed the window. Karen scooped up a pile of glass-laden dirt with the dustpan and dumped it in the trash bag, then began sweeping again. A moment later J.T.'s mother appeared at the edge of the fence. Dressed in a nurse's uniform, with a sweater folded over one arm and an umbrella in hand, she looked wary, distrusting and ready to flee at a moment's notice. ''My name is Shawntae Williams.''

Withdrawing one glove, Karen approached her, then shook hands through the iron bars. ''I met a number of the families on the street yesterday, but we missed your building. I guess it doesn't matter since you don't open your door to strangers—although maybe you would have. I was with Jamey O'Shea. Do you know him?''

''Everybody knows Jamey. Are you a friend of his?''

Karen's laughter was automatic. ''Not exactly. More a thorn in his side, I think. He thinks my being here is a very bad idea, but he can't avoid me. He can't even look out from the bar without seeing my house and me.''

''So why are you here?''

She gave her spiel on Kathy's House. Shawntae didn't look impressed. Karen sighed. ''I just need to be someplace where I can make some sort of difference, where I can do something that counts. I need to stay busy. I need to believe that what I do matters.''

''One person—one *woman*—can't make a difference.''

Karen shook her head adamantly. ''You're wrong. One person can influence one other person, who can influence still one more. This morning I'm out here cleaning alone, but tomorrow maybe you'll come out, too, and next week maybe one of your neighbors will come.''

''I have to get to work in the mornings,'' Shawntae said, apparently taking her words literally, missing her point. Her next statement, though, proved that thought wrong. "I'll tell you what—Friday's my day off. If you haven't given up by then, maybe I'll help. Okay?"

"Okay." Karen's smile made her face ache. "I'll see you Friday."

Rising from the bed, Jamey felt every year his age and then some. He hadn't slept well last night, and he had a headache and stiff neck to show for it. Wandering into the living room and out into the hall, he made his way to the bathroom, where he washed down a couple of aspirin tablets with tepid water before returning to the living room and the windows that overlooked Serenity Street.

Raindrops streaked the glass and were trapped in the tiny squares of the screen, but they didn't obscure the fact that there were no lights on across the street. He wondered if Karen was sleeping in. Dark, rainy weather like this was perfect for it. If it weren't for this damned headache, he would still be in bed himself. He would stay there until five minutes until ten, then throw on some clothes, brush his teeth and open the bar. It wasn't likely he would be busy. Rain often kept his daytime customers at home. Nothing would keep them away at night, though, with the possible exception of a hurricane. The bar had been pretty full the last time New Orleans had been threatened. If that was going to be their last night on God's earth, they'd wanted the comfort of their Scotch, their bourbon, whiskey and beer to accompany them on their way.

Jamey could think of a hell of a lot better ways to spend his last night of life than in a bar. Like with a beautiful woman whose passion was more than a match for his own, whose capacity for giving was equally strong, whose fiery hair could trap a man in a fragile web, whose sweet smile could hold him there... A scowl hardened his features as he realized that his intended description of a nameless, faceless beauty had somehow become an all-too-accurate description of his neighbor across the street.

He was about to turn away from the window when he saw her, strolling down the street as if she didn't notice it was raining. She was pulling a plastic cart behind her, filled with tools, two fat trash bags and that scrawny mutt, raising his face to the rain with the same pleasure his owner displayed. She turned into her gate, pulled the cart up on the veranda, then set Jethro on the floor. He immediately shook himself, spraying raindrops all around. She damned near did the same thing, pulling her cap off, shaking her hair free, giving her bare arms a swing or two to remove the excess water.

She'd been at the park, he realized, and his scowl intensified. Leaving the window, he returned to his room, where he dressed in jeans and a T-shirt to the accompaniment of long, low rumbles of thunder. For crossing the street where water had already started collecting, he chose his oldest, rattiest sneakers, then grabbed his keys from the dresser and left the apartment.

She was still on the veranda, seated in the rocker, her shoes and socks off, and Jethro was wrapped in a towel in her arms. "Can you believe this silly dog is afraid of thunder?" she asked as Jamey took the steps three at a time to the shelter of the porch roof.

He ran his fingers through his hair, slicking it back from his face, dislodging raindrops, then looked at the dog. All that was visible was a fluff of black fur and the tip of a tail. The mutt's head was tucked between her arm and her body, and the rest was wrapped in the towel. Maybe the dog wasn't so silly. Cradled in her arms, with his head on her breast, wasn't a bad place to be. "It's easy to be afraid of something you don't understand."

"Yeah, but it's just as easy and a lot more satisfying to learn from new experiences."

She was a new experience, but he'd already learned just

about all the lessons he wanted. He knew, as Reid had pointed out, that she wasn't his type, knew without anyone pointing it out that he wasn't her type. He knew that she wouldn't last long, no matter how determined she was. He knew it wouldn't be long until she, like everyone else on Serenity, left the neighborhood in one way or another.

Since his visit Sunday morning, she'd uncovered a bench somewhere, long enough and broad enough for a person to stretch out, and hauled it to the veranda. It was a scuffed pale blue now but showed through the scrapes and peeling where it had once been yellow, purple and, originally, white. He sat down, kicked his shoes off and got comfortable. With a pointed glance at the cart, he asked, "Make much headway?"

"I picked up the trash and enough broken glass to make a dozen windows, and I talked to Reid, a little boy named J.T. and his mother, Shawntae."

Jamey resisted the urge to warn her yet again to stay away from Reid. She hadn't listened to him any of the other times, and there was no reason to believe she would listen now. "Shawntae's a nice kid. Her father used to be a regular customer of mine."

"What happened?"

"He took off. He'd had enough of life on Serenity. One day he just packed his bags and left. She must have been about fourteen or so. She started running a little wild and had J.T. the next year. His father took off, too." His smile was sour. "Maybe it's something in the water. Maybe the men on this street are incapable of being decent fathers." After a moment he gave in to the question that was waiting to be asked. "What was Reid doing out that early?"

She shrugged. "Maybe he's an early riser. He fixed my gate before dawn, and he was already at the park when I got there at six-forty-five."

"Maybe he was up all night doing—" Abruptly, tasting the bitter guilt that too often accompanied talk of his son, he broke off, grimaced and looked away. That simple action, though, didn't stop him from feeling the weight of Karen's steady gaze.

"Doing what?" she asked at last.

God knows what. Breaking into someone's house. Stealing someone's car. Fencing property previously stolen from someone else. Meeting with the Morgans and Jimmy Falcone. Delivering warnings, threats or more ominous "messages" for the bastard. Murder and mayhem, raping, robbing, pillaging and plundering—Morgan's gang did it all.

But did Reid?

She gave up waiting for an answer. "He says you told him he was a worthless bastard."

Jamey's face burned hot with shame. He and Reid had shared eleven years of hostility, but he knew immediately the incident she was referring to. It had happened the day of Meghan's mother's funeral. It had been July and so miserably hot that the flowers over the casket had wilted, their fragrance turning sour with decay. There weren't many people there to complain, though—just a priest, a neighbor and Jamey. Her daughter, who had run away from home, from a husband and eventually from her son, hadn't shown up. Neither had Reid. The old woman had taken him in when Meghan abandoned him. She hadn't had much love for him, but she'd made a place for him, had kept him in food and clothing, and she hadn't mistreated him, but he couldn't bother with attending her funeral. He couldn't show her that one small bit of respect.

Jamey had returned from the cemetery to find Reid and his buddies having a party in the street right in front of O'Shea's. They were drinking, harassing anyone who walked by, indulging in indecent displays with their girlfriends and generally behaving like the snotty, obnoxious little bastards they were. He had lost his temper and said some pretty harsh things. Reid had offered a few sharp-edged insults of his own, and then he had avoided all contact with Jamey for weeks.

"Yeah," he said grimly. "I shouldn't have said it."

"You shouldn't have thought it."

"What else did he have to say?" He expected some curse, some expression of derision. He was surprised.

"That you were right. That he *was* a worthless bastard."

Maybe the kid felt guilty about skipping out on his grandmother's funeral. Jamey couldn't even make a guess, because he didn't really know his own son. He knew the obvious—that Reid hung out with a bad crowd, that he was one angry young man, that he'd been in trouble with the law since he was ten—but he didn't know much else. He didn't know just how involved Reid was in Morgan's shady activities—although, until recently, he'd thought he had. He didn't know how the kid felt about anyone or anything, other than his animosity for the father who had failed him. He didn't know if Reid had any decent friends or a special woman, if he'd ever had any goals for his life, if there had ever been anything he'd wanted to do someday.

"I told him you weren't," Karen said, rocking slowly and making a board underneath the chair squeak. "I told him that you're not nearly as right as you think you are."

He didn't say anything to that. He just sat and listened to the rain, falling harder now, and the thunder. Every booming clap made the puppy shudder, made his tail wag a little harder.

"Have you ever considered trying to mend your relationship with him?"

"He's twenty-six years old. He doesn't need a father."

"I'm thirty-seven, and I still need my dad. Age has nothing to do with it, Jamey. No matter how old he is, no matter how badly you neglect the relationship, it's still there. He'll always be your son, and you'll always be his father. It's up to you guys what you make of it, whether you hate each other or learn to speak politely to one another or even someday come to love each other.''

He wouldn't know how to begin such an effort. How could they possibly fix what was broken when they couldn't exchange a civil word? How could they right what had gone wrong from the beginning when there was no trust, no love and precious little tolerance between them?

He stared out at the street as two figures hidden underneath a shared umbrella hurried along the sidewalk toward Decatur. Few of the Serenity residents who held jobs— definitely a minority in the neighborhood—owned cars. They made a quick exodus in the morning to the bus stop down on Decatur, then just as quickly returned to their homes when their workday was over. There were no leisurely strolls, no friends or co-workers offering rides. It was a minor difficulty in lives filled with major ones.

''I don't hate Reid,'' he said at last, his voice flat.

''Maybe not, but you talk about him with the same derision you reserve for Ryan Morgan and the others. You call him the same names. You show the same lack of forgiveness.''

He didn't need to look for the truth in her statements. It was there. From the very beginning, there had been so much negative emotion between them. Reid had been hostile; Jamey had been defensive. Reid had been angry, bitter and resentful; Jamey had been drowning in guilt and regret. Reid had treated him with scorn and contempt; Jamey had reciprocated with the same. But Reid had been a kid, and Jamey had been an adult. Reid had been the child, Jamey the father.

He had never acted like a father—or an adult. Only like an idiot.

Weary of the conversation, the guilt and the shame, he deliberately changed the subject. ''What have you got planned for today?''

She stretched her arms over her head. ''I don't know. A

day like this is made for staying in bed, if you can spare the time.''

So they agreed on that much—although he made a conscious effort not to focus on it. Not to imagine her bedroom somewhere at the back of the house, with tall ceilings and open windows, spotlessly clean, hopelessly feminine, an oasis of comfort in this big, run-down house. Not to imagine *her* in the bedroom, her wild curls unrestrained, her passion also unrestrained. She would sleep bare in the bedroom of his imagination—it was too hot for clothes and too muggy for covers—and she would stay that way when she was awake, too. She would—

''But I can't spare the time,'' she went on, her voice even, her tone matter-of-fact. It wasn't the voice he imagined in the bedroom—throaty, husky with invitation—and it introduced reality into his fantasy before he'd had a chance to really enjoy it. ''I guess I'll start with some cleaning and, later, make some phone calls. I called the city last Wednesday about the burned-out street lamps, but the woman I spoke to didn't seem particularly interested once she understood what neighborhood I was talking about.''

''And you were surprised?'' he asked drily. ''There aren't fifty law-abiding adults in the neighborhood. I doubt a single one of us is registered to vote. We don't contribute money to political campaigns, and our incomes are so low that our taxes don't amount to anything. We don't write letters to the newspaper. We don't file complaints with the city. We don't understand our rights, and we certainly don't stand up for them.'' His voice turned cynical. ''Welcome to Serenity.''

She smiled the sort of smile that could make it hard for a man to breathe. ''You see? You need me. I do vote, I write letters, and I'm great with complaints. I know the resources available to help with the kind of problems we have here. What rights I don't understand, I can learn about, and I can certainly stand up for them.''

"You're a dreamer if you think you can change things."

The smile came back. "Maybe...but there's nothing wrong with being a dreamer. It beats being a cold-hearted pessimist."

"I prefer 'realist.' I face facts."

"So do I," she retorted. "But I don't let them interfere with my dreams. I don't let them stand in the way of what could be. Come on, Jamey. With a name like O'Shea, you must have had the ability to dream at one time in your life."

"Not since I was a child—and that was too long ago to remember."

"One dream," she coaxed. "If you could have one dream, what would it be?"

He gazed down the street where he'd spent the better part of his life. For better or worse, this place was home. It was where he wanted to be, where he belonged. He owed it a lot—but not the one dream Karen had allotted him. He wouldn't unselfishly wish for salvation for Serenity, not when he was convinced that Serenity couldn't be saved.

He had long ago quit wanting things for himself. The bar was never going to be profitable. He'd proven beyond all doubt that he was lousy husband material and even worse father material. He didn't want a woman of the permanent, till-death-do-us-part type in his life—didn't want any more people, any more responsibilities, any more troubles, than were already there.

He certainly didn't want a pretty, foolishly optimistic, redheaded do-gooder who was still mourning her perfect hero husband in his life.

Not even if some small part of him thought he did.

No, if he were fanciful enough to dream, it would probably be for Reid—a wish that the first twenty-six years of his life hadn't been so tough and a hope that the years remaining were great in both number and satisfaction. He would hope that somehow the kid could overcome the odds stacked against him and make a life for himself with a family to love him the way his parents had failed. He would look for some little bit of absolution in making things right, even at this late date.

But he wasn't fanciful. He was a realist. A cold-hearted pessimist. "There aren't any dreams on Serenity Street, darlin'," he said as he got to his feet. "Only nightmares."

Chapter 5

Thursday brought Karen a visitor at lunchtime bearing a gift of food. The smell, drifting in through the locked screen door, reached her long before she reached the door. Redolent of spices, it was enough to make her mouth water—and to bring back more than a few bittersweet memories. She'd learned to make every Cajun dish she knew from Evan's Aunt Sirena, who had lived for years across the lake in Slidell before returning to Landry, who had also taught Evan's partner the same dishes. They had spent countless hours gathered around crowded tables—just her and the guys, enjoying the food a lot and the company even more.

"Michael." She unlatched the screen door and pushed it open, then, careful of the pot he held, wrapped her arms around his neck for a long, tight hug. Of them all, he had been Evan's best friend. They had both come from small towns, from medium-sized, stable, loving families. They'd shared the same upbringing, the same values, the same way of looking at the world, the same method of working. They had been so close that Evan's death had hurt Michael almost as much as it had hurt her. Blaming himself, he had begun drinking, and he almost hadn't stopped. Thank God he had. Losing him, too, would have made a great tragedy even more so.

"You look good, Karen," he said, holding her at arm's length so he could study her. "Still as pretty as ever."

"It's nice of you to say so...though I know your tastes run to tall and blond." What a coincidence. Lately, so did hers. "How's Valery?"

"Beautiful. Busy with the shop and the kids."

Valery Bennett owned a shop in the Quarter that specialized in antique clothing, handbags and jewelry. If a woman had the money, the figure and the style to carry off the elegant dresses, she could look like a million bucks. Valery did. Karen only wished she did.

"I'd say that's Aunt Sirena's seafood gumbo in that dish," she said, taking a deep breath.

"Show me to the kitchen and we'll eat."

She waited until they were seated at the spacious built-in breakfast table, plates of steaming gumbo and rice in front of them, before she spoke again. "Why don't we take care of business first and get it out of the way?"

"What business?"

"Didn't you come to tell me that I should leave here? That this is a dangerous place? That I don't belong here?"

His answering tone was mild. "I imagine Jolie and Smith have already given you more warnings than you needed. You're a smart woman. You know this is a dangerous place, or you never would have come here."

She studied him for a long time, wondering if he was playing some sort of game, trying to somehow manipulate her into doing what he wanted. He seemed sincere, though, and not the least bit manipulative. "You don't disapprove?"

"Giving you credit for intelligence doesn't constitute approval," he pointed out drily. "I don't think you belong here. I think the sooner you get out, the better."

"You think I can't help."

He took his time answering, obviously choosing his words carefully. "You've taken on a big job, Karen. It would probably take an entire department of social workers, counselors and cops to clean up this place. If it were just you up against the problems of poverty, poor education, abusive relationships, teen pregnancy and despair, I'd put my money on you any day. But it's not that simple. It's you against some of the meanest, dirtiest, toughest sons of bitches in the city. It's you against Ryan Morgan and Jimmy Falcone. You're no match for them, Karen."

"Alone, no. You're right. But you and me—rather, your department and me... Everyone keeps telling me what a contemptible person Ryan Morgan is, how dirty he is, what a conscienceless crook he is."

"He is," Michael agreed. "He's a young Falcone."

"Then why isn't he in jail? Why haven't you guys made a case against him?"

"To make a case, we need evidence. We need a witness. But no one testifies against the Morgans or their people. People who witness their crimes or are the victims are afraid to speak up. They're afraid to cooperate with us."

"So if you can't lock him up, make him leave. Make it so hard for him and his gang to do business here that they have no choice but to go elsewhere. Make a show of force. Whenever they're trying to do something illegal, be there watching. Send a car in here for an occasional patrol. I've been here a week and a half, Michael, and I have yet to see a single police car."

"Make a request," he suggested, then immediately dampened any hope that might have sprung up. "But don't be surprised if you're told that we're too shorthanded, that we're already spread thin. We used to make regular patrols down here until one officer got shot and another half dozen were shot at but unharmed. They got bricks through their windows, threats, hostility.''

"So you backed off?" she asked, her voice rising in dismay. "You should have come in here and kicked butt. You should have found the people who fired the shots and threw the bricks and hauled them off to jail. Instead, you backed off and let them win. You told them it was all right to assault police officers. You sent them a hell of a message.''

He gave her a wry smile. "Can I point out that *I* had nothing to do with this? I didn't make the decisions. I agree with you. If it had been up to me, I would have made it impossible for them to turn around without finding a half-dozen cops watching. But it wasn't up to me, and we *are* shorthanded. Money's tight, and, frankly, there's some logic to spending it where it might do some good instead of down here.''

"So the good people who live in the neighborhood and the kids who are at risk, who will be deciding soon whether to become productive, contributing citizens or to follow in Morgan's footsteps, aren't as important as people in other less dangerous, less hopeless neighborhoods.''

His only response was a rueful shrug.

"Is anybody interested in Ryan Morgan?''

"We are. The FBI is. Does anyone have enough to make a case against him?" He shook his head. "I don't work organized crime, but I'll talk to someone who does. I'll see if anyone's interested in a little harassment—within the limits of the law, of course.''

Of course...which was part of the problem. Ryan Morgan didn't work within the limits of the law. He had no restrictions, no regulations, no laws dictating what he could do or how he could do it, while the authorities trying to stop him were restricted. The courts bent over backwards to ensure that none of his rights were violated, but who protected the rights of his victims?

"So...does that take care of business?"

She offered Michael a wan smile. "I guess so. Thanks for not trying to talk me into giving up."

"I've known you a long time. I've never seen you give up, not even when Evan..."

Died. Even after all these years, it was still hard for him to say. "I wanted to," she admitted. "I had no interest in a life that didn't include him."

"He would be proud of what you're doing."

The solemnly spoken comment sent a slow warmth through her. She had spent so much time trying to convince herself and everyone else she could do this that she hadn't given much thought to whether Evan would have needed convincing. She thought Michael was probably right. Evan wouldn't have liked the neighborhood, and he wouldn't have wanted her living there alone, but he would have seen the need, and he would have understood her need to try to fill it. He would have believed in her, supported and encouraged her.

Of course, he also would have been right at her side every moment he wasn't working. He would have protected her. He would have warned away the punks and watched out for her.

As Jamey had done. As he was still doing.

She and Michael finished their lunch with lighter talk about families and futures. He showed her the latest pictures of his daughters, sweet little girls with the delicate beauty of angels and the gleam of the devil in their dark eyes. As she handed the pictures back, she felt a twinge of sorrow around her heart. When she had married Evan and moved clear across the state from her home, his college roommates and best friends had become her family. It hadn't been just her and Evan, but them plus Michael, Remy and Smith. She had thought it would always be that way, with additions, of course. Their friends would get married, and instead of five, they would become eight. And the babies... They would all have babies, three or four or even more, and they would take weekend outings to the zoo, the park and the lake. They would celebrate birthdays and holidays together. They would be family and best friends until the end of time.

But Evan had died, and she had moved away, and there would never be any babies for her. Her dream was coming true: the guys had remained best friends, their wives and kids were best friends, too, and they celebrated everything together. They had become the family she'd wanted...but she wasn't a part of it.

After transferring the leftovers to her own dish, she washed Michael's pan, then walked out with him. "Thanks for lunch. It was good seeing you."

"If you need anything, give me a call." From his hip pocket, he removed a business card with the department number—as if she could have forgotten it—and his pager number printed on it, his home number written. "You do have a phone, don't you?"

"Of course I have a phone." She'd taken care of phone service before she'd gone to the closing. She recited the number—it was easy to remember—then gave him another hug. "Give my love to Valery and the kids. Bring them over sometime."

The look he gave her said he knew she didn't expect an acceptance on the invitation. Bring his pretty little girls to Serenity? Not even when hell froze over. She couldn't blame him. If she had children of her own, she probably wouldn't be here, either, certainly not living here. "Take care, Karen. Remember, if anything at all comes up, call me."

"I will." Standing at the top of the steps, she watched him leave, then, as if she had no willpower at all, her gaze shifted to O'Shea's. The doors were open—it seemed the only time they ever closed was those eight hours from

2:00 to 10:00 a.m. when Jamey slept—but there was no sign of him.

Impulsively she returned to the kitchen, took the leftover gumbo from the refrigerator and clipped Jethro's leash to his collar. After she locked up, they made the trip across the street and through the first set of doors. Jamey was in his usual place behind the bar, a toothpick in his mouth, watching TV with little interest. He looked sleepy, lazy...and sexy as hell.

"You can't bring that mutt in here," he remarked as she bent to loop Jethro's leash around the post supporting one ragged bar stool.

"He's not a mutt. He's my guard dog," she reminded him as she climbed onto the next stool. She set the bowl in front of him. "Here. Lunch."

He unfolded the foil and sniffed. "You make this?"

"I could have—I have the recipe—but Michael made it."

He raised one brow. "Michael?"

"Michael Bennett. Evan's partner."

"Yeah. I thought he looked like a cop."

Under other circumstances, Karen thought, a woman might feel flattered that a man had noticed her company— her very handsome, very appealing male company. She might think it meant he was a little interested—not in an it's-a-slow-afternoon-and-I-have-nothing-better-to-do sort of way, but in an also-handsome-also-appealing-man-to-woman way. But under these circumstances, it was exactly a slow-afternoon sort of way, with a self-appointed-guardian-of-Serenity watchfulness tossed in.

But it was okay. She wasn't disappointed. She wasn't interested in Jamey that way, and she didn't want him to think of her that way, either.

Right. And instead of an afternoon shower, today the skies would open up and rain pennies from heaven all over Serenity.

He fished a scallop from the gumbo and ate it in one bite. "I don't suppose he talked any sense into you."

"I'm so full of good sense that there's no room for any more."

His mouth wanted to curve into a grin, she could see, but he refused. "You're full of something, all right." He disappeared into the back, then returned with a spoon. After a couple of bites, he asked, "You can cook like this?"

"We-ell... We were taught by the same person, and we started with the same recipes, but Michael is one of those people who thinks that cooking is a perfectly reasonable way to spend a few hours of your day. The idea of making a roux or shopping for the freshest seafood or chopping a ton of vegetables doesn't faze him at all. I don't mind cooking, but I want shortcuts. Thirty minutes is more than enough time to spend preparing a meal. Do you cook?"

He shook his head. "I'm great with a can opener and sandwiches. As far as real cooking, I make excellent bacon, and my sunny-side up eggs aren't bad. I'll fix them for you some morning."

An invitation to breakfast. That could hold some promise...if they didn't live across the street from each other. If it didn't go without saying that he would be rising from his bed and she would probably be long risen from her own.

She gave an exasperated shake of her head. What was wrong with her? She had no time for fantasies, no time for any relationship more demanding than those eventually connected to the women's center. Even if she was interested in a relationship, Jamey O'Shea wasn't her type. She couldn't have found a man who had less in common with Evan if she had tried.

But Evan was dead, and the last thing she wanted to do was try to replace him. It wouldn't be fair to herself, to the man or to Evan. If she ever did get involved again, it had to be with a man who attracted her for who and what he was, not for being someone who reminded her of Evan.

Jamey didn't remind her of anyone but Jamey.

"I went by the park last night. I'm not sure you're keeping ahead of them."

She focused her attention on the physical man in front of her and away from the image of him in her mind. "I'm holding my own." Every morning she went to the park before the sun got high and the heat unbearable. She picked up trash and sprayed over graffiti. If she had time, she scraped away rust and flaking paint from a few bars on the iron-lace fence across the front and gave them a quick coat of fresh paint. Every night the kids gathered there, dumped more garbage, broke more bottles and painted more graffiti. Last night one of them had sprayed an entire can of neon orange paint across the fence.

"How long can you keep this up?"

"Longer than they can."

He shook his head. "They're younger and have more energy."

"I'm older and more stubborn." She shrugged. "It's a game to them. I clean it up, and they trash it. Eventually, someone will get tired and quit playing. They're betting that it'll be me, but they're wrong."

"Not a single young kid has walked through that gate in months—maybe years. All this work you've done, and no one has come except the kids you want to get rid of."

"I don't want to get rid of them. Lord knows, there's no other place on the street to gather. I just want them to treat the park with some respect. There's no reason why they can't use it at night and leave it in reasonably decent shape for the little kids during the day."

"No reason except they don't want to." He finished the gumbo, then drew a wooden stool close to the bar and sat down. In the space of a moment he went from his usual skeptical self to something Karen thought very few people, if any, had ever seen in him: uncertainty. Insecurity. "Have you seen Reid down there again?" He asked it casually, as if it were a perfectly normal question, as if an even vaguely friendly—well, at least not hostile—mention of Reid weren't a rarity.

"No. I think he might be avoiding the place because I've been there every morning." She hesitated, then asked, "Have you seen him this week?"

He shook his head.

"Do you worry when that happens?"

"Yeah, I do."

She would bet it cost him tremendously to answer that question honestly. She would also bet his feelings for his son were far more complex than he let on. They must have the most complicated father-son relationship east of the Mississippi. She hoped, for both their sakes, that someday they would be able to make it work. They each had a lot to lose if they didn't. Reid, with the direction he was going, could lose his life.

"For whatever it's worth, I haven't seen the Morgans or Vinnie Marino around, either," she remarked. "Maybe they took off for a few days."

"Maybe they're hiding out," Jamey said with his customary sarcasm. "Laying low."

"Or maybe they're having a little fun, like young men do. Maybe they went to the beach." Even as she spoke, she acknowledged the incongruity of the suggestion. The beach and that gang of four... More likely they had gone to burglarize the homes of people who had gone to the beach. Reaching across the bar, she laid her hand on his arm, patting reassuringly. "He's all right. He'll show up in a day or two, and you'll wonder why in the world you ever worried."

Regretting the touch almost immediately, she tried to withdraw without looking too hasty, too clumsy. Her face suddenly felt warm—which was only fair, because her fingers were tingling and her throat had gone tight. "I—I'd better get back to work." She picked up her bowl from the bar, laid his spoon on the polished wood and started out. She was halfway to the door when he finally spoke. He sounded as if his throat was a little tight, too.

"Hey, Karen?"

Expecting an awkward thanks, she turned and looked back. He pointed over the bar and to the floor, where Jethro sat watching her with a pitiful look of abandonment. "Aren't you forgetting something?"

With a sudden laugh, she hurried back and retrieved the puppy. "I'm sorry, sweet pea," she said, cuddling him in her arms. "I didn't mean to forget you."

"And you think you can take care of Serenity," Jamey said, shaking his head in a chiding manner. This time she made it all the way to the door before he spoke again. "Hey...thanks."

"For the lunch," she clarified.

"Yeah. For that, too."

The alarm went off at seven o'clock Friday, an annoying harsh beep that made ignoring it impossible. Jamey shut it off, then rolled over, intending to go back to sleep for at least two more hours, when abruptly he remembered why he'd set it in the first place. It was early in the morning, Karen's hours of choice for working in the park. Although she'd been perfectly safe without his presence for four days, he saw no reason she should push her luck. Besides, it was Friday. Weekends usually signaled more than the usual activity on Serenity, and this—a payday weekend for those with jobs—would be even more so.

He dressed, shaved, brushed his teeth and combed his hair. It was getting kind of shaggy, he noticed in the mirror's reflection. Usually he let it go until it started getting in his eyes, and then he made a trip to a barber just outside the touristy part of the Quarter. Maybe he wouldn't wait so long this time. It didn't hurt to look a little neater than the kids on the street.

Then he scowled hard at himself. Not once in his entire life had he ever gotten his hair cut, or not cut, to please a woman, and damned if he wasn't too old to start now. He didn't know whether Karen liked short hair, shaggy or ponytail long, and, more important, he didn't care. He did know that she liked respectable men, like Evan the hero cop, like Smith Kendricks and Michael Bennett, who were as upright and straight-and-narrow as any Boy Scout. She liked family men, who made a commitment when they got married, when they had kids, who were good husbands and generous, loving fathers. She liked dreamers who were willing to support her dreams.

He missed out on all counts.

After shoving his feet into a pair of disreputable sneakers, he pocketed his keys and left the bar, stopping to secure the dead bolt behind him. Early mornings on Serenity weren't so bad. The street was quiet because that was the way of nature. Everyone was either asleep or just getting up. It wasn't the unnatural stillness that often settled over the neighborhood. Things were *supposed* to be quiet at dawn.

The first thing he noticed when he turned was the sign on Karen's fence—the sign painted with the pretty rendition of her house, with the Kathy's House name in a flourish across the bottom. It was covered with paint and bent around in such a way as to make removing it difficult. The fence had been painted, too, bright wavy lines of orange, lime green and white stretching from one end to the other, and garbage bags piled beside the driveway awaiting the next trash pickup had been torn open and scattered across the yard.

So it had started. Her uneventful days on Serenity had come to an end. This was probably the punks' way of protesting the changes she was making in the park they considered their own personal property. They figured if she wanted to pick up trash, she could do it from her own yard;

if she wanted to clean up paint, she could do it on her own fence, and leave their place alone.

And where was she? The mutt tied to the wrought iron fence three blocks down gave an easy answer: back in the park. *I'm older and more stubborn,* she had told him, and she was apparently trying to prove it.

He went that way, giving Jethro a scratch under his chin before walking through the open gate. She had brought a ladder with her this time and was standing close to the top of the swing set, patiently untangling the chains and unwinding them from the top bar. He moved to a place just inside the gate, leaned against the fence and watched while he waited for her to notice him.

She was wearing the baseball cap again—amazing that it could keep all that thick, long hair tucked up out of her way—and her usual shorts and tank. The work she'd done outside here and at her own place was starting to pay off in the hint of gold that colored her exposed skin. Too bad it wasn't paying off anyplace else.

He was beginning to think she was lost in her own world, unaware of his presence and careless of her safety when she finally spoke. "Hey, Jamey, that fence you're leaning against?"

"Yeah?"

"I just painted that section about forty-five minutes ago. I don't think it's dry yet."

With a grimace, he moved away and twisted back to look. Sure enough, a loosely formed pattern of tacky black paint stretched across his T-shirt. *Now* who was unaware and careless?

She leaned way across to unwind the last chain, then climbed to the ground. "Checking up on me?"

"Yeah."

"You saw my house." Her voice was conversational, empty of any but the most casual emotion.

"Yeah. Sorry."

"You shouldn't apologize. You didn't do it."

"That sign was too big a temptation."

"That's okay." She picked up a can of spray paint and began repairing the damage he'd done to the fence. "I thought it might be. That's why I have others."

"If you put up a new sign, they'll take it as a challenge."

She smiled. "If they trash it, I'll take *that* as a challenge."

"You're fighting a losing battle."

As quickly as the smile had come, it disappeared, leaving her intensely serious. "Giving up is losing. Giving in, running away—that's losing. As long as I don't let them win, I haven't lost. No matter what, Jamey, I don't intend to let them win."

Giving a shake of his head, he moved further into the park. He didn't understand why she cared. The people down here were nobodies, losers. They meant nothing to anyone. They weren't willing to help themselves. They weren't willing to fight for themselves. Most of them weren't even worth saving. Defacing a fence, vandalizing a car, burning down a house or killing a defenseless woman—it was all the same to the punks down here. Rights meant nothing to them. *Life* meant nothing to them. So why the hell did any of them matter to her?

His wandering took him to the back wall. There was a house, long ago abandoned, on the lot behind the park. The one-story wall separated the two yards and provided some measure of privacy, but the person who'd built it some hundred years ago hadn't wanted to be cut off completely. He'd added a gate in one corner that allowed passage between the lots. Once the park had been put in, the gate had provided a shortcut to kids living on the next street or a convenient exit to anyone needing a quick getaway. Four years ago Nicky Carlucci had held a few private meetings down here with Jolie Kendricks, and the gate had been his way of getting in and out without being seen. If he'd been seen, it could have meant his death. Instead, he'd wound up in prison, placed there by his own guilty plea, because it was where he'd felt he belonged. Just as Jamey was here because it was where *he* belonged.

But Karen didn't.

"As long as you're here, you might as well help."

He turned to see her watching him. She was holding two cans of spray paint, shaking them both, making the balls inside rattle. Satisfied that they were ready, she tossed one to him. Deliberately he didn't catch it, but let it hit his arm and bounce to the ground. "I didn't come to help," he reminded her.

"I know. You came to tell me yet again that I can't win down here. I can't make a difference." She walked to the first bit of new graffiti on the back wall and sprayed a thin coat of black paint over it.

"I don't believe in what you're doing."

"You've made that clear." She moved on to the next profanity.

"I'm not a part of it."

Looking over her shoulder, she gave him an annoyed look. "I'm not asking for a commitment to the cause, Jamey. I'm asking you to spend five minutes of your time painting over a bunch of misspelled graffiti. If that's too much, fine. Go back to O'Shea's. Give up, give in, and get out. Let them win."

He scowled at her, though she didn't have the decency to notice as she turned her back on him and went back to work. *Give up, give in, and let them win.* In other words, be a loser, like everyone else on the street. He was—he knew he was—but he didn't feel like admitting it this morning. He didn't feel like giving in. Irritably he picked up the can, moved to the opposite end of the wall and followed her lead, spraying a light coat of paint first, then returning when it was slightly dry to go over it again. At this rate, in another few days, the entire wall would be covered with black paint—not a particularly appealing sight, but better than the obscenities that filled it now.

"Well, well. Isn't this a sight? Jamey, I do believe the paint is supposed to go on the wall, not on your back."

Jamey turned to see Shawntae Williams, dressed in shorts and an old stained shirt—as if she'd come to work—standing in the gateway. She had come to work, he realized as she came inside and pulled a pair of brown cotton gloves from her pocket. He watched as she picked up a garbage bag lying on the ground and started the job of trash pickup that Karen hadn't yet finished, then murmured, "I'll be damned."

A few feet away, Karen gave him a faintly smug look. "Most likely," she agreed, her voice just as soft. Louder, she said, "Shawntae told me Monday that if I was here today, she would help."

"If I'd thought you really would last, I wouldn't have said it," the young woman remarked. She looked at the brick wall, liberally dotted with long black smudges and gave a shake of her head. "I admit, I like it better this way than having my son learning the kind of words from his bedroom window that get him a spanking. But don't either of you have any artistic talent? Can't you make it look like something more than a brick wall with dirty words painted over?"

"Something like a mural," Karen suggested. It was a thought she'd obviously already had. "Maybe Serenity Street the way it used to be."

"Well, if it's going to be outside *my* bedroom window, I was thinking maybe something like Hawaii or Tahiti or a cruise ship to Paradise," Shawntae retorted. "But yeah, Serenity would be an improvement over this."

"I can't even draw a straight line," Karen said without hesitation, "and Jamey's only doing this because he can't back down from a challenge. Even if he could draw, he'd be too stubborn to do it."

"You know who's got some real talent?" The woman looked from Karen to Jamey. "Reid Donovan. I've seen some pictures he's done for J.T. He's good."

So Reid had artistic talent. That was news to Jamey. He certainly hadn't gotten it from his parents. The only thing Meghan had ever drawn was a welfare check and the wrath of all the creditors she'd skipped out on over the years. Jamey was pretty good at drawing a beer, but give him a pencil, marker or paintbrush, and he didn't have a clue.

He almost missed the cautious look Karen gave him before she spoke. "I thought J.T. wasn't allowed to speak to Reid."

"Well, he's not supposed to, but J.T. spends so much time in his room and Reid spends so much time here. Sometimes they talk."

Reid, whose favorite emotion was anger, whose reaction to everything was hostile, who should be kept away from small children, liked to talk to and draw pictures for an eight-year-old boy. The image didn't jibe with the Reid he knew...but hadn't he finally admitted that he didn't really know his son at all? Wasn't this just further proof?

"But if we paint a mural," Karen was saying, "won't they just paint over it?"

"There's supposed to be this paint that's, like, graffiti-proof," Shawntae replied. "Besides, maybe if one of their own did it, they'd leave it alone."

"What makes you think he would do it?" Jamey asked.

The young woman smiled. "Just have Karen ask him. I bet he'd do it for her."

He turned back to the job he'd been given. Finally, something he and Reid had in common: the things they would do for Karen. His only hope was that painting was the extent of them. The last thing in the world he wanted was to find himself in competition with his own son for any woman's affection.

Then, with a furtive long look at Karen, he rephrased

that. The *last* thing he wanted was to compete for this woman's affection. Not with the people on the street. Not with her dead hero husband. Certainly not with his own son.

Not *anyone*.

After spending the entire morning outside, first at the park, then in her own yard, Karen decided to devote the afternoon to patchwork inside. In the last week and a half she had painted the main rooms upstairs—her bedroom, the bathroom and the living room—from the ceiling all the way down to the baseboards. She had even, with the roller mounted on an extra-long extension pole, managed the twenty-foot walls in the entry, and all of those spaces, if she said so herself, were looking better than livable. The bathroom and the bedroom were downright pretty.

Now it was time to start the downstairs rooms, but not before the holes in the plaster were patched—and there were a ton of them. It seemed that either the previous owners or, more likely, the kids who'd hung out in the empty house before she bought it, the ones responsible for the same sort of trash she'd been collecting from the park, had had little regard for the plastered walls. Whether the cause had been accidents, fistfights, fits of anger or just plain boredom, the result was the same: holes in every wall, in all sizes and shapes, sometimes damaging the lath underneath and, in one case, going clear through to the next room.

She had gathered all the necessary tools and supplies, along with her how-to book, in the gentleman's parlor and was in the process of scraping off her first effort to try again when a knock sounded at the door, then the screen swung open. "Hello?"

Darn, she'd forgotten to latch the screen door again. At least it was a woman's voice. If it'd been Jamey, instead of a greeting, he would be lecturing her, and she'd had enough lectures lately.

She moved close enough to the big double door to see her guest. Trying to hide her surprise and pleasure, she offered a casual smile. "Hi, Alicia. Come on in."

The young woman hesitated in the doorway. "Are you busy?"

"Not with anything important. Come in and have a..." She glanced around the big empty room. "Well, there's not a seat to have, but you're welcome to the floor."

"No, thanks." Alicia patted her stomach. "I might not get up again." She gave the room a wide-eyed look. "This is a nice house."

"It will be when I'm done." Bending over the bucket of patching plaster, Karen made a face at her response. Even in its current sorry condition, this house *was* nice compared to the others on the street. It was an improvement over the substandard shelter offered by most of the apartment houses, with too little space, too few windows and too little comfort. At least she had plenty of light, air circulating through the open windows and room to move without bumping elbows with someone else.

"I saw what they did outside on my way to work this morning. Too bad."

"Was that supposed to be some sort of message from Ryan?"

The girl shook her head. "I'm sure he thought it was funny, but I don't think he did it. He was with me most of the night." She shifted as if she were uncomfortable—probably tired, Karen thought. She had walked to work before six this morning, had put in a complete shift, then walked back again. Excusing herself, Karen went out to the veranda, picked up the rocker there and came back.

"Here, sit down. Get off your feet."

"Thanks." She sat carefully, bracing herself with one hand on the rocker's arm, settling in awkwardly with a heavy sigh.

"When is your baby due?"

"Three weeks."

Two months, maybe three, Reid had guessed, and Karen had placed her own guess at two. She wasn't very big to be so close to delivery. Maybe that was normal for her—after all, she wasn't very big herself—but it could mean a problem. Affordable prenatal care was unknown in neighborhoods like Serenity, and low birth weight was one of numerous unfortunate results.

"You must be excited. Are you hoping for a boy or a girl?"

"A pretty little girl," Alicia replied with a dreamy smile.

"What about Ryan? What does he want?"

Just one mention of her baby's father was enough to dim the light in her eyes. "For it to all be over with. He says I'm no fun when I'm pregnant. Yeah, well, let him carry around an extra fifteen or twenty pounds in the hottest months of the year, when he's on his feet all morning, and see how much fun he is." Folding her hands over her stomach, she set the chair in motion. "He thinks everything will go back to the way it was before. He's such a typical man—so stupid. Before there was no baby. Now there is. Who does he think is going to take care of her, to feed her and change her and walk with her when she's cranky and can't sleep?"

"You are," Karen answered matter-of-factly. Stepping back, she studied her second patch and decided it was good enough. Fortunately, with the textured surface of the plaster, she didn't have to be perfect. "Of course, you're also going to make her magically disappear when he wants to be alone with you. You're going to take care of her all day and through half the night and still be pretty, fresh and eager whenever he comes around. You're going to devote yourself to her except, of course, when you're devoting yourself to *him.* Naturally, he'll come first. She'll come second, and you just might place a distant third."

Alicia looked at her for a moment. "You had a man like that?"

"No. My husband was the sweetest, kindest, most loving man I've ever known." Before the girl could ask the obvious question, she went on. "He died six years ago. He was shot by a man he was trying to arrest."

"You were married to a cop?" She asked it with the same skeptical disapproval that most people on Serenity probably felt for cops, and who could blame them? The police department was failing to protect the good people, and, according to Jamey, all the others had troubles with the law. "From a cop to the owner of a seedy bar. That's a change."

Karen finished the second patch, then glanced at her. "Jamey and I are..." Exactly what were they? Not exactly friends, but a little more than acquaintances. But how much more? "Just neighbors," she said at last.

Alicia's laughter was easy and loud. "Yeah, right. He's a very handsome man—"

"Who's old enough to be your father."

"And old enough to be your man. They tease Reid about it. They say that maybe one day you'll be his stepmother."

Be careful what you wish for, the saying went, for you might get it. All her life she'd wished to be a mother, but she'd been thinking along the lines of a sweet, innocent baby, not a twenty-six-year-old man with more troubles than anyone should ever bear. Not that it mattered. While she couldn't figure out exactly what she and Jamey were, what they weren't was certain. They weren't involved. They weren't sweethearts. They weren't going to become lovers. They certainly weren't going to get married someday, and even if hell froze over and they did, it wouldn't mean a thing to Reid. He already had a mother somewhere. He didn't need another.

"I haven't seen Reid lately," she said, eager to change the subject. "Is he okay?"

"He's around. Sometimes no one sees much of him."

Karen put down the putty knife she was using, wiped her hands on a towel and went to crouch in front of her guest. "Can you tell me something?"

Shrugging, the girl waited expectantly.

"Is Reid as bad as Ryan and the others?"

"Ryan isn't..." Her defense died unfinished. Because she suspected Karen had already decided to believe everyone else's assessment of her boyfriend? Or because she didn't quite believe the denial herself? "Nah. Reid's a good guy—as much as anyone who's been raised the way he has can be."

"Why does he hang out with Ryan?"

"Because he doesn't have anyone else. His mother doesn't want him. Jamey doesn't want him." She shrugged again. "That's what holds us all together. No one has anyplace else to go or anyone else to care about them. We don't have anything but each other."

"You have your baby," Karen said softly, and Alicia's face lit up.

"Yeah, I have my baby. And right now I'm going to get her and me home and get some sleep. It's Friday, and Ryan always likes to stay out late on Fridays."

"You know, you don't have to stay out late with him. It's perfectly all right for you to stay home and get some rest. Heavens, you're going to give birth in three weeks. You're entitled to a few quiet evenings at home."

"Yeah," she agreed mockingly. "Explain that to Ryan." She scooted to the edge of the chair, then stood up. "You mind if I come back sometime?"

"Not at all." Karen followed behind her to the door. "If you see Reid, ask him to come by, will you?"

"I'll tell him, but don't count on seeing him. His old man would raise hell if he saw him over here, and that's something Reid tries to avoid."

Karen watched her leave before wandering back into the

parlor and picking up the putty knife. There were so many questions she would have liked to ask Alicia, about everything from her medical care to her plans for the future, about Ryan and Reid, about who it was that hadn't wanted her. Who had failed to care about her? Who had left her so needy of affection that she accepted Ryan Morgan's sorry version of it and allowed herself to be satisfied with it?

Parents. Many of Serenity's problems came from poverty, crime and just plain bad luck, but a depressing number were caused by bad, absent or uncaring parents. Too many parents refused responsibility for their children but instead let them run wild, getting into trouble, breaking the law, using drugs, turning to crime and, all too often, ending up dead years before their time. As Jamey had pointed out, the kids around here didn't talk about *when* they grew up but *if* they grew up.

Maybe some of the parents had tried. Maybe Ryan and Trevor Morgan's father had given them a better example to follow. Maybe Vinnie Marino's mother had done all she could to keep him on the straight and narrow. Maybe Alicia Gutierrez's parents had counseled her to get away from Serenity, to get an education and make a better life for herself. Maybe the parents of every one of those lost souls who met in the park at night had done their very best to guide and support their children, but they had failed.

Or maybe they had found the job of raising children in a place like this too difficult and had given up. Maybe none of them had cared from the start.

Maybe Jamey didn't believe it, but that was one problem she and her staff could help with. Parenting skills could be taught—always had been, back when the world was different, when most families stayed geographically close. For generations mothers had advised daughters on how to care for their own babies; fathers had taught sons by example to be fathers themselves. Too often now the family support system was gone, but that didn't mean the support had to disappear, too. The women of Kathy's House would provide the support, advice and assistance that had once been taken for granted, and maybe, when the next generation of Serenity teenagers came along, they would have a street full of parents who were more than up to the challenge.

And then, she thought with a stubborn scowl, maybe Jamey would believe in her.

It was a busy night in the bar and a busy night on the street. Jamey had seen the Morgans drive by a half-dozen times, the speed always as slow as a stroll. Trevor was driving, while Ryan sat beside him in the front seat, like a king surveying his kingdom. Jamey had seen Marino's ugly face in the back seat on one trip by, but he hadn't been able to identify one of the other bodies inside as Reid. He hoped none of them was Reid…but if they weren't, then where *was* the kid?

After turning the last chair upside down on a table, he shut off the front lights, then stepped outside. There was a party going on in the park. Music filled the air, along with shouts and laughter and the smell of wood smoke. There had been only one bench left intact there; he assumed it wasn't anymore. He could excuse the fire if it was seriously cold, but it was eighty-seven degrees tonight, the air thick with 90-plus-percent humidity. The punks had lit the fire out of sheer meanness, too stupid to realize that, in destroying the last bench in the place, they were not only depriving anyone else of a place to sit, but themselves as well.

He hated to admit that he shared any of Karen's naiveté, but to some extent, on this subject at least, he did. He just didn't understand why the kids insisted on trashing the park. Surely the little bastards could appreciate a nice place to hang out the same as anyone else on the street. Surely sitting around talking in a clean environment with benches, grass and flowers was more enjoyable than in a glass-littered dirt lot, and he knew for a fact that the more intimate pleasures they indulged in were definitely better with grass for a cushion and shrubs for privacy.

No one was asking them to stay out of the park, although, no doubt, the neighbors nearby would appreciate a quiet night once in a while. Karen just wanted them to leave it in a condition that could be enjoyed by others. That wasn't too much to ask…or maybe it was. Maybe, when your life held no promise of a future, when you valued nothing but your own momentary pleasure, when you had no goals but to have fun right here, right now, showing respect for public property was out of the question. Maybe they trashed the park each night because none of them knew if they would be alive the next night to come back. Maybe living in the moment made looking ahead to the future impossible.

Down by the park the party had spilled out into the street. The Impala was parked there, right in the middle, its stereo system—worth more than the car itself—booming. In the buildings around it, there were lights on in different apartments, in spite of the late hour. No use trying to sleep when music was blasting through the walls. Across the street, though, the house was dark. Maybe the house provided enough sound-blocking material to Karen's rear-facing bedroom that she was one of the lucky few able to sleep. More likely, she was sitting in the dark up there at one of the bay windows or…

He stared hard at the porch. It was deep in shadows, but he could make out a faint movement back and forth. That damned rocker. Awake and uncomfortably hot, she had decided to sit outside, where she would make a perfect target for anyone with a gun and a grudge. Too many Serenity residents had both.

He locked up the bar, then crossed the street, entering her yard through the driveway, ignoring the wide central steps for the smaller set at the near end of the porch. She was sitting there, all right, one foot propped high on the porch rail to keep the chair rocking. Worse, she wasn't alone. Someone sat on the floor facing her, his back against the elaborately turned spindles, his arms resting on his bent knees. Reid.

The desire to send him away with one final warning was strong. He didn't trust the kid as far as he could see him, which, right now, was about eight feet. He'd believed the worst of him far too long to give up all his suspicions, doubts and distrust easily. But he didn't suggest Reid should get lost and, as far as Karen was concerned, stay lost. It was hard to resist, but saying anything would only offend Karen, and, honestly, he was no longer 100-percent sure that such a warning was necessary. Ninety percent, maybe, but not a hundred. Instead, he approached them, took a position against the rail but facing the park and said, "This isn't the best place to spend a late Friday night."

"That's what Reid said when he came," she replied evenly. "I see you sitting out on the sidewalk often at night, three feet from the street and in bright light."

"Yeah, but I haven't been spending my time making enemies the way you have."

"You made your enemies a long time ago. Old enemies are no less dangerous than new ones." She raised one hand in gesture toward the bench. "Sit down."

"No, thanks. I'm faster on my feet." Finally he turned his attention to Reid, sitting on the floor, pretty well hidden from the street. He couldn't remember a time he had ever gotten within twenty feet of the kid that he hadn't actually felt the anger and resentment radiating from him. Even the very first time they had met, it had been there, real, palpable. Tonight was no different. "Did she ask you?"

There was a slight shift of the younger man's head, but he didn't look at Jamey. "About the mural?" He sounded suspicious, antagonistic. "It's a stupid idea."

"He says Ryan would tear the back wall down before he'd leave a mural on it undamaged," Karen explained.

"Maybe he's right."

"And maybe someone needs to tear Ryan down." Her tone was conversational, as friendly as the expression he could see now that his eyes had become accustomed to the dark, even though her words weren't.

"The only person Ryan Morgan is afraid of is Jimmy Falcone," Jamey warned, "and Jimmy isn't going to make him leave your park alone. If by some off chance, you do make a difference here, Jimmy will want to get rid of you as much as Morgan does."

She smiled. "I think you underestimate the man. Falcone has money, power and every corrupt official in the state in his pocket. What he doesn't have—and what he's always wanted—is respect. Not from people like Ryan Morgan, but from people like us—the everyday, average, common people of Serenity."

"He *used* to want respect," Reid said derisively. "After barely avoiding prison a few years ago, he's decided that more money, more power and more corrupt officials are a perfectly fine substitute. For all he cares, the everyday, average, common people of Serenity can go to hell."

Jamey had no doubt about the correctness of Reid's assertion—after all, he worked for the bastard from time to time. He was glad, though, to hear the contempt. He'd heard the Morgans and their buddies talk about Falcone before. It was *Mr. Falcone* this and *Mr. Falcone* that, in an almost reverent voice. They admired their boss. They all wanted to be just like him someday. Obviously, Reid didn't. Thank God for *something*.

"So forget Ryan and Falcone," Karen suggested. "If I get the paint, Reid, will you paint the mural?"

"It's a waste of time and money."

"So what better things do you have to do with your time?"

He looked away, down the street toward the park where his friends were gathered, where his part-time girlfriend

Tanya was performing a provocative, inviting dance on the hood of the Impala, to the loud, lewd pleasure of the young men gathered around. When he looked back, there was a tension in his face that hadn't been there before. "I don't know what Serenity was like thirty years ago."

"I doubt that it's changed much," she pointed out mildly. "Most of these houses and buildings are sixty to a hundred and sixty years old. But for any details you might need, you could ask your father. He lived here then. He probably remembers."

Your father. A curious stillness followed those words. To Jamey's best knowledge, no one had used them—at least not in front of both of them—since Meghan had walked into the bar and said, "There's your father, Reid—the man who never wanted you." He had wondered at the time if that was the way she had always referred to him. Reid's go-to-hell response suggested that it had been.

With a sudden surge of energy, Reid got to his feet. "I'll think about it. But it won't last. They'll destroy it." He took the steps to the cracked sidewalk, then glanced back. "Around three-thirty or four, Ryan's going to be drunk enough to get mean. I wouldn't advise being out here when that happens."

Jamey and Karen both watched him walk down the street toward the park. Before he got too close, though, he turned into the building where the apartment he shared with the Morgans was located on the second floor. Only a moment later, to the great disappointment of the punks in the street, Tanya slid off the hood of the car, adjusted her clothing and headed that way. Jamey didn't realize how severely he was frowning until Karen spoke. "Maybe she's not so bad one-on-one. Maybe this is all just an act."

"Maybe her reputation is all fluff and no substance?" he asked dryly.

"A great deal of Reid's reputation is without substance." So she insisted. He hoped she was right.

Stepping past her, he turned the bench around so he could lean back against the wall and stretch his legs out in front of him, then settled in. "Why are you out here?"

"It was too noisy to sleep, so I thought I'd come out and see what was going on. Then Reid came by. I had asked Alicia this afternoon to tell him that I wanted to see him."

Jamey shook his head in dismay. "You're determined to make this personal with Ryan, aren't you?"

"What do you mean?"

Her innocence, he knew, was an act, one that he wasn't foolish enough to buy. Neither would Morgan. "You've already got Reid, who's the closest thing to a best friend Morgan's ever had, hanging around, and now you're going after his girlfriend—the mother of his baby. If you win both of them away from him, you think he's not going to take it personally?"

"I'm not trying to take anyone away from him. If Alicia finds other ways to spend her time and other people whose company she enjoys more, that's not my fault. Ryan can't blame me because he treats her like property and she doesn't like it."

"Darlin', Ryan can blame you for the state of things in China. Even if you'd never met Alicia, if she dumped him, he would find a way to put it on you. Common sense and reason don't enter into it."

She twisted in the chair until she was facing him. "You worry too much, Jamey."

"Go away," he said with a scowl, "and cut my load in half."

"Half? I'm flattered."

"You're foolish."

"You're a pessimist."

"I'm a realist."

"I appreciate your concern. I really do. It makes me feel safer. But it would help us both a lot if you'd just have a little faith."

"You want to know who I have faith in down here? The Morgans. Vinnie Marino. Tommy Murphy." He added a few other names for good measure: the Rodriguez brothers, Mitch Campbell, Tyrone Block, the Rossellinis, Pete Carletti. There were more, a couple dozen more if he chose to waste the time. "They're the people who do what they promise. They're the ones who stand up, who never back down, who never hide."

"I haven't backed down yet."

"Only because they haven't yet put you in a situation where you have no choice."

Instead of further argument—or maybe just changing the angle of the argument—she remarked, "You didn't name Reid."

It didn't pain him to answer. "I don't know about Reid."

"A week ago you were convinced that he was as bad as the others. Now you're willing to admit that you may have judged him unfairly."

"I'm willing to admit that maybe it's not so black and white. Maybe he's not just like the company he keeps."

She rewarded him with a smile. "You're making progress. Maybe next week you'll see that a lot of his behaviors are defense mechanisms. He expects you to meet him with hostility and resentment, so he approaches you that way. If you were less predictable, maybe he would be a little more open."

He did always assume the worst with Reid, he had to admit. Maybe part of it was simply taking the realistic view. The kid had already been well on his way to juvenile detention when he'd come from Atlanta. But maybe the larger part was Jamey's own defense mechanisms. He had never felt guilty or ashamed of anything...except his treatment of his own son. He had blown off the most important relationship in his life for his own convenience. He hadn't wanted to be a father, and so he had accepted Reid's disappearance with relief, even though he'd known Meghan wouldn't be much of a mother, though he'd known the kid would need *somebody.* He'd felt tremendous guilt, although he'd denied it. By treating Reid like a punk, by convincing himself that he must *be* a punk, he had in some small way validated his failure as a father. The kid had been beyond saving and so there was nothing for Jamey to do, no responsibilities to accept, no guidance to try to offer.

But maybe, he acknowledged now, he'd been wrong. Terribly, irreparably wrong.

An angry shout from down the street drew his attention. The natives were getting restless. Someone's temper had reached the boiling point. At least Reid was inside his apartment, removed from the crowd. It was time for them to retreat, too. Rising from the bench, he opened the screen door and held it, silently waiting.

Karen sighed. "I guess that's my cue to go inside, cower and hide." She stood up, leaving the rocker still rocking, and made it as far as the doorway before stopping. "A week from tomorrow I'm having a neighborhood party— probably around six, when it's not yet dark but a little cooler. Maybe you could find someone to take over the bar—or, better yet, close it up and bring your customers over."

"No one will come," he warned.

"That's what Reid said. You two are more alike than you realize. You certainly think alike." She stepped inside, pulled the screen door shut and latched it. "You were surprised when Shawntae joined us at the park this morning. Maybe you'll be surprised next Saturday when you see how many of your neighbors are willing to venture out for a little celebration."

"We'll see," he said cynically. If even one showed up— Shawntae, maybe—he would be surprised.

Just before she closed the door, she echoed his words but gave them an entirely different feel. Optimistic. Confident. Downright cheerful. "That's right. We'll see."

Chapter 6

Over the following week Karen managed to convince virtually everyone she came into contact with that she was either incredibly brave or incredibly stupid. Anyone put to a vote, she thought late Saturday afternoon, would probably choose stupid. Although street parties had been common a generation ago, no one had hosted one in years, and no one felt safe attending one. Even Shawntae, who'd spent hours Saturday, Sunday and the next Friday and Saturday mornings working with Karen in the park, thought the idea outrageous. Even she, who recognized and even shared a little of Karen's stubbornness, wasn't convinced that attending the cookout wouldn't put her and her son's lives in danger.

Maybe no one would show up, as Jamey and Reid had insisted. Maybe she was going to the effort for nothing. Maybe she would be disappointed. That was why she'd bought food that could be easily frozen—hamburger meat, wieners and buns—or would last indefinitely—pickles, mustard, canned soda. If no one showed up, she would eat salad every day for lunch and dinner until the pounds of lettuce, tomatoes and onions were gone, and then she and Jethro would eat burgers and hot dogs for the next year or so until all the meat was gone, too. She wouldn't be out anything but the ice.

She had set up a folding table on the side porch, with the charcoal grill she'd bought and assembled yesterday at the bottom of the steps. Bags of potato chips, jars of condiments and foil pans filled with brownies covered most of the table. An ice chest held cold soda, and the hamburger patties were chilling in the kitchen, along with the vegetables. She was laying out paper plates and napkins when her first guest arrived.

The young woman didn't look familiar, which meant nothing down here. There were plenty of people in the neighborhood she'd never seen or had caught only glimpses of when they'd refused to fully open their doors to her or when they scurried out on their way to work in the morning. This woman, though, didn't look like a Serenity resident. Her clothes were different. Her manner was different. She had a level of elegance that no one on the street could come close to matching, including Karen herself. She was even more of an outsider, if that was possible, than Karen.

"Can I help you?"

"I'm looking for Karen Montez."

"That's me."

The woman's gaze shifted to the party preparations. "You're expecting guests. I'm sorry. I didn't meant to interrupt—"

"You're not interrupting anything. I'm trying to host the first monthly Serenity Street cookout, but I've been warned repeatedly that no one will come. What can I do for you?"

"I'm Cassie Wade."

Karen looked blankly at her for a moment, then the name clicked. "Jolie's sister, the youngest Wade. How nice to meet you." She offered her hand, and Cassie took it in a firm shake. "I take it your sister has no idea that you're down here this evening."

Cassie's smile was dry. "She would have used her connections to have me arrested if she'd known. I would appreciate it if you don't tell her about my visit. I'm not asking you to lie," she said hastily. "Just don't volunteer the information." She glanced around, first at the house and the shabby yard, then at the street. When she turned back to Karen, her expression was calm, steady and, deep in those brown eyes, just a teensy bit intrigued. "Jolie told me about your project down here. We may have moved from Serenity when I was a child, but the entire family still finds interest in it—from a safe distance, of course. I understand you'll be relying on volunteers, and I would like to offer my services. I have a degree in English but no particular skills for this type of work. However, I can answer the phone and take messages. I have my own car, so I could play chauffeur. I can entertain the children. I work eight to five, but my evenings and weekends are usually free, so I would be available then."

That was a shame, Karen thought. Cassie Wade was entirely too pretty to be sitting home alone nights. The men of New Orleans were definitely losing out. "I would be happy to accept whatever help is offered," she said, "but nighttime isn't exactly the best time to be on Serenity, especially for a young woman alone."

"What neighborhood *is* safe at night for a woman alone?" Cassie asked with a shrug. "I know Serenity. I've heard the stories. My brothers and sisters have all lost friends here. They've all sworn never to come back here."

"Why are you willing to?"

Another shrug as the woman turned to look across the yard to the street. "I have a good job. I make decent money—good money, in fact," she said with a wry smile, "since I live in Smith's condo and don't pay rent. I have friends with good jobs. We take vacations together—we went to London after Christmas, to Paris last summer. I live a very comfortable life...and I feel as if something's missing. I'm doing a lot of receiving and very little giving, and I believe it's time to change that.''

"You could do volunteer work in other places that aren't so dangerous.''

The smile turned cool, dismissive. "The level of need isn't the same in other places that aren't so dangerous.''

Karen studied her for a moment. For the sake of her friendship with Jolie, she felt that she should seriously try to dissuade the younger Wade, but Cassie was an adult—with a brilliant mind, if Karen recalled Jolie's proud boasting correctly—and she certainly seemed to have given her decision some thought. She wasn't acting on impulse. She wasn't walking into a situation blind. She was aware of Serenity's problems and wanted to be part of the solutions. Karen wasn't going to insult her by treating her as if she were ill-informed, naive or foolish. She had gotten enough of that herself.

As movement across the street—Shawntae and her mother, holding tightly to J.T. between them—caught her eye, she smiled and extended her hand once more. "Welcome to Serenity Street and Kathy's House. Your first official duty will be attending the cookout this evening. Even if only three people come, we'll consider it a success and try harder next time.''

The Williamses joined them a moment later. Karen introduced everyone, then went inside to bring out the chairs from the dining room. When she came back out, Alicia had joined the group, along with a quiet, white-haired woman named Rosa. While they waited for the coals to burn down, they chatted, just like guests at any number of cookouts in the city this evening, but there was an uneasy air, as if everyone was ready to bolt on a moment's notice. J.T.'s play with Jethro was confined to the back third of the yard, away from the fence and the street, and the women sat facing the street, ever vigilant.

Six-fifteen came and went. By six-thirty, the coals were ready. While Cassie brought out everything else, Karen got the burgers and hot dogs for J.T. on the grill. The meat was almost done when her next guests arrived: Jamey and eight customers from the bar, each carrying a chair. As the men settled in the yard, Jamey joined Karen at the grill.

"I didn't expect to see you." Though it was true, she would have been disappointed if he hadn't come. More than anyone else on the street, she had wanted him to have enough faith in her to show up.

"I didn't intend to come," he admitted. "But I figured everyone can use a free meal from time to time."

Especially since he knew some of his regulars might be hungry, knew that, even so, they never would have come on their own. "Thanks for bringing them." She accepted a platter of hamburger patties from Cassie, then motioned to the younger woman to wait. "Jamey, this is Cassie, one of our volunteers. Cassie, this is Jamey O'Shea, who owns the bar across the street, looks out for the people of Serenity and has little faith in our ability to accomplish anything here."

Cassie acknowledged him with a polite nod before disappearing inside again. Maybe she was shy, but more likely she hadn't counted on meeting so soon anyone with a tie to her family. Remembering how quickly Jamey had called Jolie on *her,* Karen thought retreat was probably the wisest move Cassie could have made.

"Another do-gooder, huh?" Jamey was looking after her, but all he could see was the screen door and a few feet of hallway. "I have a suggestion. Once Morgan's gang gathers in the park tonight, just send *her* down there for a stroll. She could lead them all away, like the Pied Piper— preferably to the river, where they could fall in and drown."

"She *is* pretty, isn't she?"

"Too pretty to be down here. Too smart, too young, too delicate." He grimaced. "I forget. Am I talking about her or you?"

Karen blamed the grill for the heat that moved through her face. Pretty, smart, young, delicate. She would settle for any one of the four adjectives to describe herself. To be favored with all four of them was enough to go to a woman's head. Before she could bask too long in the glow, though, he turned serious again.

"She doesn't need to be down here, Karen."

"No one *needs* to be here, Jamey. Come on, don't start, please. This is a party. People took a chance to come here and enjoy themselves. Let's not spoil it with your argument that never ends."

He hesitated, then shrugged. "All right. Now you can say 'I told you so.'"

She raised one brow.

"About people coming. I honestly didn't think anyone would show."

She mimicked his shrug. "That's because you don't have faith. *I* do."

"Too often faith isn't justified. Look at Reid. Look at that black wall in the park. Look at the bags of trash you picked up there this morning and imagine the bags you'll pick up tomorrow morning. Look at all the people you invited to this, all the dozens who didn't come."

"But look at the ones who *did* come," she pointed out before taking exception to an earlier comment. "As for Reid, he hasn't let us down. He said he would think about it, and that's what he's doing. Eventually he'll come to the right decision, and we'll have our mural."

"And in the meantime he's staying out all night with the Morgans. He's drinking too much and spending too much time with Tanya Stanford."

"Some people won't change willingly. They wait until

their conscience drags them, kicking and screaming. Maybe Reid's rebelling against change. Maybe he's trying to convince himself that he *is* as worthless as people say. When he accepts that he's not, he'll come around.'' She transferred a couple of burgers to a platter, then offered him a smile. "Grab a plate. Have some dinner. Mingle."

The look he gave her was dry and just the slightest bit mocking. "I don't 'mingle', sweetheart. But I will take you up on the food. It smells good."

She was counting on that, hoping that the aroma would entice a few neighbors into joining them. If the people in the apartment house next door smelled the food and saw that her guests were eating, talking and having a good time without any problems from outside, maybe they would come over, and maybe they would bring their neighbors here with them. The bigger the crowd, the safer they were. Bullies like Ryan Morgan liked the odds in their favor. They liked to boast and threaten, but they wouldn't try to carry out those threats when they were outnumbered.

At least she hoped so.

Over the next half hour, they did get a few more guests— a mother dragged along unwillingly by her two eager sons and the elderly woman who lived next door to them. The final tally, including Cassie and Karen, came to twenty. Karen had bought enough food to feed fifty or more, but she was happy with twenty. Heavens, she was downright ecstatic.

The only tense moment of the evening came from the street, predictably from Ryan. He directed his brother to stop the beat-up car right outside the fence, and they all climbed out. It was the first good look Karen had gotten at Trevor Morgan. He wasn't as handsome as his brother or as tall. Five eight, maybe five nine, wearing dark glasses and mimicking Ryan's macho posturing, he looked like exactly what he was: a kid brother, with the emphasis on the kid part. He was maybe eighteen, and, according to Jamey, he liked to use knives.

Not much of a *kid*.

Jamey approached the fence. Karen followed, stopping a safe distance back, and Cassie came to a stop beside her. "What do you want, Morgan?" Jamey asked.

"You're having a party, huh? And you didn't invite us. My feelings are hurt." Ryan laughed, then, in a heartbeat, turned deadly serious. "Alicia, it's time to go."

Karen glanced at the young woman, sitting in the rocker Cassie had brought around for her, her head ducked, her hands folded tightly together over her belly. "Maybe she's not ready to go," she said, looking back at Ryan. "Maybe she would rather stay here."

Morgan fixed a malevolent stare on her. "Maybe I'll make her ready. And maybe while I'm at it, I'll make you damned sorry."

Though the muscles in her legs were unsteady, the ones in her stomach taut, she didn't move. She didn't take a few steps closer to the safety of Jamey. She wasn't going to hide from this punk, and she certainly wasn't going to hide behind Jamey. Instead, she stood her ground, her gaze unflinching.

His anger inflamed by her refusal to shrink back, Morgan slammed the door and started around the back of the car. He was bluffing, she thought—she hoped. He wouldn't come onto her property and try to take his pregnant girlfriend by force. He surely wouldn't try to do anything to *her*, not with Jamey and everyone else here. But a quick glance behind her showed that everyone else was wishing they were anywhere else. They looked so withdrawn, so apprehensive and timid. Only Jamey, Cassie and Karen were even looking at the four young men. The others were staring docilely at the ground, praying to go unnoticed.

Reid caught Morgan's arm. "Let it go, Ryan," he advised, his expression dark with wrath that Karen had little doubt was directed toward her. "Alicia's coming. Don't start trouble here."

"I haven't started anything. The red-haired bitch did. But I'll finish it." He addressed his next words, along with a steely gaze, to Karen. "You'd better take O'Shea's advice and get out of here. You won't get many more chances to walk out alive."

Ignoring the shiver that raised goose bumps on her arms, Karen moved forward. "Is this how you got your reputation, Ryan? Intimidating weaker, smaller women? Do you pick on us because you're afraid to face someone more your equal?"

"Shut up, Karen," Jamey ordered, his voice too low for anyone else to hear, his tone too taut with anger for her to ignore—but ignore it she did.

"I plan to make these parties a regular thing," she announced. "Everyone in the neighborhood is invited. There are a few rules, though: no booze, no drugs, no weapons, no trouble, no bullies." Sarcasm crept into her voice. "Gee, I guess that leaves you out, doesn't it?"

Ryan tried to jerk away, but Reid held him tighter, forcibly restraining him until Alicia hurried out to the car and coaxed him back into the front seat. Karen turned back to find Cassie's gaze fixed on the car. It was good that the young woman had seen this tonight, she thought regretfully. An in-person dose of Ryan Morgan was worth more than all the words in the world. If anything would scare the girl off, it was him.

But she didn't look scared. She seemed to be simply observing an interesting scene...and if Karen wasn't mistaken, the part of the scene she found most interesting was Reid. Opposites attract, the saying claimed, and she couldn't think of many people more completely opposite Cassie Wade than Reid. She was so elegant, so coolly composed, and he... She felt a moment's guilt for the incompleted thought. So he wasn't polished, well educated or respected. He had the potential to be a good, decent, honorable man. What more could a woman want?

As the Impala drove away, she turned her attention to her remaining guests. They were rising from their chairs, preparing to leave. The party mood was broken, and all the cajoling and pleading in the world couldn't restore it. Morgan's little scene had reminded them of the danger that had temporarily moved from center stage in their lives. They wanted to go home, lock themselves in and restore their false sense of security, and she could do nothing but let them.

"Shawntae, will I see you at the park tomorrow?"

J.T.'s mother sighed heavily without answering. With a little more regret, Karen laid her hand on her arm. "It's okay. I understand."

"No." Shawntae shook her head as if confused by her own feelings. "I'll be there. I never did like Ryan Morgan. He was a punk in school, and he's still a punk. I would like to help someone put him in his place."

"Thank you. And thanks for coming tonight."

She said goodbye to every guest but Jamey. When there was no further excuse for avoiding him, she looked, but he had already returned to the bar. The doors were open, the lights on, and his customers were inside drinking. She was relieved to have escaped his anger, but none too thrilled at the prospect of facing it later, especially knowing that, to some extent, she deserved it. Her behavior could have caused serious problems here tonight. But not saying anything, backing down and silently watching while he claimed his property and intimidated everyone else would have caused even more serious problems in the future. She didn't regret anything she'd said.

Alone with Cassie and a table full of food, she offered the young woman a tight smile and repeated her earlier words. "Welcome to Serenity Street." Then, as an afterthought... "Are you sure you want to be here?"

* * *

When the last of his customers wandered out a few minutes before midnight, Jamey closed the bar. He didn't bother putting the chairs on the table to make Monday morning's sweeping easier, didn't give a thought to washing the glasses and returning them to their place behind the bar. He shut off the lights, locked up and went straight across the street to Karen's. The mutt was asleep in front of the screen door, as if, while waiting to go inside, he'd gotten too tired to keep his eyes open. Karen was sitting motionless in the rocker, her feet drawn up on the seat, her hands clasped around her ankles.

He stood in front of her, leaning against the rail, folding his arms over his chest. For a moment they simply looked at each other; then she sighed. "I know. You think I'm an idiot who doesn't have the sense to avoid a confrontation with Morgan. You think it's guaranteed that he'll start harassing me now, that he'll try to make my life down here impossible."

"If Reid hadn't stopped him—"

"But he did."

Jamey muttered a curse. "If you're not concerned with your own safety, then think about Reid's. Think about mine. You keep pushing Morgan like that, you're going to get one of us killed."

Guilt flashed across her face before giving way to that damnable stubbornness. "Ryan Morgan is a coward. He isn't going to come after me unless he's reasonably sure of success. That means catching me alone, when you're not around, when Reid's not around. He wasn't going to try anything this evening, not with all those people there. He'll look for me when I'm by myself, which means neither you nor Reid will be in danger."

"You're by yourself most of the time! For God's sake, Karen..." He looked away, dragging his fingers through his hair, making an effort to control his frustrated anger.

"You're right. He's not going to do anything when you're with me, but I can't spend twenty-four hours a day with you. Neither can Reid."

She sighed again. "What am I supposed to do, Jamey? Hide inside this house? Never venture out unless I know he's out of the neighborhood? Let this punk control my life? Exactly what is it you want me to do?"

"Leave." He offered the solution with more reluctance but no less conviction than the other dozen times he'd suggested it. He would be sorry to see her go. He would miss her presence, her arguments, her relentlessly optimistic nature. He would regret what Serenity would lose in her going—what he would lose—but he still wanted her to go.

"That's not an option."

"That's the only option. You heard what Morgan said. He's not going to give you many more chances."

"Morgan can go to hell!" she said hotly, rising from her chair, taking the few steps necessary to confront him, to get right in his face. "I have a right to be here! These people need *me* a hell of a lot more than they need *him*. If he doesn't like it, that's too damned bad, and if you don't like it—"

Reaching up, Jamey touched her face. It was nothing much, just his palm to her cheek, but it was enough to make her words dry up in midsentence. Enough to make her go suddenly still. Enough to send a shot of heat along his skin. More than enough to make a sweet breath hard to come by.

They stood that way a long time, staring at each other, barely touching, touching too much. After a moment, she drew a breath that made her shudder, but she didn't retreat, didn't back down. She knew he was going to kiss her, as surely as he knew she was going to let him.

As surely as he knew it would be a mistake.

As surely as he knew he would never be able to walk away from it.

He raised his other hand, cupping her cheeks in his palms. Even in the shadows, her skin was pale against his. Even with the care he took, she felt fragile underneath his hands, as if he could crush her with no effort. But the fragility was an illusion. She was a strong woman, a strong, courageous, beautiful and hopelessly foolish woman. He'd never suspected he might have a weakness for strong or foolish women, had never suspected a weakness for the two combined, but the proof was in front of him, inside him, all around him.

Heat and humidity flushed her face, but it wasn't responsible for her dazed expression, for her labored breathing or the moistness of her lips, slightly parted. He brushed his thumb across them, and her eyes closed, then opened again, in the laziest, sexiest flutter he'd ever seen. She looked exactly the way he felt: wary of what was about to happen but helpless to stop it. Utterly helpless.

He slid his fingers into her hair and swore for an instant that it did burn, just as he had once suspected it might. Then he touched his mouth to hers, and he stopped thinking, swearing, suspecting. He damn near stopped breathing. His kiss was demanding, hers accepting. There was nothing tentative, no hint that this was a first kiss between two people who hardly knew each other, who were on their way to knowing each other too well. He didn't dance around it—didn't brush his mouth across hers, didn't start out gently, hesitantly, giving her every chance in the world to stop him, didn't give her a sweet kiss that eventually grew more insistent. He simply claimed her mouth and thrust his tongue inside, as if he had kissed her a thousand times before, and she welcomed him, as if she had a thousand times before.

His arousal sizzled to life, a little heat that, in the space of a moment, flared out of control. His body was hard, his skin damp, his chest tight, all with no more contact than his mouth against hers, his hands buried in her hair. If he touched her, really touched her—wrapped his arms around her and held her tight enough to feel her breasts against his chest and her hips pressed hard against his, if he held her close enough to feel her heat, her need... God help him, he might not survive.

She groaned, and he realized that her hands were on him, catching his T-shirt in tight little fists, tugging it from his jeans with a slowness that made his muscles tremble. He felt an instant of cooling when the hem slid free, exposing his middle to the night air, then searing heat as she slid her hands underneath the fabric and across his stomach. Her kiss became far more than merely accepting, merely welcoming. There was a greediness to it, a demand as relentless as his own. She was as aroused as he was, as needy as he was, and she was making him burn.

At first the sound down the street barely penetrated his dazed mind. In the next instant he was breaking away, then catching hold of her arm. "Get inside," he ordered, pushing her ahead of him to the door. Protesting, she stopped long enough to scoop up the puppy, then went in. He followed, closing the screen door silently behind him. "Take the mutt to the kitchen and stay there."

"But—"

"*Go.*" He watched until her shadow blended with other shadows in the darkened hall, then turned his attention back to the street, staying out of sight, watching covertly through the screen door. The sound that had distracted him had been a badly tuned engine and the relentless thud-thud-thud of a stereo powerful enough to vibrate the entire body of a rusted-out old wreck like the Impala. They were coming from Decatur, headlights off, going slower the closer they came to the house. They came to a full stop out front, the engine settling into a rough idle, the music reverberating through the walls of the house.

The doors opened, and the occupants spilled out. Alicia, wearing a white dress that gave her an ethereal look, whirled around, pointedly ignoring Morgan, and started for home a half block away. The younger Morgan, Marino and one of the Rodriguez boys waited at the rear of the car while Ryan opened the trunk. On the other side, Reid stood watching, a dozen feet between him and his buddies, his hands in his hip pockets and that business-as-usual scowl of his firmly in place. At least it didn't seem he would be taking part in their devilry...but he wasn't doing anything to stop them, either.

"What's going on?"

Startled, Jamey spun around, then sank back against the wall. "Jeez, Karen, I said stay in the kitchen!" he whispered, pulling her to the side, away from the door.

"I left Jethro in there. He'll be fine." She turned and twisted, trying to see what was happening outside. "What is it?"

"I'm not worried about your damned dog. Even Morgan doesn't mess with strays." Although Vinnie Marino would probably find almost as much pleasure in tormenting a puppy as he did a person. "You've got company, and they're not feeling too neighborly. Go back to the kitchen, stay quiet and keep the dog quiet."

She'd gone about a foot when the sound of shattering glass sounded off to the right, followed by a thud on the wood floor. In the thin light from the streetlamps Jamey could see a brick in the middle of the parlor floor. Then came Morgan's voice. "Hey, Karen. You in there?"

Jamey pulled her back, holding her tight against him with one arm around her waist and one hand over her mouth. She had confronted Morgan out in the yard this evening. Damned if he would let her try again.

"Come on out, Karen. We know you're there. We want to party. We want to welcome you to the neighborhood."

There were more crashes on both sides of the hallway, more bricks hitting the floor, followed by the clang of something hitting metal. Probably a baseball bat coming into contact with Karen's car. She should keep those damned gates closed and padlocked, Jamey thought grimly. A secure eight-foot-tall fence wouldn't stop the little bastards, but at least it would make things harder for them. On the other hand, though, as long as they could destroy her property without any trouble, maybe they wouldn't be tempted to come after *her*.

She was trembling in his arms—from helpless anger, he suspected, rather than fear. Less than three weeks ago she had replaced all the broken windows, and they'd just destroyed at least four of them. More work, more money, and they would just come back whenever the mood struck and break them again.

After another moment the sounds of mischief faded away, along with the pounding of the music. Unnatural stillness filled the air, broken after a time by Morgan's voice. There was no false friendliness or good humor this time. Just malice. Pure, icy hatred. "Listen up, bitch. You stay away from my woman, and you stay out of my business. We don't want you down here. We won't let you stay down here. You can leave on your own, or you can be carried out. It's your choice."

The slamming of car doors echoed in the night. Counting only two, Jamey pushed Karen behind him and shifted just enough to see out. The right passenger doors were still open, and Ryan stood on the sidewalk, talking to Reid. Their words weren't audible, but it wasn't a friendly conversation, judging by the shove Ryan gave him before climbing into the front seat and jerking the door shut. The force knocked Reid back against the brick wall of the bar; then he straightened, gave a disgusted shake of his head and walked away.

After the car drove away, long after silence returned to the street, Jamey exhaled deeply, then left his cover to examine the damage. Every window in the two front rooms was broken. There was spray paint on the fence, the garbage from tonight's cookout was dumped on the driveway, and the car was in need of a new trunk, fender and four tires. He straightened from examining the knife slashes in the right rear tire to see Karen standing silently on the porch. Even in the shadows, her face was a shade paler than normal. She looked stunned, shaken.

He climbed the steps and stopped in front of her. "Get whatever you need for the night. You're coming over to my place."

She shook her head numbly. "I won't let them chase me out of my house."

"You can't stay here with all these windows broken. The place is even less secure than usual."

"And I can't leave it unsecured. Some other little punks will come in and take whatever I have."

"Damn it, Karen—"

"If you want to spend the night over here, that's fine. But I won't leave. I can't."

He stared at her. Hadn't spending the night been exactly what was on his mind before those bastards showed up? But this would hardly be what he'd wanted. The mood had been shattered, and he wasn't sure he could get it back tonight. She was looking terribly fragile, and he was feeling that way. "All right. Let's get inside and see what we can find to fix the windows for tonight." She had plenty of supplies around. Maybe there was some plywood or something else suitable until morning.

"I'm going to call the police."

"They won't come," he warned.

"I'm going to call anyway, and if they don't come, tomorrow I'm going down to talk to Evan's old commander to find out why. I'm going to file charges against them. I'm going to demand that the police arrest them."

Jamey shook his head. "Darlin', you didn't see them." He had kept her away from the door for her own safety— not just at the moment that the bricks were flying, but later, too. If pressed, she couldn't swear under oath who had thrown the bricks, bashed in her car or slashed her tires. All she could say was that Ryan Morgan had been with the vandals, that even though she didn't see him, she thought she recognized his voice.

"But you did. You can tell them..." Her voice trailed off, then that stunned look came back. "*Will* you tell them?"

People didn't speak out against Morgan and his gang, he'd told her before. It wasn't the best way to stay healthy. He didn't want to identify them to the cops. He sure as hell didn't want to testify against them in court. That was more deeply involved than he cared to be.

It was also more cowardly than he cared to be.

She was waiting for an answer, and instinct told him that whatever he said just might determine the future of their relationship. If he agreed, Morgan's enmity would extend to him and, quite possibly, to his customers, who were poorly equipped to defend themselves against anything. But if he refused, the police would do nothing. The punks would get away with it, and they would come back again whenever they needed something to do. If he refused, the next time they might not be satisfied with breaking windows or damaging her car. The next time instead of bricks they might use bullets. Instead of slashing tires they might slash *her.*

If he refused, he would be little better than they were.

Muttering a curse, he shook his head in dismay and said, "Yes, I'll tell them. It'll probably cost me a dozen or so sets of doors, but I'll tell them. Satisfied?"

For the first time in what seemed like forever, she smiled, just a faint curve of her mouth. "It takes more than that to satisfy me," she said in a soft voice, "but it's a start."

While Jamey patched the windows with the two-by-sixes she'd bought for shelving, Karen called the police. The dispatcher took the information, said an officer would be by and hung up. She didn't really expect a patrol car to pull up in front of her house any time in the near future, but she was awake—*wide* awake. She would wait and see.

After sweeping up the glass in the parlors, she wandered out onto the porch where Jamey was hammering the last board in place. For all her brave talk, she was glad he'd been here tonight. She probably would have been foolish enough to stay outside when she'd recognized Morgan's car, and if they had seen her, they might have done a lot more than smash a little glass. Ryan might have made good on his threat to make her sorry. He might even have left her dead.

Instead, because Jamey had been there, because she'd known he would keep her safe, she hadn't felt more than a shiver of fear—and a wealth of anger. Those punks thought they could chase her away with a middle-of-the-night visit? Think again. She wasn't going *anywhere.*

He sank the last nail, then turned to face her. His gaze went past her, though, to the steps by the driveway, and his expression hardened. She turned to see Reid standing at the bottom of the steps. He looked as hostile as Jamey, as if he would rather be anywhere else than here. But he was here. He'd come because he had to, because he couldn't *not* be here.

"Are you okay?" he asked grudgingly.

She nodded, but Jamey chose to answer, too. "Hell, yeah, we're fine. Everything's fine...no thanks to you." His words answered a question Karen hadn't asked. She hadn't wanted to know whether Reid had been out there on the street with the others. She hadn't wanted to know that he might have taken part in this.

Reid's frown tightened. "I don't put my neck on the line for anyone," he said harshly. "She brought this on herself. Any idiot would have expected this after what she did at the damned party."

"Did you have fun standing back watching?" Jamey demanded.

"I tried to talk him out of it—"

"Yeah, I could see you were trying real hard."

His movements jerky from the tension that held him rigid, Reid made an angry, frustrated gesture. "I don't need this," he muttered, his expression so bitterly hopeless that it threatened to break Karen's heart. "I don't give a damn what you think or what you believe. I don't give a damn about you at all."

When he turned to leave, she started toward him. "Reid, wait a minute, please."

He stopped and turned, but not to listen to her. "Why don't you take everyone's advice and get the hell out? No one wants you here except him, and he's just looking to get into your bed, and then he won't care, either. Go away before Ryan or Vinnie or Mr. Falcone *makes* you go away."

"Reid…" She sighed as he stalked off, his back straight, his animosity a protective shield about him. With a wistful sigh, she turned back to Jamey.

"He's right."

"About what?"

"You should leave. They will try to make you leave." His grin came slowly and was charmingly, disarmingly crooked. "And I am looking to get into your bed."

She looked at him for a long time before managing a faint smile of her own. "I kind of guessed that from that kiss." All that heat, all that hunger…and so much of it her own. Just a few weeks ago she had insisted that she wanted nothing from Jamey but friendship, that she didn't care if she remained celibate and alone the rest of her life. Tonight she had only one thing to say to that.

Ha.

Obviously she had been in some sort of denial. She had forgotten how incredibly steamy a kiss could be. She had completely forgotten the sweet aches of arousal and the sweeter promise of satisfaction. In the years since Evan's death, she had lost touch with the purely feminine, sexual side of herself, had convinced herself that it had been buried right alongside him. After all, hadn't he been the great love of her life? The only lover in her entire life? The other half that had made her whole? How could she possibly be with another man the way she had been with him? How could she ever want another man the way she had wanted him?

Damned if she knew, but she wanted Jamey.

She wanted to feel alive. She wanted to feel powerful. Desirable. Special. She wanted to be a part of him, one with him. She wanted. Needed. Craved.

She gestured toward the lone board that remained leaning against the wall. ''Are you finished?''

He nodded.

''Then let's go inside.''

He followed her in, hooking the screen door when it closed, locking the dead bolt when he closed the wood door. The first floor was brightly lit, with lights reflecting off the piles of glass in both parlors, illuminating the hall and all the way back to the kitchen. While Jamey waited at the foot of the stairs, she shut them off one at a time, then circled around him and led the way upstairs.

It was hotter up there—one reason why she spent part of her nights outside. Though she hadn't admitted it to herself, she suspected the man behind her was another. She was always looking for a glimpse of him, like a schoolgirl with a crush. But tonight she didn't feel like a schoolgirl. After that kiss—that one single, breath-stealing, exquisite kiss—she felt like a woman, with a woman's fantasies, a woman's needs and, in Jamey, a woman's dream.

She wasted no time on coy behavior but turned down the hall and straight into her bedroom. A single lamp was burning on the night table—pale pink frosted glass, with glass bead trim around the edge of the round globe. Offering very little softly diffused light, it served as her nightlight, so that she never awakened unexpectedly to a dark room. It was perfect for what they were about to do.

She stopped in front of the dresser and removed her jewelry—simple earrings, an inexpensive silver ring and her watch—while watching Jamey in the mirror. He glanced around the room at the open windows and the sheer pink curtains that fluttered every time the fan turned their way, at the pale pink coverlet and the lace-edged pillows, at the deep rose-hued walls, the lace doilies and the ruffled slipcovers on the overstuffed easy chair. It was all so utterly feminine, but he wasn't uncomfortable. He didn't look out of place.

He approached her, not stopping until he was close behind her. When she started to turn, he held her in place with his hands on her shoulders. When she started to protest, he lifted her hair and silenced her with a kiss just below her ear. She gave a little sigh, or meant to. The sound somehow got lost inside her, trapped by all the feelings his simplest touch aroused.

She tilted her head to one side, giving him better access to her neck, and let her eyes close. There was so much heat in the room, nearly unbearable, heavy in the night air, radiating from Jamey's body, from her own. Her skin was damp, her blood hot. Every brief, shallow breath scorched, and every place his mouth touched seemed to steam.

When he ended the kisses, it took a moment to gather the strength to open her eyes. He was gazing at her in the mirror, just looking. The intensity of his gaze sent a shiver through her and stirred a longing as potent as any she'd ever felt. It was sharp-edged and raw, starting deep in her belly and spreading its unsettled, restless energy through her entire body. She took a step back, closing the distance between them, pressing against his chest, his hips, his thighs.

Murmuring her name, he touched her then, not just his hands resting on her shoulders but undeniably sexual, sensual touches, down her arms, across her stomach, to her breasts. His hands were big, his fingers long and oddly graceful, a creamy deep gold against the pale blue of her shirt. They curved over her breasts in a gentle caress before sliding to the buttons, unfastening each one, pushing the fabric away to cup her bare breasts. Such contrasts, she marveled. He was dark. She was pale. His palms were rough. Her skin was sensitive. His caresses were soft, making her nipples hard.

He pulled her shirt away, turned her to face him and bent to kiss her, taking her mouth, thrusting his tongue deep inside. His hunger fed her own, making her press closer, wriggling and writhing as if she could become a very part of him. She tugged at his clothing, pulling his shirt halfway up his chest, unbuttoning his jeans, sliding the zipper down, sliding her palm inside.

Muttering a curse, Jamey withdrew her hand, slid her arms around him and positioned her hands in a clasp at the small of his back, then held her tightly, resting his cheek against her hair. "Not too fast," he whispered, his voice thick and husky. "We have all night."

Rubbing her entire body against his, she insisted, "Fast this time. We have all night for slow."

He wrapped his hands in her hair and used the hold to tug her head back so that she was gazing up at him. His face was damp, his skin glowing a warm, rosy gold where the lamplight touched it. "You feel so fragile."

"I'm not going to break."

His smile was slow and sexy. "I know. I've never known anyone so strong...." Releasing her hair, he slid his hands down to her bottom, lifting her hard against his hips, against his arousal, and kissed her once more, hotter, hungrier, more demanding than ever. They covered the distance to the bed, removed their clothing, shoved aside pillows and sank down onto the mattress, coming together quickly. He moved between her legs, seeking, finding, sliding deep inside, filling her, and he took her the way she wanted, fast, needy, damn near desperate, bringing her to completion with a helpless cry, making every muscle in her body go rigid, making her entire body tremble as release washed over her. Only a heartbeat later, he came, too, emptying inside her, sending new little tremors through her.

Just as she'd wanted, he didn't stop. He continued to kiss her, caress her, move inside her. Only the wildest, neediest edge of their arousal had been sated. Now they could take it slower. Now she could stroke him, and she did, gliding her hands over his slick skin, exploring taut muscles, feeling quivering nerves, learning new lessons. Though he was lean and powerful, he was as sensitive to gentle caresses as she was. The brush of her fingers over his nipples made him shudder. The rough scrape of her tongue made him swear, and the tender nip of her teeth turned curses into tortured groans. There was a place on his belly where her lightest touch set his skin rippling, and when she glided her hand between their bodies to where they were joined and lower in an intimate caress, he lost his tightly held control. His thrusts came harder, faster, driving her, driving him, beyond thought, beyond reason to pure sensation, pure sweet pain and finally pure sweet pleasure. Pure, sweet satisfaction.

Oh, yes, she thought as her heart finally slowed its thudding, as her lungs admitted a breath or two of air, as her muscles settled into a lazy quaveriness. The purest, sweetest satisfaction.

Chapter 7

Jamey lay on his back, catching his breath. With Karen beside him, her head on his shoulder, her hand on his stomach, he watched the ceiling fan overhead as it and the oscillating fan across the room did their best to cool the air. Maybe if it were just August heat and humidity, the fans could do a decent job, but the heat in this room had been generated by something far more potent than a Louisiana summer night, something so potent that he didn't care to examine it too closely. Calling on the first distraction that presented itself, he broke the quiet to bluntly—and belatedly—ask, "Should I have used a condom?"

The instant the words were out, the instant he felt the tension that streaked through her, he wished he could call them back, wished he could rephrase the question so that his meaning was clear. She had told him several times that she was infertile, and he knew without being told what a sorrow that was. He wasn't insensitive enough to remind her of it now, not deliberately.

But before he could say anything else, she blew out her

breath in a deep exhalation, then laughed unsteadily. "You're a little late in asking, aren't you? Is this how Reid came to be? You waited until it was over to suggest some form of birth control?"

"There are other reasons for using condoms," he said with a scowl before giving her hair a playful tug. "For your information, darlin', we *were* using birth control. Meghan was on the pill, and I always used condoms. Reid came to be anyway."

"Double protection," she teased. "Were you just cautious, or didn't you trust her?"

He took a moment to consider it. He wished he could choose only one answer—caution—but it wouldn't be true. He had known Meghan all his life, had dated her, seduced her, married her and had a child with her, but he had never fully trusted her. He had never fully trusted anyone. Life on Serenity Street wasn't conducive to building trust, to having faith or believing in others...but Karen was determined to change that. For the first time he was beginning to think that she might succeed—at least, with him. "A little of both, I guess."

She sobered and scooted back just enough to allow a breath of air between them and so she could see him better. "You know, that means Reid was *meant* to be here. Only you and Meghan could have created that particular child, and since you weren't cooperating, fate took over."

"Meant to be here," he repeated, his tone more than a little scornful. "For what? To become what he is?"

Raising herself on one arm, she fixed her most serious, social-worker gaze on him. "What he is, Jamey, is a young man who has never had anyone to love him, to teach him right from wrong, to encourage, support and protect him. Did you see the way he looked at you tonight when you blamed him for not stopping Ryan? He wants your approval. He wants you to look at him the way a father looks at a son, not with loathing and derision, not with regret for

his very existence. He wants you to give him the benefit
of the doubt once in a while, to not automatically assume
the worst. I have no doubt that he did try to talk Ryan out
of coming here tonight, but you just assumed that he was
lying about it.''

He felt uncomfortably guilty—because she was right,
damn it—but stubbornly he clung to his hostility. ''I *saw*
him standing there watching, doing nothing.''

''Come on, Jamey,'' she chided gently. ''You know
those guys. You know the mood they were in. If Reid had
tried out there on the street to stop them, what would they
have done?''

Unwillingly he recalled that moment before the bastards
had left, when Ryan had confronted Reid on the sidewalk,
when he had shoved him against the wall, no doubt for his
refusal to participate. If he had not only refused but had
tried to stop them... He scowled hard at her, hating the
answer he was about to give because it made him look—
and feel—so damned detestable. ''They would have turned
on him.''

''He talked to them before they came, he stood back and
didn't take part, and after they left, he came back to make
sure everything was all right. He did all he could, Jamey.''
She settled in beside him again. ''Reid's in a tough place
right now. I don't believe he's like Ryan Morgan and the
others, and I don't think he wants to be like them, but
they're all he's got. He can't get away from them until he
finds someone to take their place in his life, but he can't
find someone to do that—to accept him, to support him and
be a friend to him—until he gets away from them. He's
facing some really difficult choices, some crucial choices.
It would probably make a world of difference to him to
know that his father would be there to help him with the
right one.''

He wished he could believe that she was right. If she
could prove to him that Reid wasn't like the others, that he

was worth saving, if she could show that he was open to some sort of father-son relationship... But she couldn't provide proof. All she had were her instincts, and they were too optimistic by a mile—didn't her very presence on Serenity prove that? Her instincts hadn't lived with eleven years of Reid's contempt, his defiance and insolence. Her instincts didn't fully comprehend all the failures between them. "He's spent his entire life hating me," he said flatly. "That's not going to change."

"I don't believe he hates you."

He believed it. Their entire relationship consisted of nothing but antagonism, bitterness and resentment, suspicion, distrust and disdain. Meghan had fed Reid hatred for his father along with strained carrots and baby formula. She had taught him little beyond the fact that Jamey was responsible for the misery of their lives, that Jamey had never wanted him, that Jamey was happy to be rid of him.

To some extent she had taught him the truth. Jamey could have been a better husband. He *should* have been a better father. It was no wonder Reid had learned to hate him. It was no more than he deserved—no more, he'd thought for a long time, than he'd wanted. He had never wanted a son, had never wanted the obligations, the burdens, the responsibilities of another life. He'd been satisfied with the hostile non-relationship between them...until lately. Lately he worried. He wondered. He had doubts.

He had Karen to blame for that...or maybe to thank for it. He wasn't sure which.

After retrieving a pillow from the floor, he turned on his side to face her. She was a lovely woman, all pale skin and fiery red hair—and the color was her own, he now knew. The first time he'd seen her, he had been foolish enough to dismiss her as not his type, but at the moment he couldn't remember why. What was so great about legs a mile long, short dark hair and large breasts? Who wanted athletic and hard-muscled when he could have deceptively delicate?

Who needed other women when he could have *this* woman?

At least for a time. Until Serenity defeated her. Until the Morgans and the Marinos and the Falcones and the Donovans—and yes, the O'Sheas—succeeded in driving her away. Until she left for some other place that wasn't so hard on the spirit, that didn't take such a toll on the soul. Until she left him alone.

That just might be one more loss than his spirit and soul were willing to bear.

Raising one hand to his face, she brushed her fingers lightly across his jaw. "In answer to your earlier question, birth control isn't an issue for me, as you already know. As for those other reasons for using condoms, they're not an issue, either. My only other sexual relationship was monogamous. There was never anyone but Evan, and I believe he was faithful to me."

Of course he was, Jamey thought with more than a little jealousy. Evan had been perfect, and what kind of perfect hero husband would be unfaithful to his wife?

"All of my relationships have been monogamous," he said, keeping his voice carefully empty of envy. "I always took precautions, and there hasn't been anyone in a long time."

"Why?"

"I was waiting for you."

She smiled swiftly at his flippant answer, then repeated her question. "Seriously, why hasn't there been anyone?"

He slid his hand over her hip to her waist, then to her breast, watching as his fingertips closed around her nipple, watching as the soft rosy flesh immediately began to harden. "When you live on Serenity Street, you lose a lot of people. After a while, the losing can be worse than the having. It becomes easier to be alone."

"No," she softly disagreed. "I've been alone for six years, and there's nothing easy about it."

Which helped explain why she was here with him. He dealt with his losses by staying alone. She dealt with hers by settling for less.

He'd known all his life that in the ways that counted, he was less than men like Evan Montez, Smith Kendricks and virtually everyone else she knew, and it had never bothered him. He'd never had much ambition, had never cared much about respectability or money or success. He had never wanted things he couldn't have.

Until now.

Reaching behind him, he found the brass key that turned off the lamp, then pressed a kiss to her forehead. "It's late," he said quietly. "Get some sleep."

She pulled away long enough to find her own pillow, then kissed his cheek and snuggled in close. "Good night, Jamey."

Though she fell asleep almost immediately, he lay awake a long time, listening to her even breathing, to the settling of the old house and the street. There was no party in the park tonight. Maybe trashing Karen's place had fulfilled Morgan's need for destruction. Maybe, with his girlfriend angry with him and being angry himself with Reid, he hadn't been in the mood for the usual gathering. Maybe, if the world was lucky, God had struck him dead somewhere.

Restless and edgy, after a time he gently pulled away from Karen and left the bed. He tugged on his jeans, then wandered through the dark house to the living room across the hall, to the big bay window that overlooked the street. Music came from somewhere, not too loud, distant and lonely. The blues. Perfect for his mood.

He never should have made love with Karen, never should have kissed her, never should have befriended her. He never even should have looked at her long enough to decide whether he might lust after her. She didn't belong with him any more than she belonged on Serenity.

He had once boasted that he'd never had a regret he

couldn't live with, but that was no longer true. Reid was a major regret. Karen threatened to be the biggest regret of his life.

A glint of moonlight drew his attention to the opposite side of the street, to the old house that stood next to the bar. It had been empty for twenty years and was as ramshackle a structure as any he'd ever seen. Even the kids stayed away from it, well aware of the danger represented by its precarious state. With every storm that swept down Serenity, the residents expected to look out and find that the place had collapsed, but so far it had surprised everyone.

But it wasn't the house that interested him tonight. It was Reid, sitting on the steps, his head down, his shoulders bowed, as if his burdens were just too great to bear. Maybe he'd just needed a quiet place to think. Maybe after the scuffle with Morgan, he hadn't wanted to go home or felt he couldn't go home. Maybe he had no place else to go.

Reid had some crucial decisions to make, Karen had said, and she was probably right about that, but not the rest. Jamey couldn't help him make them. His only influence on Reid had always been negative. Hell, he didn't even know how to talk to the kid without making things worse. He didn't know how to treat him, how to react to him.

He didn't know how to get past his own guilt.

He stood there a long time before, eyes gritty, bone tired and soul weary, he returned to the bedroom. Being careful not to disturb Karen, he shucked his jeans, then slid into bed beside her, moving to lie close behind her. It shouldn't take him long to go to sleep this time, because he felt every single one of his years.

And then some.

In spite of the late night, Karen awoke at her usual early hour Sunday. For a time she indulged herself and simply lay there, watching Jamey in the thin morning light. He was sleeping soundly, though she had little doubt that any sound out of place would penetrate his slumber and bring him wide awake in a heartbeat. Living on Serenity did that to a person. But it was a quiet morning, and there were no sounds out of place, nothing to disturb his sleep or her pleasure in watching him.

In all the years since Evan's death, she had never contemplated an affair. After all, he had been her husband, her best friend and her one true love, and making love with any man who wasn't him would constitute a betrayal of that love...or so she had thought. But she'd been wrong. Making love with Jamey hadn't diminished her love for Evan in any way, just as all those years loving Evan didn't diminish what she felt for Jamey. She had no regrets, no guilt, no remorse—just an incredible feeling of being alive in a way she hadn't been in six years.

Reaching out, she touched his jaw, rough with morning stubble. Even in sleep, he looked like a man with problems. The incidents with Ryan Morgan last night had angered and, in some small way, frightened him. Reid troubled him deeply. Probably what they had done here in her bed, no matter how much he'd wanted it, had disturbed him as well. *After a while, the losing can be worse than the having,* he'd said. *It becomes easier to be alone.*

She understood his reasoning. Losing Evan, the children she had hoped would brighten their future, and her sister Kathy had been almost more than she could bear, but she still had the rest of her family and a bunch of very good friends. Jamey had lost his parents and too many of his friends. In a very real sense—even though he still fought for his little piece of it—he'd lost the neighborhood that was his home, that was a tremendous part of who and what he was. He had a bad marriage behind him, relationships that hadn't worked out and a son who probably did hate him almost as much as he wanted to love him. Now here he was with her, fully expecting her to give up, walk away from Serenity—away from him—and never look back.

But it wasn't going to happen.

At last, with a sigh, she got up, gathered work clothes from the dresser and went into the bathroom to prepare to face the day. If she'd had any idea last evening that she would wake up with six feet of gorgeous male sprawled across her bed, she would have told Shawntae to forget about working at the park this morning and she would pull the armchair closer and spend the next hour or two simply watching him. Then, when he awakened, she would crawl back into bed with him and concentrate on making the heat rise to unbearable again.

Instead, she left a note folded on the jeans he'd discarded on the floor last night, telling him that she was at the park, inviting him to stay where he was and reminding him of that offer a week ago to fix her breakfast some morning. Then she went downstairs, where she found Jethro looking fat and happy in front of a newly emptied food dish, had a quick snack of brownies and soda, then left the house.

Last night had apparently been quiet in the park. When she arrived with Jethro and the utility cart in tow, she found little new damage—a few bits of trash scattered about, a half-dozen empty beer cans and a new form of graffiti on the back wall. There was no profanity, just pictures apparently done by different artists. On the right side was a gun, drawn much larger than life, with sparks flying from its barrel and, a few feet away, a bullet speeding to its small, defenseless target. The target was a much cruder representation, a stick figure with arms and legs spread-eagled, with a round face and bright red corkscrew curls sticking out in all directions.

As messages went, she would rate this one as effective. It made goose bumps rise on her arms and created a chill that made her shiver in spite of the morning heat.

For a long time she simply stood and looked. Then she

picked up Jethro, pushed the cart to one side of the gate and headed back to her house. Making an effort not to disturb Jamey upstairs, she went to the kitchen, where Michael Bennett's business card was tucked in the molding of the cabinet door closest to the wall phone, and dialed his home number. When he answered on the second ring, she identified herself, then said, "I'm sorry to bother you so early on a Sunday morning, but you said if I needed anything..."

The call was short. He said he would come over; she agreed to meet him at the park. Acknowledging that she would feel more comfortable waiting at the house, she went back to the park for that reason. She wasn't going to let Ryan Morgan scare her, no matter how many threats he made, no matter how many windows he broke, how many little drawings he and his goons painted on the walls.

When she returned to the park, it was no longer empty. Reid stood inside the gate, as she had done earlier, looking at the wall. As she came to a stop beside him, she lightly touched his arm, startling him, making him jerk away. "Sorry," she apologized, then tried to make light of the painting. "It's better than the usual obscenities, isn't it?"

He stared down at her. "This isn't a joke, Karen. When I came in and saw that and saw your stuff... Why the hell did you come back?"

"I went to the house to call a friend of mine who's a cop. He's going to meet me here."

"Why don't you meet him at your house, where you can at least lock the damn door?"

"Jamey's there. He was angry enough last night. I don't want him to know about this."

He gave her a narrowed, speculative look, then, with color creeping into his face, he turned away. He knew, she thought, a little embarrassed and a whole lot curious. He knew that his father had spent the night with her, that they had shared a bed and a lot more. *How?* She had seen her own face in the mirror this morning, the same unchanged face she saw every morning. How had Reid guessed, and would anyone else—like Michael, who had been Evan's best friend and partner, who had felt a love and loyalty for Evan so intense that Evan's death had almost killed him? Not that she was ashamed. She wasn't, not in the least. But didn't everyone deserve the chance to fall in love in private?

"About last night..." She touched his arm again. He wasn't startled this time, but he still pulled away. Was it because of her new relationship with his father, because in the macho posturing of the young men of Serenity, last night had officially made her Jamey's woman? Or was he simply unused to casual, friendly contact? She doubted that a woman who could neglect, then abandon her son, as Meghan Donovan had, had ever displayed much affection for him. Other than young women like the miniskirted Tanya who had clung to him as if he were the grand prize in a contest that *she* had won, he'd probably never received much physical affection, if any at all. "Thank you for coming by last night."

He scowled. "Yeah, right."

She let her gaze settle on the brick wall again, but she didn't really see the drawings. "Jamey's been a lousy father—there's no denying that—but he regrets it. He just doesn't know how to tell you, how to show you."

His glower intensified, but he didn't say anything scornful or mocking.

"Your grandfather wasn't much of a father, either. He didn't set an example for Jamey to follow, and Jamey set a bad example for you to follow. When you have children—"

He gave her a sharp, disbelieving look. "Why the hell would I do that?"

"It may be an accident," she said with a shrug. "No form of birth control is a hundred percent effective, you know. Or someday you might meet a young woman, fall madly in love and decide that your lives won't be complete without children of your own.''

He looked at her as if she were speaking a foreign language. Maybe she was, she thought sadly. No one had ever loved him—not even his mother and father, the two people whose love and devotion every baby should be guaranteed—and it was doubtful that he had ever loved anyone. How could he imagine a woman who would change that, who would become more important to him than his own life, who would treasure him more than her own life? How could he even begin to understand the love two people could share, that filled all the empty spaces, eased all the hurts and made each a better person? When all he'd ever known was rejection and resentment, abandonment and betrayal, how could he ever consider bringing another helpless, innocent child into the world?

She sighed, an unhappy sound that faded away as a car came to a stop behind them. Turning, she saw Michael and Remy Sinclair climbing out. She glanced back at Reid, who was heading for the back gate. "Reid, come over for dinner tonight, will you? About seven?"

He glanced at the two men, then at her and shook his head.

"I'll fix something anyway, in case you change your mind."

He disappeared through the gate, and she walked out on the sidewalk to meet her friends. "Remy." Stretching onto her toes, she gave the tall, blond man a hug.

"Karen." He was gazing distractedly at the back gate. "Was that Reid Donovan?"

She nodded. "I suppose you've heard of him." After all, Remy was the Bureau's authority on Jimmy Falcone and all his people. He'd been in charge of the FBI's investigation into Falcone's organized crime activities until the bastard had almost killed him five years ago.

"Yeah, I have a file on him," Remy replied, none too pleased.

"I've arrested him several times," Michael added while he studied the drawings.

It was time to change the subject, Karen decided, and remarked in careless, unconcerned tone, "I don't think it really looks like me."

"Funny." Michael pulled her cap off, spilling her hair down her shoulders, then looked from her to the painting and back again. "I think it looks exactly like you: little, skinny and red-haired."

"Who did this?" Remy asked.

Before Karen could answer, a shocked gasp came from the sidewalk near the end of the fence. Shawntae stood there, staring at the wall. Beside her, J.T. was trying to free himself from his mother's tightening grip to go to Jethro, and behind her more bad news was coming down the street in the form of Jamey. Even from a distance she could tell he was annoyed, most likely by her insistence on coming out here after last night's run-in with the Morgans.

"Oh, Karen." Shawntae stopped near the gate. "I didn't hear a thing last night. I thought everyone had stayed away. Oh, no..."

Feeling a headache coming on, Karen stuffed her hair back under her baseball cap, then pulled a can of black spray paint from the cart. "I don't know who did it," she said with a scowl, "but I'm going to get rid of it."

Remy caught her arm as she headed through the gate. "Not so fast. Michael's going to get some pictures."

She gave Jamey, less than a block away now, a faintly desperate look. Maybe she shouldn't have called Michael. Maybe she should have simply painted over the scene the minute she'd seen it, and then no one would know about it but her and the artists. Reid wouldn't have been concerned, Michael and Remy wouldn't be looking like worried cops at a crime scene, Shawntae wouldn't be staring in shock, and Jamey...

"What the hell are you doing here?" he demanded, ignoring the others, focused only on Karen. "Didn't last night teach you anything? Didn't Ryan's message get through that thick skull of yours? You admitted yourself that he'll be looking for you when you're alone and then you traipse off..." His gaze moved at last to the back wall, and he broke off and stared. After a moment, he swallowed hard, blinked and looked down at her again. He looked as if he wanted to take her in his arms, to hold her tightly, keep her safe and never let her go. She wished he would. She could use a strong dose of security right now, and not even Michael and Remy, who were both surely armed, or Shawntae, J.T. and Jethro could provide it as easily or effectively as Jamey.

But he didn't reach for her. He didn't hold her. He simply looked at her.

"Your reference to last night..." Remy glanced over his shoulder as Michael took a camera from the trunk of the car and went into the park. "I assume you mean the broken windows at the house and the damage to her car?"

Jamey nodded.

"What happened?"

In an unnaturally subdued voice, Jamey repeated the same details Karen had given the dispatcher last night. He named names, including the two witnesses she had left out: Alicia Gutierrez and Reid.

"You figure the Morgans did this, too?"

"Them or their punks," Shawntae said with disgust.

"Why didn't you call the police, Karen?" Remy asked, ignoring the other's woman amused snort.

"You think the police would come to Serenity Street in the middle of a Saturday night for anything less than multiple homicides?" Karen blew her breath out in a heavy sigh. "I did call. They said an officer would be by, but no one came."

"I don't suppose you've considered taking their advice about leaving." This came from Michael, returning from the wall with three developing Polaroids in one hand.

This time the snorts, varying from amused to derisive, came from Karen and Jamey as well as Shawntae. Michael's response was a faint smile. "I didn't think so. Well...I'll take a report on both this and the vandalism at your house. I'll need a statement from you—" he nodded toward Jamey "—and addresses for Donovan and the girl."

"Reid lives with the Morgans. You can't talk to him there," Karen protested. "It would be too risky for him. Besides, he's not home. He left the park just as you were arriving."

"Then if he shows up for dinner tonight, let one of us know," Remy said with a hint of sarcasm. "Maybe we could make an appointment with him then."

"Or maybe you could leave him alone. He saw the same thing Jamey did, heard the same thing I did. You don't need to interview him. You don't need Alicia, either. She's Ryan's girlfriend. She's going to have his baby any day now. Bringing her into this will just cause problems for her with him." Reaching out, she clasped Jamey's hand tightly in her own. "Jamey's the most reliable witness you'll find on Serenity. He knows everybody, and he's not intimidated by them. Take his word for it. Don't cause trouble for Reid and Alicia."

Remy and Michael exchanged glances, then Michael shrugged. "Okay, Karen. We'll do it your way this time. Jamey, want to step over here?"

Jamey stood beside the car, hands in his hip pockets, and watched as Karen and Shawntae sprayed third and fourth coats of paint over the graffiti. Next to him, Michael Bennett—the cop who had made the seafood gumbo, who had been Evan Montez's partner—closed the notebook he'd taken from the glove box and turned his own gaze on the two women. "She's got a stubborn streak a mile wide."

Jamey responded with a brief word of agreement.

"She said you're not intimidated by the people down here."

He never had been before. He had had run-ins with every punk on Serenity until he'd built a reputation as a man to avoid. Even Jimmy Falcone, who'd taken over every business on the street, legitimate or otherwise, had left him and O'Shea's alone. But that was before last night. Before Karen. Before he'd had something to lose. Now he felt pretty damned intimidated. Powerless. Furious.

"Can you look out for her?" the other man asked. Bennett had introduced him as Remy Sinclair, an FBI agent. That Sunday afternoon by the river, Karen had mentioned that Sinclair, along with Smith Kendricks, had been close to Evan, so close that the two of them had notified her of her husband's death.

"Can I handcuff her to the bar?" Jamey asked dryly. "She equates being careful with cowardice. She believes in her God-given right to be here. She honestly feels that she can make a difference by not backing down or showing fear—which, down here, means taking your life in your hands. The kids come down here and trash the park every night; she's here between six-thirty and seven every morning to clean it. In front of a crowd last evening she accused Morgan of picking on women because he was too much the coward to confront a man. She's made friends with his girlfriend and his best friend. She's in his face, literally or figuratively, all the time. So far they've only threatened her property. Someday they'll go after her."

"Any chance they'll back off and leave her alone?"

Jamey shook his head. "The last do-gooder we had down here didn't back down, either, until she found herself alone with a fifteen-year-old bastard who was pretty good with a knife. She got carried out in a body bag. Karen's convinced it won't happen to her, but she's made enemies a lot faster than she's made friends.''

"So what would persuade her to leave?"

He looked at her, laughing as J.T. and Jethro ran in circles around her, tangling the mutt's leash around her ankles. "Nothing that I can think of." God help him, he had tried.

Bennett put the notebook, camera and photos on the back seat, then sighed. "I'll see if I can get a few patrols in here. A lot of the guys remember Evan. They'll try to help her out because of him. In the meantime, try to rein her in a little—which I know is easier said than done."

Amen to that, Jamey thought with a scowl.

"Karen, we're finished here."

She came out to the sidewalk, smiling as if she didn't have a care in the world, and slid her arm around Jamey's waist. Even though he automatically slipped his arm around her shoulders, her action took him by surprise. He had figured she wouldn't want any public displays of affection, especially in front of Evan's best friends. That was why he hadn't touched her when he'd first arrived, why he hadn't gathered her so close and so tight that no one could ever hurt her. It had been harder than he'd imagined to not claim her, to not make a silent declaration to her cop friends and anyone who might be watching out their windows that she belonged to *him*, that messing with her would bring far more grief than anyone on this street could handle.

"Thanks for coming out, guys. I'm really sorry to bother you on a Sunday morning, especially when there's really nothing you can do."

"We're going to stop at your house and get some pictures of the damage there," Bennett said. "I'll write up a report and take it to the D.A.'s office tomorrow morning. Once they review it, it'll go to a judge. We should have a warrant for the Morgans, Marino and Rodriguez by tomorrow afternoon. Any suggestions where we'll find them?"

Jamey shrugged. "Sometimes they're around. Sometimes they're not."

"I'll ask Reid at dinner," Karen volunteered.

"What makes you think Reid won't warn them?" Sinclair asked.

"You people," she muttered. "A troubled kid breaks a few laws, and he's branded as no good for life."

"Don't come out alone for a while, Karen—at least until this settles down." Bennett raised his hands to stall her inevitable protest. "I'm not saying pack up and leave, though I think everyone but you agrees that would be best. I'm just asking you to show some sense. Don't be one of those idiots who gets badly hurt or killed and leaves everyone around them shaking their heads saying, 'She was asking for it.' Be a little more careful. Keep your mouth shut. Stay a little closer to your friends."

Sinclair took up the argument. "Maybe you *can* make a difference, Karen. Maybe you can help these people solve their problems and take back their neighborhood—but not if you're dead. You're no good to anyone if you're dead."

"All right," she said grudgingly. "I'll be more careful. I'll show some sense. I'll cower like Jethro in a storm."

Jamey didn't believe her for a minute. He wasn't sure the other two men did, either, but they accepted her concession—most likely because they didn't want to call her a liar outright. He had no such qualms. After the cops left, turning around where the street dead-ended, then heading back up to Karen's place, Jamey drew her into his arms and gazed down at her. "Liar."

She smiled sunnily. "Name one thing I said that wasn't true."

"You won't cower. You didn't last evening, when you called Morgan a coward in front of his boys, or last night, when he was threatening you, when they were throwing bricks, breaking out windows and tearing up your car."

"I wasn't scared last evening or last night."

"You should have been. You should have been scared right out of town."

"But you were there. They never would have stopped the car out front if they'd known that. They're scared of you."

"Right," he scoffed. "Most of them are bigger than me. They're *all* meaner than me."

"Yeah, but they're tough in an immature, hot-tempered, impulsive sort of way, while you're tough in a cold, dangerous, grown-up sort of way. They grew up hearing that if they screw around with you, they'd better be prepared to pay the price. They may not be one-hundred-percent convinced that you're tougher, but they don't have the courage to find out."

Hoping they didn't find that courage, he glanced at the wall, mostly black now, and felt a renewed jolt of the shock that had blasted through him when he'd first seen it, in that first instant when he'd understood its meaning. Looking back at her, he held her tighter. "Karen—"

"Don't ask me to leave, Jamey," she pleaded softly. "I can't do it, and I can't fight with you about it."

"Then live someplace else. Come down here during the day and work, but go home to someplace safe. Don't give them another chance at you. You're right," he said, before she could interrupt. "They probably wouldn't have stopped if they had known I was there last night, but they didn't know. What happens tonight or tomorrow night or next Sunday night when they come back and you *are* alone?"

Her smile returned, sweet, sensuous, full of promise. "Maybe we should make certain that I'm not alone tonight or tomorrow night or next Sunday night." Cupping her hands to his face, she pressed a kiss to his jaw. "Come on, Jamey. It's your day off. Let's not spoil it with talk of the Morgans or standing on the sidewalk arguing. Let's go back to the house, have breakfast—"

"Fix the windows."

''Then spend the rest of the day being lazy and doing nothing that we both don't want to do.''

His own smile was rueful. ''In all the time you've been here, I think we've only agreed on one thing that we both wanted.'' He wanted *her*. He wanted to undress her, kiss her, make her hot. He wanted to touch her all over, wanted to watch her nipples tighten, her muscles quiver, her skin ripple. He wanted to bring the hazy, lazy look of arousal into her sweet blue eyes, and then he wanted to bring the damp, heated flush of pleasure to her sweet, slender body. He wanted to seduce her and satisfy her, and he wanted to be seduced by her.

''Why don't we go back to the house and I'll try to guess what that might be?''

Before he could answer, Shawntae called from the park. ''Okay, Karen, unpeel yourself from his body. I'm bringing my innocent little boy out.'' She tied a knot in the trash bag she was carrying and dropped it in the cart, then came through the gate. ''Whew,'' she said, fanning her face with exaggerated motions. ''Like it's not already hot enough out here? You guys need a cold shower or something.''

They needed something, all right, Jamey acknowledged as Karen stepped back a few inches, but a cold shower wasn't it. Not yet, at least. Not until after.

''You need any help cleaning up at your house?''

Karen shook her head. ''Thanks, Shawntae, but it won't take any time at all.''

''Well, don't forget that this is supposed to be a day of rest. Do whatever has to be done, then forget about work for a while. Relax. Enjoy.'' The younger woman grinned. ''Somehow I doubt you'll have any trouble at all with that. I'll see you later.''

J.T. handed the mutt's leash to Karen, said his goodbyes and raced after his mother. When the door to the apartment house swung shut behind him, Jamey released Karen completely and pulled the utility cart onto the sidewalk.

"Breakfast first," he suggested as they started toward her house.

She gave him an amused smile. "In your dreams. If you're so hungry, you should have gotten up when I did."

Three blocks ahead, the car parked in front of her house drove away. Jamey was glad to see them go. Maybe Karen felt comfortable together with Evan's best buddies, but he didn't. It took only one glance at Michael Bennett and Remy Sinclair to remember that he didn't fit in, to remind him that she belonged with someone like them—the good guys, the successful ones, the winners. She deserved better than the best Jamey O'Shea of the Serenity Street O'Sheas—of the Serenity Street losers—could ever provide.

But right now she wanted nothing that he couldn't provide: lust, desire, passion, heat, sex and protection. Right now that was enough for her. Right now it had to be enough for him.

At her house, they returned the fence to its original black and pried the boards from the windows, then she brought out the extra window panes stored in a back closet. Jamey had never replaced a window before, but he didn't mind being her assistant. He liked watching her, liked the tremendous satisfaction she took in a job well done. He liked the desire her efficiency aroused deep inside him. There was something sensual about a strong, capable woman...especially when she looked so china-doll beautiful.

Maybe she was right, he thought as she finished with the last window. Maybe breakfast *could* wait.

She stood up, tossed her baseball cap to the floor and held her hair with both hands, lifting it high on her crown. "How would I look with hair up to here?"

"Cute, in a pixie sort of way."

"Pixie?" she repeated with mock scorn, as if the word were an insult. She came to where he still sat on the floor in front of the window, moved to sit on his lap and wound her arms around his neck. "A *pixie?*"

"You know, a sprite. A fairy. A leprechaun."

"I bet Jamey O'Shea doesn't believe in leprechauns, the way a good Irishman should."

He shook his head. Good Irishman or not, he didn't believe in anything he couldn't see, while Karen believed in all sorts of things she couldn't see. He was a cynic. She was an optimist. He was a realist—a pessimist, she insisted—and she was a dreamer.

At odd times, though, he found himself wanting to share her dreams.

He buried his hands in her hair, gathering it, clenching his fingers around it. "Your hair is sexy as hell—the color, the length, the curls." It was wild and unrestrained—exactly the way she had been last night—and the color of passion. Practically from the first time he'd seen her, it had made him think of heat and light and intense desire. "But if you cut it all off, you would still be beautiful." He would still want her. She would still take his breath away.

She shifted her hips, rubbing sensuously against him. "Let's make love, Jamey," she murmured, her lips brushing his ear, the soft husky tones of her voice sending sensation—need, raw hunger, steamy, red hot desire—through his body.

"Right here?" His own voice was husky, thick. "On the floor?"

"Right here."

"In front of the window?"

That stopped her, as he'd known it would. She might be bold, but never that bold. Unlike the kids who filled the park at night, she would never risk an audience for something so intimate and private. With that pleasure-promising smile of hers, she got to her feet and offered him a hand. He let her pull him up, then followed her upstairs to the bedroom.

They had never made it under the covers last night, so the bed was still made, though badly wrinkled. The windows were still open, the fans still turning. There was little light in the room. The sun wouldn't touch it until early afternoon, if it came out from behind the dark clouds gathering. With luck, it wouldn't make an appearance until they'd had a little rain to cool the day. Normally in August, thundershowers were practically a daily event, but these last few weeks had been hot and unusually dry.

The room was hot.

They were hot.

Stopping at the foot of the bed, she removed her clunky white tennis shoes, then peeled off matching socks and dropped them to the floor. He watched from his seat leaning against the windowsill as she drew her shirt over her head and dropped it, too. Her shorts came off next, along with a scrap of lacy panties, and then she approached him. She wasn't the least bit shy with her nudity, but why should she be? She knew he thought she was beautiful. He'd just told her so downstairs in the parlor. He'd told her last night as he'd kissed her, caressed her, filled her.

When she came close enough, he drew her between his widespread feet, pulling her snug against his groin. The heat generated by that small contact threatened to burst into flames that would consume them both and would burn into eternity. It robbed his muscles of strength, sapped the energy right from his body and seared his lungs with every breath. It was unbearable, yet he craved it. He *wanted* to burn. He wanted to be destroyed by need, to be shattered by satisfaction into a million pieces that could be put back together to create a new man. A different man. A man deserving to love a red-haired dreamer.

She raised her hands to his face, branding his damp skin with her touch, and kissed him. Her hunger fed his, making it stronger, increasing its intensity until the desire became a physical ache, a torturous throb that made him groan.

Pleasure became pain, and pain became pleasure. Hurt—tight, demanding, relentless—gathered in his body from his hands where they rested at her waist. From his legs that, through jeans, touched hers. From his chest, rubbed sensuously by her breasts. From his groin, where his swollen flesh strained without success against her. The pain centered deep in his belly and made his wordless pleas harsh, made his response to her kisses savage.

When she opened his jeans, he moaned. When she wrapped her fingers, soft and gentle, around the length of him, he swore aloud and pushed her away long enough to kick off his shoes, to yank off his clothing with such impatience that he half expected the fabric to tear. Then he was on the bed, on his back, and she was settling over him, taking him deep, deeper, inside herself.

Satisfaction came that quickly. He was that needy. She took him, and he filled her. But it wasn't over yet. Heaven help him, it was never going to be over between them.

She sat astride him, her head tilted back, her hair falling in wild curls to brush against his hip. Her skin gleamed in the thin light, milky and pure. Her breasts were swollen, her nipples taut, inviting his attention, his hands, his mouth. He raised his hands, covering her breasts, feeling the erect nubs of her nipples even against his callused palms.

Looking down, she covered his hands with her own, pressing them, moving them in hard, slow caresses, and she moved her hips, withdrawing, sinking deep, pulling back again. Her rhythm was slow, deliberate, her body accepting his intrusion with a tight, convulsive little welcome. She was stimulating him as well as herself, her pace quickening, her breathing growing ragged, her need—like his own—spiraling out of control. Faster, deeper, wilder, her muscles straining, his hips rising to meet hers, until at last it was too much. Too much sensation. Too much stimulation. Too much need. Too much heat. Too much to bear.

Her cries echoed in the high-ceilinged room as her body

clenched convulsively around his. It was those last movements, those intense little quivers deep in her belly, that
sent him over the edge, his voice ragged, his words unintelligible even to himself—maybe a plea, maybe a curse,
maybe a prayer.

Or maybe a confession of love.

Chapter 8

A few days of being more careful, as she'd promised Michael and Remy, left Karen feeling vaguely unsettled. She still went to the park each morning, but only after Jamey was awake and dressed to accompany her. She stayed inside the house working, with the doors closed and securely locked, all day, relying on windows fixed so they opened only so far and fans to stay reasonably cool. She stayed inside evenings, too, working with Cassie Wade the last two nights, spending the evening before that across the street at O'Shea's—escorted there and back, of course, by Jamey himself. All in all, it was an unsatisfying way to spend her time.

The nights, though... Ah, the nights were exquisitely satisfying. Whether she and Jamey made love, talked or simply shared the same bed with nothing more intimate between them than a good-night kiss, she always awoke with a feeling of complete contentment.

It was because she was in love, she acknowledged to herself as she used an extender and a roller to paint the tall walls in the parlor. She certainly hadn't come to Serenity looking for love—in fact, after losing Kathy, she'd thought that she might have lost the capacity for it—but she wasn't foolish enough to deny it simply because she hadn't expected it.

She loved Jamey O'Shea.

Nothing in the past had prepared her for this. Falling in love with Evan had been so easy. She had known him all her life. She had loved him all her life—friend to friend, girl to boy, woman to man, wife to husband. It had been so simple. She had known everything about him. There had been no secrets, no getting acquainted, no doubts. She had loved Evan, and Evan had loved her. Plain, simple and easy.

There was nothing plain, simple or easy about Jamey. His life on Serenity had been as far removed from her own as any she could imagine. By his standards, she had been privileged, given everything her heart desired, both materially and emotionally. She hadn't known—to this day didn't know—what it was like to go hungry, to have parents who required the child to parent them, to go through a bad marriage, to be estranged from your only child. She didn't know what it was like to live in a place without hope, to expect to lose everyone you cared for, to be resigned to living a life governed by despair, fear, despondency and futility.

Loving him would be no magic cure for their problems. He still wanted her gone. He still believed she didn't belong down here. He believed her life was in danger as long as she stayed. He thought she was a dreamer, and he didn't believe in dreams.

But no one had ever said love had to be easy. She and Evan had lucked out. He had been one great gift for her to treasure.

Jamey was a gift, too, but she was going to have to earn it.

Dipping the roller into the paint pan, she removed the excess paint, then raised it to the wall again. Always work with a wet edge, her how-to book recommended. Even in a room this size, that wasn't a problem. With the humidity hovering in the high 90s, the paint wouldn't even think about drying until she was showered, perfumed and powdered and watching at the window for Jamey.

She watched for Reid, too, but with no luck. He hadn't come to dinner Sunday night, and she hadn't caught even a glimpse of him in the four days since. Maybe he felt uncomfortable knowing that she was sleeping with his father. Maybe he thought she would take Jamey's side against him. Maybe it was really Jamey he was avoiding; it was hard these days to find her without him. Or maybe it was all those visits from the police that kept him out of sight.

Although the judge had issued warrants for the arrest of the Morgans and their partners in crime, it hadn't happened yet. Michael and other officers had made a number of trips to Serenity looking for Ryan and his gang. They drove through the neighborhood, knocked at his door, asked the neighbors about their whereabouts, but they hadn't yet succeeded in locating them. If the threat of arrest was keeping them from showing their faces on the street, Karen hoped the cops *never* found them. The neighborhood was more peaceful without them. The younger punks seemed at a loss without their guidance. Serenity was a little bit nicer place to live.

Finishing with the roller, she picked up a paintbrush to fill in around the trim. All the rooms had elaborate crown moldings and base and door trims. She had painted those early in the week, a soft creamy white that provided a wonderful contrast to the deep rose hue of these walls. It had taken several hours to tape the wood this afternoon, using a special tape that wouldn't strip the paint underneath or leave its sticky residue on top. Once she got the second coat of paint on the walls tomorrow, she would remove the tape. It was a lot of work, but the room would be beautiful, in her oh-so-unbiased opinion.

A knock at the door sounded as she reached the corner. Cassie's timing was perfect, she thought with satisfaction as she balanced the brush on the edge of the paint can, then got to her feet.

Instead of her young assistant, she found Alicia Gutierrez on the veranda. Her eyes were damp, her expression distraught, her clothes disheveled. Noticing the dark red splotch that extended across one cheek, Karen felt an old familiar sickness deep inside. How many times had she seen Kathy looking like this? How many times had she ignored it because that was what her sister had wanted? How many times had she lost a chance to do something because she'd been too polite to call her sister a liar, too afraid of endangering their relationship, too sure that if she forced Kathy to face the truth, *she* would lose, not her bastard brother-in-law?

"I see Ryan's back in the neighborhood."

Alicia's hand went to her cheek. "No, no, this is nothing. I just—"

"Walked into a door? Got clumsy? Didn't see that fist aimed at your face?"

The girl sighed. "Can I come in?"

Karen unlatched the screen door, then stepped back. As soon as Alicia cleared the threshold, she closed and locked the door. "What happened?"

Tugging her clothes into place, Alicia wandered into the broad doorway of the parlor. "This is pretty."

"I bet he used to punch you in the stomach or the chest so it wouldn't show, didn't he? But he can't do that anymore because of the baby."

Alicia faced her, her manner defensive bordering on belligerent. "He doesn't hit me. I forgot I left a cabinet door open when I was fixing dinner. I turned and walked into it."

Karen crossed the foyer to her, tilting her face to the light. "That's one solid door. My cabinet doors aren't anything like that. Are you hurt anywhere else?"

The girl shook her head. Turning away from the parlor and its strong odor of paint, she went to the stairs and carefully sat down on the third one. She drew her feet close and leaned forward, huddling as much as a heavily pregnant woman could. "You know the police are looking for him. He says it's your fault."

"I'm the one who called them," Karen said with a shrug. "But if he hadn't broken the law, they wouldn't have a warrant for his arrest. He has no one to blame but himself."

Alicia's smile was rueful. "Ryan doesn't think that way. He thinks you're a problem that's gotten out of control. Mr. Falcone—the man he works for—he's wondering if maybe Ryan can't take care of things the way he used to. He heard about the cookout last week, about your plans and about the cops coming down here Sunday."

"Tell Ryan to tell Mr. Falcone that there'll be another cookout Saturday. Tell him he can come and meet the neighborhood he's trying to run, as long as he leaves his goons at home. Same time, same place. You come, too, Alicia." Until that moment she hadn't made any such plans, but why not? There were dozens of hamburger buns, patties and brownies in her freezer, dozens more in Cassie's freezer, and frankly, she was getting a little tired of salads and burgers every day. Even Jethro was starting to turn up at his nose in disdain at the mere scent of a hamburger.

Seeking a more comfortable seat, Alicia moved closer to the wall so she could lean against it. "Some of my friends who didn't come wished they had. They said maybe next time they could drop by. And my grandmother said she would make a pot of her special chili to bring."

The words brought Karen pleasure. Change came slowly, but it did come. Some of the other young women on the street would come, and maybe they would bring their

friends or, better, their families. And Rosa Gutierrez, wh
had sat quietly and hardly spoken to anyone, was not onl
willing to come again but also to contribute. In the lon
run, that was her goal: everyone bringing a dish or two
sharing food and good times with their neighbors. *That* wa
a real community party.

"Tell your grandmother I would appreciate that." Sh
sat down on the bottom step and leaned against the railin
where it started its fancy finishing curve. "She seems lik
a very sweet lady."

"She is."

"What does she think of the baby?"

"She's happy, but she wishes I had a husband...just no
Ryan. She thinks he's no good."

A smart lady, too, Karen thought privately. "Do you liv
with her?"

"Most of the time. Sometimes I stay at Ryan's, but fou
people in two rooms gets cramped. There's no privacy
People are always coming over...lately the cops."

"Does your grandmother know that he hits you?"

Her question was met with silence—no denial, no ar
gument. Rosa knew, Karen suspected, and didn't approve
Those were probably the times—when she bore bruises o
other evidence of his abuse—that Alicia stayed at his place
Maybe she preferred not to lie to her grandmother, o
maybe staying away until her face healed was simply a wa
of avoiding the issue with the old lady altogether.

"Ryan loves me," Alicia said at last. "He just loses hi
temper sometimes. I do stupid things that make him mad
He doesn't mean to hurt me. He just forgets that I'r
smaller and weaker than him."

"He forgets? Have you ever seen him confront someon
who *wasn't* smaller and weaker than him?"

The girl remained silent.

"I told you when we met about my sister, Kathy. Sh
used to say the same things. 'It isn't Davis's fault. He love

me. I screwed up. I made a mistake. I did something stupid. I deserved to be punished. He just lost his temper. He didn't mean to, and he swears it won't happen again.' But it did happen again and again, until he killed her. She was my sister—his wife, the woman he claimed to love more than life itself—and he beat her to death." She paused. "Strange love, huh?"

"Ryan's not like that," Alicia said, her voice muted, her lips barely moving. "He *loves* me. He loves our baby. We're going to be a real family."

"And what if he gets tired of hitting you, Alicia? What if he hits your baby?"

She looked appalled. "That won't happen. He would *never* hit a little girl."

"You're a little girl," Karen pointed out softly, "and he hits you."

For a long still moment, they stared at each other, then Alicia struggled to her feet. "I've got to go."

"Go where? Back to Ryan so he can treat you like a piece of property until he gets mad and punches you again?"

"I'm going home. It's been a long day."

"Are you still working?"

She nodded, her long hair swinging around her.

"What does your doctor think of that?"

The touchy look came back. "I don't have a doctor."

There were no doctors' offices located nearby. Transportation to the nearest clinic was often a problem; so was the time needed for the interminable wait at low-cost or free clinics. No one had health insurance or the money to pay up front. Health care wasn't a regular part of their lives; when they got sick or injured, getting medical help wasn't their first, second or even tenth thought. Being pregnant wasn't the same as being sick; why waste precious money on a doctor? Karen had heard all the reasons before. Which, she wondered, was Alicia's?

"I don't need a doctor," the girl said, challenging Karen to disagree. "I'm healthy, and my baby is healthy."

"Probably so. But listen, Alicia, I have a friend who's a nurse-midwife—a nurse who delivers babies. If you have any questions about labor, giving birth and taking care of your baby, she'd be happy to answer them for you. Just let me know, and I'll give her a call." Elly had already agreed to donate her services one day a week once Kathy's House was up and running. Karen was positive she wouldn't mind getting a little head start.

"I'll think about it." Alicia unlocked the door and opened it, then breathed deeply. "It's raining."

Karen stood beside her and mimicked her inhalation. "It smells good, doesn't it? This house stinks of paint all the time. Even in my sleep, I smell it."

"Just keep reminding yourself how nice it will be when it's finished."

Karen accompanied Alicia onto the veranda, stopping at the top of the steps and watching as the girl started across the yard. At the front gate, she turned back. "About that friend of yours…"

"The nurse?"

"Yeah. All I know is what my friends say, and none of them has ever had a baby. Maybe if she just has something I could read explaining what happens…"

"I'll call her tomorrow."

"Thanks."

She passed through the gate, then started toward Serenity's dead end. Karen watched for a moment before directing her gaze across the street. What little she could see of O'Shea's seemed busy, and why shouldn't it be? In the bar with people who cared—at least with a bartender who cared—was a better place than most to spend a rainy August night. In fact, if Cassie didn't show up in another minute, she just might lock up, leave a note on the door and head that way herself.

Sixty seconds passed with no sign of the young woman. Karen was turning away toward the door when a sound down the street caught her attention. Half cry, half groan, it resonated equal measures of pain and fear. Returning to the top of the steps, she peered in that direction but saw nothing. Maybe it was nothing…but it had certainly sounded like something. It had sounded like a wounded animal, like someone in pain. Maybe a very pregnant woman.

Without hesitation, she left the veranda, crossing the yard in the rain, letting herself out the gate onto the sidewalk. The street was deserted except for a figure in the next block, supporting herself against the abandoned storefront there. Karen started that way, walking at first, then picking up the pace until she was running. "Alicia!"

The girl was leaning against the rusty security gate that covered broken plate-glass windows, her head bowed, her hands pressed to the sides of her belly. Looking up, she pushed to her feet, shook her head vehemently and extended one hand, palm out. "No! I'm all right," she insisted. "Go home. Go back home and lock your doors."

Out of breath, Karen slowed to a walk again a dozen yards away, but she didn't stop. "You're not all right. Is it the baby? Are you having cramps?"

"Please," Alicia cried, her voice taut with desperation. "Go home *now,* please, before it's too—"

Late. That was how she would have finished it, if she'd been given a chance. If Ryan Morgan hadn't stepped out of the shadows of the recessed doorway halfway between the two women.

Karen stopped short. It was only a block or so to O'Shea's, but it was a long block. Covering it the first time had left her breathless. There was no way she could run it again, no way in the world she could run it faster than Ryan Morgan could. He would catch her before she'd gone thirty feet.

"What's up, Karen?" he asked with a grin, so handsome and so damned evil. Tall, dark and dangerous, she had teasingly referred to him her first day on Serenity. There was nothing even slightly funny about the thought now. "I understand you've had people out looking for me all week, but now that you've found me, you look like you want to run the other way."

She forced air into her lungs and prayed that her voice would be steady. "The police are still looking for you, Ryan. You mess with me, they'll never stop."

"You've got it all wrong, bitch. *You've* been messing with *me*. I don't like that. I don't like people coming in causing trouble for me."

"Makes you look like you're not in control anymore, doesn't it?" she asked mildly. "I understand that Mr. Falcone doesn't like that."

His expression turned colder, darker, more dangerous. "No, he doesn't," he agreed, his tone just as mild but a million times more menacing. "But I assured him that I would take care of this little problem."

"You feel confident taking care of *little* problems, don't you? Hitting your little pregnant girlfriend. Threatening me."

He came closer. She backed away, but he followed until a post that had held a rusted No Parking sign was at her back. Catching her chin in a cruel grip, he leaned close. "Someday your mouth is going to get you killed, bitch...and today just might be the day."

Choosing one of the chairs nearest the doors, Jamey sprawled comfortably, his spine rounded, his legs stretched out all the way to the next table, and gazed out the door toward Decatur. It was only about seven, but it seemed later, thanks to the dark skies and the rain that was falling a little harder with each passing moment, bringing with it a little relief from the day's heat. This week had been paricularly miserable. Karen had complained every night about not being able to open the doors or slide the windows all the way to the top. He didn't blame her. Painting, sanding and patching holes was miserable work in this weather.

Headlights sliced through the rain as a car approached from outside. He wished it would be Ryan Morgan, so he could pick up the phone, call the police and watch them take him away. More likely, it was the cops themselves, come by in another futile attempt to locate the little bastard, or Karen's young friend, Cassie. She was usually here by six and gone by nine, but he'd seen no sign of her car this evening.

"Jamey!"

He didn't recognize the voice that called from outside, but he did recognize the alarm. Jumping to his feet, he stepped outside as Cassie pulled into the driveway across the street. It wasn't Cassie who'd yelled, though, but Alicia Gutierrez, hurrying up the street as quickly as her unaccustomed heaviness allowed.

"Jamey, my God, hurry...!"

He glanced toward Karen's house, saw that the front door was open, the interior lights shining brightly onto the empty porch. His nerves tightening, he started toward Alicia, meeting her in the middle of the street, catching her as she stumbled forward. Her words were almost unintelligible, shaky with fear and punctuated with great, heaving gasps for air. "It's Ryan! He's mad about the police, and he blames Karen. He says it's all her fault that he's in trouble, that Mr. Falcone is losing faith in him. He says he's got to be stopped, got to be punished. I tried to stop him, I tried to talk to him, but when he gets like this, he doesn't listen, he doesn't—"

Jamey gave her a little shake as Cassie came toward them. "Where is Karen?" he demanded.

Alicia abruptly became still, then drew a deep breath and

burst into tears. "With Ryan," she sobbed. "Down the
street, by the Laundromat. He was hurting her…"

Jamey shoved her into Cassie's arms. "Take her to the
bar and stay there. Call the police and tell them to get in
touch with Michael Bennett. Tell him what happened."
Breaking free of Alicia's grasp, he headed down the center
of the street at a full run. His heart pounded in his chest,
and his lungs ached, but neither response was due to physical exertion. It was fear. Pure, relentless fear.

There was no activity around the old laundry. The street
was quiet, the shadows empty. Slowing to a jerky walk, he
looked around the area, then shouted Karen's name. There
was an instant of silence, then a sound—soft, familiar, flesh
hitting flesh. It was followed by a grunt, another bone-
crunching punch, then a curse and the sound of running
feet. He headed toward the alley on the far side of the
building just as his call was answered, though not in the
voice he was expecting, hoping—praying—to hear. "Over
here."

Jamey paused in the darkness, letting his eyes adjust;
then he saw them. Karen was on the ground, on her side,
her knees drawn up protectively, and the other figure—the
man who had spoken—was kneeling over her. His back
was to Jamey, but even in the darkness he could recognize
Reid's blond hair. Even in his panic, he had recognized his
son's voice.

As Jamey dropped to his knees beside her, Reid moved
away, getting to his feet, simply standing and watching.
Reaching for her hand, Jamey checked the pulse in her
wrist, more thankful than he'd ever been in his life to find
it strong and steady. Bending low, he whispered, "Karen,
it's Jamey. You're going to be okay, sweetheart. Everything's going to be okay."

She offered no response. She was mercifully uncon-
scious.

Without debating the wisdom of what he was doing, he

carefully scooped her into his arms, rocked back on his heels and stood up. He knew it could be risky moving her when he had no idea what injuries she'd suffered, but it could be just as risky leaving her there to wait for an ambulance. The paramedics had quit answering calls on Serenity before the cops had.

"Come with us," he commanded Reid, his voice as cold as the anger inside him. He had never been so frightened, so furious. He had never felt so dangerously close to losing control. He had *never* felt so murderous.

Barely feeling the burden of Karen's weight, he carried her out of the alley and toward home. In the light from the streetlamps, he could see that her lip was split, that one eye was already swelling and turning darker shades, that one cheek was scraped raw as if it had come into hard contact with a brick wall. Judging by the shallowness of her breathing, there were other injuries as well.

"I'm going to kill him." His low words were a fierce promise. He was going to get Karen taken care of, make sure that she was safe, and then he was going to come back here, find Ryan Morgan and beat the very life out of the bastard. Let him see what it felt like to be used as a punching bag. Acquaint him with the sort of pain, fear and helplessness she must have felt. Make him suffer before he ended it, before he left the punk dead or dying.

"I wasn't part of this." Reid's voice was as low as Jamey's, as empty of emotion. "I didn't know he was back."

Jamey glanced at him. Fear hadn't allowed him a moment to wonder about Reid's presence in the alley. Even now he didn't. A month ago, even a few weeks ago, he would have automatically suspected that the kid was involved, but not this time. While he hoped his son was too much a man to ever physically harm a woman, he *knew* Reid was too fond of—too attracted to? too affected by?—Karen ever to hurt her, ever to stand by and let someone else hurt her.

"I was up on the roof," he continued in that flat, dead voice. "I heard them talking. I heard Ryan say that her mouth was going to get her killed, maybe today. By the time I got down there, she was already on the ground, and he was kicking her."

As they reached the beginning of Karen's fence, Jamey gave him a long, dark look. "You have a hell of a best friend, Reid." Then, after a moment's heavy silence, "Go across to the bar. Ask Cassie if I can borrow her car."

The kid took off, returning a moment later with a set of keys. He opened the back passenger door, then stepped back so Jamey could carefully lay Karen on the seat. Straightening, he closed the door, then took the keys. "Stay at the bar, would you? Keep an eye on Alicia and Cassie. Don't let either of them leave."

The next two hours were a blur—the reckless drive across town to the nearest hospital, the nurses and doctors hurrying in and out, the questions he was asked and the forms they wanted him to fill out, the arrival of her friends. Jamey didn't wonder how they found Karen. They were a cop, an FBI agent and a U.S. Attorney; they could probably find out anything—including, he hoped, where Ryan Morgan was. He just told them what he knew, and Bennett and Sinclair left immediately for Serenity.

Finally, when the waiting had become almost more than he could bear, a doctor approached Jamey and Smith Kendricks. "Mr. Montez?"

Mention of Karen's husband—of Kendricks's good friend—who had died six years ago in one of these hospitals made Jamey swallow hard. Kendricks didn't react at all. "No Mr. Montez," he said. "Jamey O'Shea and Smith Kendricks. We're friends of Karen's. How is she?"

"Bruised and battered, but nothing's broken. We would like to keep her overnight, but she insists that she'll rest better at home. Is there someone who can stay with her?"

When Kendricks didn't answer, Jamey did, though with

reluctance. "Yes." If she went back to Serenity, of course he would stay with her...but he didn't want her going back. He didn't want her to ever set foot on that damned street or in that damned neighborhood again.

The doctor didn't seem to notice his hesitation. "You can see her if you'd like. We'll take care of the paperwork, and she'll be free to go soon."

Together they followed the doctor to the room where Karen lay on a gurney, her head turned in the opposite direction, looking so small and vulnerable. Kendricks hung back, though, gesturing to Jamey to go in alone. He did so, approaching the bed slowly, reaching out when he was beside her to gently touch her hand. Immediately she turned and tried to smile, but the effort was painful. "How do you feel?"

"Numb." She turned her hand so her fingers could wrap around his. "I'm sorry, Jamey. I knew I wasn't supposed to go out, but I heard a cry, and I saw Alicia looking as if—"

"Shh. It's okay. I'll yell at you later." Bending closer, he brushed his hand over her hair, still damp and caked in places with mud. Her clothes had also been muddy, he remembered, and bloody. In the hall while he'd waited he had noticed that her blood was on him, too, a red stain the rain hadn't washed away. "Are you sure you want to leave tonight? Why don't you let the doctor keep you, like he wants?"

She shook her head. "I'm going home, Jamey. If you don't take me, I'll call a cab."

"Cabs won't go into Serenity."

"Then I'll go as far as they'll take me, and I'll walk the rest of the way."

He was surprised that he could manage a halfway decent grin. "You're stubborn enough to do it, aren't you?"

She tried another awkward little half smile, half grimace.

"You bet." Growing serious again, she touched her face gingerly. "Do I look as bad as I feel?"

"If you feel like death warmed over. You're twice as pale as normal and about two dozen shades of purple, black and blue. The colors don't exactly go with your hair, but you're still beautiful."

Her laughter was unexpected, and it ended in a pained wince as she raised one hand to her ribs. "That's quite a line of blarney, Jamey O'Shea. My clothes are over there. Will you help me get dressed?"

"I kind of like your gown."

"Oh, yes, it's so fashionable. Please?" She nodded toward the countertop and the small pile of clothing, but he still hesitated.

"Karen—"

Raising one hand, she covered his mouth. "Please don't argue, Jamey. I want to go home. I want to lie in my own bed. I want to go to sleep beside you, and I want to wake up beside you. Please, I need that. I need you."

Without another word, he got her clothes, helped her sit up and pulled the gown from her shoulders. Her shirt was wet and made her shiver when he pulled it over her head and down to her waist—at least he hoped it was a chill and not pain. He had never dressed an injured woman before, certainly not in damp clothes that clung and dragged instead of simply sliding into place.

He completed the job without causing her too much discomfort, then settled her on the bed again. "You have company," he said, going to the door before she had a chance to speak.

Kendricks came in, moving to the opposite side of the gurney. She greeted him, then chided, "You didn't have to come down here."

"Yeah, right. Jolie wanted to come, too, but she's with the kids." Kendricks touched her chin lightly. "Maybe next time maybe you'd better pick on someone your own size. I think this guy got the better of you.''

"Only because I wasn't prepared."

"Oh, yeah? How do you prepare for someone like Ryan Morgan?"

"You hang around someone like Jamey O'Shea," she replied, squeezing his hand tightly.

"It didn't do you much good tonight, did it?" Jamey asked grimly. "I wasn't there in time to stop Morgan."

Kendricks spoke up again, the teasing gone, his tone totally serious. "Michael and Remy and about half the NOPD are out looking for Morgan. Until they arrest him, Karen, come and stay with Jolie and me. We have plenty of room, and we both really want you there."

Although he knew it was irrational, some part of Jamey wanted to object to the invitation. If Karen went home with anyone, it should be him. *He* should be the one to take care of her. After all, he was more a part of her life than the Kendrickses, the Bennetts or the Sinclairs. But he didn't belong in her life, just as she didn't belong in his. She did belong with people like the Kendrickses. She belonged anywhere away from Serenity. Away from him.

"I appreciate the invitation," Karen said, "but I've got to go home. Jamey will look out for me. It's one of the things he does best."

"You're sure?" At her nod, Kendricks shrugged. "Then can I give you a ride?"

"I have…" Jamey hesitated as she inconspicuously squeezed his hand hard enough to numb his fingers. "…a car," he finished, giving her a puzzled look.

"Then I'll see you soon." Bending, the other man brushed a kiss to her forehead. "Until they get this guy in custody, be careful, will you?"

"I will."

As soon as Kendricks was gone, Jamey freed his hand and flexed his fingers. "What was that about?"

"I was afraid you would mention Cassie. It is her car you have, isn't it? No one else on Serenity owns a car, and I haven't gotten my tires replaced yet, and she was supposed to come over this evening."

"Yes, it's Cassie's car, but what does that matter?"

"I never told you her last name, did I?" She swung her legs over the side of the bed, waited a moment to equilibrate, then slid to the floor. "It's Wade. As in the Wades who lived on Serenity Street. As in Jolie Wade's baby sister and Smith's favorite sister-in-law."

He gave a dismayed shake of his head. He had never guessed that Cassie and Jolie were related, but why should he? He must have been away in the Army by the time Cassie was born, and her family had moved off soon after he'd returned. As far as he knew, none of them but Jolie had set foot back in the old neighborhood, and even she had done it only for a series of award-winning articles and, more recently, for the sake of a friend.

"See why I didn't want you to mention her?" Then, trying to look innocent, she reached for his hand and asked in a small voice, "Can we go home now?"

Trying to stifle a groan, Karen shifted on the bed, seeking some position where her bruises didn't hurt, but such a position, she suspected, didn't exist. Her body ached in places where no one had even touched her—not Morgan, the doctors or the nurses. Even her toes were sore.

From the darkness outside her room, Jamey appeared in the doorway. "Are you all right?"

It was around four o'clock in the morning, and he had asked the question repeatedly—when he had carried her in from the car, when he'd lain down beside her, when he'd gotten up soon after for fear his closeness might make her more uncomfortable, every time she sighed, every time she groaned... She would smile if it didn't hurt too much. It was nice to have someone so concerned for her. There was a certain comfort in it, and she needed all the comfort she could get.

"I'm fine," she lied. "You can quit watching the street, Jamey. No one's coming around here tonight." Michael, Remy and the others had searched, but there'd been no sign of Morgan or his gang anywhere. They had interviewed Reid, who had saved her from further injury and had gotten a black eye, swollen knuckles and a few scrapes of his own for his efforts, and Alicia, who had finally calmed down and had gone home with Cassie. Now the street was quiet, the buildings dark, showing no sign of life.

Except Jamey, prowling like an edgy, hungry cat seeking prey.

"Why don't you take the pain medication the doctor gave you? Maybe you could get some sleep."

"In a little bit. You know what would help more? I need to take a bath, wash my hair, get clean." She wanted to wash away the smell of the hospital and the dirt that had escaped the nurse's perfunctory cleaning. She wanted to wash off the residue of mud that had caked her hair, and most of all she wanted to wash away the residue of Ryan Morgan. She needed to be cleaned of him.

She waited hopefully but expected him to argue, to insist that she stay in bed. To her great gratitude, he didn't. He thought about it a moment, then nodded. "I'll run the water. You wait here."

She waited until the bathroom light came on, spilling out into the hallway, then she carefully eased to her feet. Movement was painful and slow, but she managed to make it halfway to the bathroom before he came back for her. He helped her into the bathroom, then left her leaning against the sink for support while he checked the temperature of the water and added sweet-scented bubble bath. Drawing a breath, she turned to face herself in the mirror. She hadn't caught a glimpse yet, but she knew exactly what she would look like.

One moment passed, then another and one more. Jamey shut off the water and came to stand behind her, his hands resting on the basin's lip beside hers, his gaze locked on her reflection. "Do you know how many times I've seen this?" she whispered.

His blue eyes shadowed with bewilderment, he shook his head. "It's not so bad."

She raised one trembling hand to touch the battered, swollen face in the mirror. "That's what Kathy used to say," she murmured. "She would come to our parents' house looking like this, and she would say, 'It's not so bad. It doesn't hurt. It looks a lot worse than it is.' And my mother and I...we let her pretend. If we told her it was bad, she shut us out. For days she refused to have anything to do with us. And so, to keep peace with her, we let her lie. We supported her lies. We told her no, it wasn't so bad...but *maybe* it shouldn't have happened. *Maybe* Davis had a problem. *Maybe* she should get help." Her eyes grew damp, and her voice began to quiver. "One day the police chief—my dad's best friend—came to the house. He'd been at the hospital, where Davis had taken Kathy after one of their fights. She was dead. In one of his uncontrollable rages, her husband had beaten her to death."

Jamey cautiously slipped one arm around her waist. When she didn't wince, he slid the other one around and held her. "I'm sorry."

"We were twins. Identical twins. She was a part of me, and I stood back and did nothing while her husband killed her one punch at a time." Her smile was crooked, thin and bitter. "When we were kids, she used to tease that I was wearing her face. This is how she looked the last time I saw her alive." The tears started then, stinging the raw scrapes on her cheek. "Oh, Jamey..."

He held her gently and let her cry, murmuring soft words and softer sounds. When she was finished, he pulled her nightshirt over her head, then lifted her into the great old claw-foot tub. As she settled with a weary sigh, he pulled the ladderback chair to the side of the tub and sat down, leaning forward, elbows braced on his knees, to watch her. Finally he spoke. "That's why this place is so important to you."

She nodded.

"But it's not worth dying for, Karen."

She stared down at the bubbles that covered the steamy water in a froth. She'd known this was coming. From the moment Ryan had dragged her into the alley, before the first punch had landed, one of the few thoughts that had penetrated her fear had been that Jamey was going to use this to bolster his arguments in favor of her leaving. He couldn't have asked for better ammunition, and through her foolishness—and her concern for Alicia—she had handed it to him on a platter.

"You're doing this for Kathy, but do you think she wants you to suffer the way she did? To endure the same abuse that she did?"

"I'm doing it for *me*, Jamey. All the plans I ever made for my life involved a family. I was going to be a good wife and a wonderful mother. That was going to be my life. But Evan died, and I'm never going to have babies of my own. I have to have something to want, to fill my time, to care about and dream about, to work for. I have to make a new future for myself in a place where I'm not Evan's widow, Kathryn and Robert's daughter or Kathy's twin, where I can be just plain Karen. The crazy lady. The do-gooder. The dreamer. The fool."

"The red-haired bitch." His tone was curt as he repeated Ryan Morgan's insult.

"That, too. I don't expect everyone to think kindly of me. I would know I was doing something wrong if Ryan did," she said with a hint of a smile before turning serious again. "If I left, Jamey, where would I go? What would I do?"

"You could go home. You could go to some other neighborhood that's not so dangerous. You could find some other place with people who need your help."

"And give up all of this?" she teased. "Jamey, I can't afford to go someplace else. All my money is tied up in this house, in these plans. If I walk away from here, I'll be walking away from everything I have."

"And if you don't walk away, Morgan or some other punk just might make good on his threat to see you carried out. Nothing here is worth dying for."

He was wrong, she knew. Plenty of people on Serenity were worth dying for. They were certainly worth living for. But she didn't argue the point with him. She was too weary, too sore, for arguments. "Let's just agree to disagree," she said with a sigh.

The slight curve of his mouth was more grimace than smile. "That shouldn't be hard. We've been doing it from the beginning."

Sinking a little deeper, she tilted her head back so that her hair fell from the rim of the tub where she had gathered it earlier and floated, then sank below the surface of the water. Closing her eyes, she slipped lower until only her face remained out of water, wetting her hair completely, then sat up again. Without being asked, he got the shampoo from the small table nearby, knelt beside the tub and squirted some into her hair. While she lathered the length of the curls, his long, strong fingers kneaded and massaged her scalp, then her neck, sending heat and relaxation through her body. "You do that well," she murmured with a yawn.

"Maybe I missed my calling. Maybe I should have been a hairdresser instead."

The idea of Jamey, with his own shaggy, carelessly unstyled hair, standing behind a salon chair instead of a bar amused her. "You're a good bartender and a good friend.

Your customers need that far more than they need a decent haircut."

He rinsed the shampoo from her hair, then pulled the plug and helped her from the tub. While she stood dripping on the rug, he got a towel from the wicker table. When he turned back, for a moment he simply stared at her body. She didn't need to look. She felt every one of the bruises that appalled him. "Because I'm so pale," she said softly, "what would be an ordinary bruise on you looks spectacular on me."

He touched one mark that extended across her ribs, his fingers so light that she barely felt them. Abruptly pulling back, those gentle fingers curled into a threatening fist. "I'm so damned sorry...but not as sorry as that bastard's going to be when I get hold of him. I'm going to kill the son of a bitch."

"No, you're not." She wrapped her hand around his and held it tightly. "You're too good a man to resort to vigilante behavior...but I appreciate the desire."

He wound the towel around her dripping hair, wrapped another around her body and lifted her into his arms. She didn't need to be carried—the hot bath had done wonders for her aches and pains—but she didn't say so. She didn't protest at all. She simply rested her head on his shoulder and allowed herself to feel pampered. Treasured. Even a little bit loved.

Ten o'clock came and went, but O'Shea's stayed locked up. Jamey had dozed for a few hours in the easy chair beside Karen's bed, then had sat there another few hours, simply watching her, before he finally headed downstairs. As he popped the top on a soda from her refrigerator, he wandered out onto the porch, feeling the force of the morning heat with his first step. If God was feeling merciful this morning, He would turn the skies dark, stir up cooling winds to chase the heat and humidity to the east and send an easy, steady rain all day and into the night to make the weather bearable. But the sky was blue, without a cloud to be seen, the smooth pale color broken only by shimmering, shifting heat waves.

Across the street Reid was sitting on the stoop of the rickety house next to the bar, his back braced against one post, his feet resting on the other. A white pad was balanced on his knees, and his head was bent over it. A sketch pad? Jamey wondered, suddenly curious about the kid's talent. It was wrong that a son should display as much drawing talent as Shawntae said Reid did and that his father had never seen so much as a line of it. Of course, *this* father and son's entire relationship was about as wrong as could be. It had gone wrong from the very start...but that didn't mean it could never be righted. Karen was convinced that there was hope for them yet, if they both wanted it. If they both tried.

Lately, he'd found himself wanting to try, but so damned unsure how to go about it. A friendly gesture might be a good start. "Hey, Reid, want a Coke?"

Even with two yards and a street between them, Jamey could see the surprise and wariness in the kid's expression before he slowly closed the pad, got to his feet and started toward the street. Jamey went in to get the drink, returning just as Reid reached the top of the steps.

"How's Karen?"

"She's sleeping. She was pretty sore last night." He sat down in the rocker and stretched his feet out. Reid chose to sit on the bench, his back against the wall, his gaze directed toward the street. Whatever he was staring at, he wasn't seeing it too clearly, not with his right eye swollen even worse than Karen's. His right hand was swollen, too, and the knuckles scraped. It looked like Morgan had gotten the better of him, even though they were pretty equal in size and strength. Maybe Reid just hadn't been able to compete against Morgan's rage, or maybe—hopefully—he lacked Morgan's killer instinct.

"About last night..."

Reid looked at him, and Jamey looked away. Gratitude was a new feeling for him—there wasn't much to feel grateful for on Serenity—but he owed it to Reid. The difference in time between his arrival in the alley and Jamey's could have been the difference between Karen being bruised and sore or dead. Most people in the neighborhood would have ignored impending trouble, and not one of them would have stepped between an angry Ryan Morgan and his victim. It had taken courage for Reid to intervene. As Karen had pointed out before, Morgan and his pals were Reid's only friends. Protecting Karen had done nothing for their friendship, and while Jamey didn't want the kid to have friends like that, he sure as hell didn't want them for Reid's enemies. If they perceived that his loyalties now lay elsewhere, they wouldn't hesitate to turn on him.

They wouldn't hesitate to kill him.

"Thanks for helping her out," he said in a rush, uncomfortable with the words but a hundred percent sincere in the sentiment.

Reid was uncomfortable, too. With little more than a grunt of acknowledgment, he looked away.

"Have you given any thought to Karen's mural?"

After one still moment, Reid picked up the pad he'd laid on the bench, flipped it to the middle and offered it to him. On the open page was an unfinished sketch of Serenity Street, three blocks of storefronts, apartment buildings and houses, along with a rendition of the park. With its grass, trees, benches and playground equipment, the place would be barely recognizable to the younger people on the street, but it was uncannily familiar to Jamey. He remembered the time when the park had looked almost exactly like that, the neatest, cleanest, prettiest little piece of property anywhere around.

"Karen will be impressed." Inwardly Jamey winced at the words. Why hadn't he said that *he* was impressed? Shawntae hadn't exaggerated. The kid had talent. Why was it so hard to say so?

Jamey started to flip to the front of the pad, then hesitated. "Do you mind?"

He would bet that Reid wanted to say yes, to take the pad back and protect its contents. Instead he shrugged as if he didn't care, as if whatever Jamey or anyone else thought of his work on these pages meant nothing to him.

Some of the drawings were done in watercolor, some pastels, some pen and ink. Most of the scenes were familiar—Serenity, the Quarter, the river—and all of them were harsh. Soft colors did nothing to lessen the bleakness that pervaded the drawings. Hopelessness, despair, desolation—that was the world Reid sketched. It was the world he lived in. In large part he had Jamey to thank for that. He and Meghan had owed their son so incredibly much more than they'd given him.

"The cops didn't find Ryan last night," Reid announced, staring at the street once more. "They wanted to know every place we've ever been, every friend he's ever had."

"Do you think he'll come back any time soon?"

"I don't know. Alicia's due sometime in the next couple of weeks. He'll probably come looking for her before then."

"Funny. He doesn't strike me as being much concerned about her or the baby." Karen had told him on the way back from the hospital last night that Morgan had hit Alicia, that he routinely did so. Just the way Karen's brother-in-law had beaten her twin. It was no wonder she felt compelled to put herself between the two, to try any way she could—physically, intellectually, emotionally—to reach Alicia.

"Of course he's concerned. He owns them. They're his property, just like his clothes, his stereo, his TV."

"Does he own you?"

He expected anger, hostility, an outright denial or a challenging admission. Instead, he got another shrug. "In a sense. I live at his place. If I don't do what he says, I'm out on the street." His expression turned cynical. "I've been there before. I'd rather not go back."

Before he had a chance to consider the suggestion he was about to make and deem it a bad idea, Jamey said, "The other apartment over the bar is empty. If you want to use it, I'll give you a key." The place was nothing fancy—one decent-sized bedroom and a large living room, with a shared bathroom in the hall and the kitchen downstairs—but it was clean and private. It couldn't be any worse than where he lived now.

Reid gave him an odd look—as if he didn't trust Jamey's offer, his motives or anything else—but neither accepted nor rejected it. Instead he nodded toward the street. "Looks like Karen's got company."

Jamey looked and saw a young woman coming down the street. Her name was Marina, and she had come to the cookout last weekend, with two little boys who were thrilled by the prospect of a party, by having a yard to play in and J.T. and Jethro to play with, by simply being outside without worry for a time. She walked swiftly, her head down, her arms wrapped protectively around something wrapped in foil. She turned in the gate and was halfway up the sidewalk before she realized that they were sitting on the veranda. Abruptly she stopped, looked as if she wanted to duck her head and take off again, but with a deep breath, she came to the top of the steps and settled her gaze on Jamey. "I heard about what happened to Karen. Is she all right?"

"She'll be fine. She's resting now."

"Have they arrested Ryan yet?"

"Not that I know of. Not unless it was just recently."

"She's not going to leave, is she? She won't let them

chase her away, will she?'' There was more than a hint of panic to the woman's voice. Why did it matter to her? What had she seen in those few hours she'd spent here Saturday evening that made her care?

He didn't blurt out that he *wanted* Karen to leave. No matter how much he would miss her, no matter how bleak his life would be without her, no matter that she would take his heart with her when she left, he wanted her gone. He would rather live the rest of his life missing her than risk a replay of last night, possibly with a more bitter ending. ''I don't know, Marina,'' he hedged. ''She needs to recover before she thinks about staying or going.''

She didn't look satisfied with his answer, but on Serenity, people didn't often expect satisfaction. ''I made this for her.'' She thrust a foil-covered pie plate into his hands. ''It's apple. She said she likes apple pie.''

''I'll give her a piece when she wakes up. Thanks.''

She smiled tautly, then turned and left in the same manner—head down, shoulders rounded, stride rushed. She probably thought that if she looked small and insignificant, no one would bother her, and she might be right. Karen had never appeared small or insignificant in her life, and look what it had gotten her.

''*Is* she going to leave?''

He looked at Reid. ''If I can talk her into it.''

''Do you plan on going with her?''

He had never considered it. He'd assumed that when Karen did leave here, she would return home to Landry, to her parents and Evan's, and that was sure as hell no place for him. *His* place was across the street—O'Shea's. He couldn't sell it—only a fool would buy it—and he couldn't just walk away from it. Besides, what could he do off Serenity? He had no job skills, not much of an education and no ambition at all. He belonged on Serenity Street. He'd been born here, and he would die here. If he was successful in persuading Karen to leave, he would die alone here.

"Ryan's not going to be around forever. He'll be dead or in prison before long. Maybe when he's gone, she can do what she wants. Maybe she can help."

"Maybe," Jamey conceded. "But at the risk of losing her life?"

"She could fall off the roof when she's cleaning the gutters and break her neck. She could be driving down Decatur when the next drunk driver comes through. This place could get swept away by a hurricane, or she could just not wake up one morning due to a heart attack." Reid set down his empty soda can, picked up his sketch pad and rose from the bench. At the top of the steps, he looked back. "There are plenty of ways to die, O'Shea. Serenity's not the only one."

Chapter 9

Karen sat at the breakfast booth in the kitchen, a salami sandwich with potato chips on one plate and a big slice of warm apple pie on another. While Jamey fixed glasses of ice for their soda, she debated, then pushed the sandwich aside and reached for the fork with the pie. The dish was sinfully delicious, the apple slices tender, the spices rich, the flavor sweet with just the right hint of tartness.

Jamey grinned when he sat down across from her and saw that half the slice was already gone. "What's the saying? 'Life is uncertain. Eat dessert first'?"

She licked the thick gooey filling from the back of the fork. "Life *is* uncertain. Look at us. Did you ever think the day you came over and helped me hang the sign out front that a mere few weeks later we would be where we are now?"

"In your kitchen eating lunch?" he asked dryly.

With all the bruises and swelling, she figured her scowl should be extra fierce, but it made him look regretful, not chastened. "For all intents and purposes, living together. Sleeping together. Making wicked love together."

"No," he acknowledged. "Though I do admit to a thought or two of a sexual nature when you came into the bar that night in tight jeans with your hair all wild."

"You hid it well. Until last Saturday night, when you kissed my socks off, I was convinced that the only thoughts you had of me were of my departure."

"You weren't wearing socks that night...or much of anything else. Besides, wanting you and wanting you to leave aren't mutually exclusive."

She left the rest of the pie for dessert and reached for the sandwich instead. After swallowing one spicy bite, she asked, "How long do I have to live here before we quit having this conversation? Six months? A year? Ten years?"

He avoided answering and instead sent the discussion on a slightly different tangent. "Marina doesn't want you to leave."

"Marina is thirty-one years old. She's got those two little boys and two older kids who live with their grandmother. Her first husband went out with his buddies one night and never came back. He was found a few days later, dead from a drug overdose. Her second husband works, pays the bills, puts food on the table and believes in swift and harsh discipline for her *and* their children. Marina is exactly the sort of woman Kathy's House is intended for. Of course she doesn't want me to leave."

"You learned a lot in one short evening."

Karen shrugged. Part of her information had come from Marina herself, desperate for female adult conversation. The rest had been filled in by the gossipy neighbor who had accompanied them on the short walk over from Divinity.

"Reid doesn't want you to leave, either."

She would have smiled smugly—heavens, she would

have grinned ear to ear—if her mouth weren't too sore to allow more than a slight lift of her lips. As it was, she settled for that small upturn and the delectable feeling of satisfaction spreading through her. "Reid's a smart young man."

"And talented, too. He's going to do your mural in the park. I saw a sketch."

"I knew he would. I've just been waiting for him to realize it."

Her brash boast made Jamey laugh. "You're awfully sure of yourself, aren't you?"

She finished the last bite of her sandwich, then called Jethro over and fed the leftover crusts of bread to him before shifting carefully on the bench. "I know what I like," she said quietly. "I know what I want, and I know what I need."

His amusement faded, leaving him serious, grim and just the slightest bit uncertain. He started to speak but closed his mouth, tried to look away but was drawn back again. "And what do you want, Karen? What do you need?"

She drew a deep breath that made her ribs throb. "You. Even if I lost my commitment to Kathy's House, even if I didn't feel compelled to be here for Reid, Alicia, Shawntae, J.T., Marina and the others, I couldn't leave, because of you. I need to be close to you. I want to be a part of your life. I love you, Jamey, and that's not going to change whether I live here or in Landry, whether I die tomorrow or fifty years from tomorrow. How long will it take to convince you of that?"

Moment after moment passed in silence. Maybe that hadn't been the best way to break the news to him. Declarations of love should be more romantic, offered under intimate circumstances, soft whispers in moonlit rooms punctuated by kisses. She didn't regret the words, though. Under intimate circumstances in moonlit rooms, a person could be seduced into making such a confession even though it wasn't true, because the words sounded right, because the partner expected them, because she—or he—got carried away by the moment.

That wasn't the case here. The words did sound right, but Jamey obviously hadn't expected them, and she just as obviously hadn't been swept up in the moment. She was thinking clearly, feeling clearly, her mind not clouded by anything—not passion, not the pain medication he'd given her before dawn or the long hours of daytime sleep the pills had induced. She knew exactly what she was saying, and she meant it with every breath in her body.

After a time, he blew out his breath. The exhalation sounded loud in the room where only the hum of the refrigerator disturbed the silence. Finally he answered her question: How long would it take to convince him that she loved him? "I don't know." Then, before she had even a moment to mourn his lack of faith, he went on. "Stick around. When I figure it out, I'll let you know."

Her mood lightened. Her eyes widened. Her smile darn near split her lip open again. "Stick around?" she echoed. "Did those words come from the mouth of Jamey O'Shea, who usually sounds like a broken record saying, 'Go away. Leave. That's your only option'?"

He scowled at her. "Don't press your luck, darlin'. You can stay—but on my terms."

Straightening on the bench, she folded her hands on the tabletop and put on her most obedient expression. "And what are those terms?"

"I'll spare you the arguments about leaving, about being in danger, about going back where you belong. I won't try to convince you that the people down here don't need you." He allowed a faint grin. "I won't try to convince you that I don't need you. I won't even call you a do-gooder anymore. But it comes with strings attached. I hope you enjoyed those hours in bed, because that's the last time in a long time that you're going to be alone. When I'm working, if someone can't stay with you, you have to come to O'Shea's. You don't go anywhere by yourself, not for any reason. I don't care if Alicia gives birth in the middle of the street in front of this house, you don't set foot outside without me.''

Although her instinct was to protest, she nodded instead. He was talking about temporary measures. Once Ryan Morgan and his fellow thugs had been arrested, his restrictions would no longer apply. Her enemies—the most dangerous ones, at least—would be locked up somewhere, and she would be free to go where she wanted.

But Jamey wasn't done. ''There won't be any more work done on the park without me or Reid—not even with Shawntae. And before you do any more work on this house, I want you to get new doors, new locks and security grates on the windows. I also want the gates kept shut, chained and padlocked at night. If those little bastards—or any other little bastards—come around again, I don't want them getting any thoughts of coming inside.''

Her momentarily hopeful mood faded into dismay. ''But if I lock the gates, no one else can come over, either. Jamey, I can't turn Kathy's House into a fortress. To do any good, it's got to be a place where women feel welcome, an inviting, open, friendly place.''

His scowl returned. ''Maybe inviting, open and friendly works up in Landry, but not here. You want to help women whose husbands or boyfriends or pimps are beating them. They don't need an open, friendly place. They need a place where they can feel safe, where nobody can kick down a door or break out a window and walk right in. They need a fortress.''

''I'll feel like a prisoner in my own house.''

''It'll give me peace of mind.'' He shook his head bleakly. ''My parents are dead. My friends have either moved on or gone to jail, or they're dead, too. I can't lose anyone else, Karen. I can't lose *you*. So if you want to stay, if you want to be close to me, if you want to be a part of my life, you have to do it my way."

She sat quietly, considering his demands—no, his requests. No matter how he phrased them, that was what they really were. She had spent plenty of time alone in her life—long hours while Evan had worked during their marriage, dark days privately grieving after his death. She really didn't mind giving up her solitude for a time. And, although she hated to admit it, the extra security sounded pretty good. It had been easy to talk about not being afraid, about taking care of herself, when nothing was happening, when no threats were being carried out. After last night, though, the mere idea of a strong, solid, unbreachable door between her and the Ryan Morgans of the world gave her a sense of added protection. Besides, Jamey was right about the prospective clients of Kathy's House. Eventually, she hoped to turn one or two of the smaller rooms into an emergency shelter. Any woman who had finally found the courage to flee an abusive man, even if only for one night, would surely feel safer behind locked gates and steel bars.

Kathy's House could be inviting, open and friendly on the inside, the sort of place where any woman could feel at home. On the outside, though, she owed it to herself, to her clients, and yes, to Jamey to make it a fortress.

"All right," she said at last. "If you could call a security company and make arrangements…"

Relief darkening his blue eyes, he nodded.

"You expected an argument, didn't you?"

"You've given me one every other time we've talked."

She carefully slid to the end of the bench, one hand braced protectively across her ribs, then stood up. "It's kind of hard to argue about security when you're black, blue and hurting. I think I'll hobble back upstairs and crawl into bed." She got a few feet away, then came back and claimed the saucer holding the rest of the apple pie.

"You're going to eat that pie in bed?" he teased, following patiently as she slowly made her way toward the stairs.

"It's comfort food," she retorted over her shoulder. "It's best eaten in bed."

"Yeah, well, keep your crumbs on your side. I don't want to sleep with bits of crust all over."

She reached the bottom of the stairs, transferred the plate to her left hand so she could use her right hand on the banister, then gave him a disdainful look. "Obviously, you've never seen me eat pie. There are no crumbs when I'm finished."

For a moment, she stood where she was, gazing at the hallway up above. She ran up and down these stairs a dozen times a day. She'd carried loaded baskets of laundry, gallons of paint, armloads of supplies and a sturdy eight-foot ladder up and down again. This afternoon she couldn't even find the energy to lift her foot to the first step.

Jamey's sweet, sympathetic voice came from behind her. "Hold on to your pie, darlin'." He lifted her carefully, one arm around her back, the other under her knees, and started up the stairs. Last night he'd managed masterfully. Of course, she admitted with a mischievous smile in thought if not in reality, last night he'd been operating on adrenaline. This afternoon, as they neared the top of the steps, she could feel his muscles straining.

"This is the last time you'll have to carry me," she promised as he turned down the hall toward her room. "I'll be fine tomorrow."

Bless his heart, he didn't argue with her. He didn't remind her what she'd been through, didn't point out every one of the bruises Ryan had given her. He very gently laid her on the bed, then collapsed face down beside her. After setting her pie aside, she brushed her fingers through his hair. "Why don't you lock up downstairs, come back up here, take your clothes off and lie down?"

He opened one eye to look at her. "I don't believe I've

ever gotten an invitation from a beautiful woman to get naked with less chance of getting lucky than I've got right now.''

"You got lucky the day you met me," she teased, but he didn't smile. He didn't offer that sweet grin. He reached for her hand and pressed a kiss to the center, a light, damp, erotic kiss, and he agreed.

"Darlin', I surely did.''

Jamey stood on the veranda, hands on the railing, staring out at the street. It was Monday, the first day of September, Labor Day. The month on the calendar might have changed, but the weather remained the same—hot and muggy. It was a day fit for sitting in an air-conditioned room and doing not much of anything, but nobody on Serenity had air-conditioning, and there was always too much of something to keep a body busy.

Behind him by the side door, the women were keeping busy—Karen, Cassie Wade, Shawntae and Marina. It was a holiday, and holidays, according to Karen, were meant for celebrating. He had tried to talk her out of this cookout. It was too soon after her run-in with Morgan. She should be resting. She should forget the parties until cooler weather, until the police caught the local hotheads and locked them away from her. Of course she hadn't listened. He would have been disappointed if she had.

He grew still, considering that last thought. It would have been nice if she had agreed, if she had postponed the party until she was completely recovered, but that wasn't Karen's way. Backing down, doing only what was safe, not taking chances—if that was the way she did business, he never would have met her. He never would have fallen in love with her.

Turning, he leaned against the rail and watched the women. Karen claimed all of his attention, of course, in a yellow sundress, her hair pulled back from her face with a matching yellow headband. She was as bright, beautiful and welcome a sight as the first daffodil must be after a long, hard winter. She was so beautiful that the injuries on her face—the fading bruise, the healing lip, the improving scrape—weren't even noticeable until the second or third look.

Feeling his gaze, she paused in the task of arranging the table, looked up and slowly smiled. It was a sweetly intimate gesture, as potent as the afternoon sun, as full of promise as the most solemn vow, as lovely and vital as anything he'd ever seen. It made the muscles in his stomach tighten, made his breath catch and brought his blood to a slow simmer. It made him wonder what excuse could entice her away from her friends and upstairs for an hour—or two or three—of his exclusive company.

None at the moment, he admitted regretfully as she turned away in response to one of the other women; then slowly his own smile came. There was always the night. Tonight and tomorrow night and twenty thousand nights to come.

Footsteps on the porch drew his attention toward the front of the house. Rosa Gutierrez had arrived. Behind her, Reid was carrying her contributions to the meal. The kid took them to the table, then came back to lean against the next section of railing. "I started on Karen's mural this morning."

Jamey smiled faintly. Karen's mural, Karen's party and Karen's friends. Soon it would be Karen's neighborhood. In no time at all, she would have transformed a bleak, miserable little corner of the city into her very own perfect place to belong. "She'll be happy to hear it."

After a brief silence, Reid spoke again. "Alicia had her baby this morning. A boy. She named him after Ryan."

Labor on Labor Day, Jamey thought. Fitting. "Any word from him?"

"No." Reid looked around, uncomfortable with what he

was about to say. Finally, his gaze on floorboards badly in need of painting, he got the words out. "That offer the other day...about the apartment... Did you mean it?"

He'd had plenty of time over the weekend to decide that letting Reid move into his building was a bad idea, but he hadn't. Considering that he'd never provided a home for his son when he was a kid and needed one, doing so now was the least he could do. "Yeah. Come over when this is finished and I'll give you a key."

Looking relieved—and embarrassed by it—Reid simply nodded, then silence settled again as they watched the women. The grill was smoking, J.T. and Marina's kids were playing near the back wall, and the others were exclaiming over Polaroids of Rosa's great-grandson. How hard was it for Karen to be happy for Alicia, he wondered, when she'd been denied the same pleasure herself? It said something for her strength that her excitement was genuine, though tinged with well-hidden sorrow.

Over the next half hour, more guests arrived. Some were his regulars—Eldin and his wife, who rarely set foot outside their apartment since the drive-by shooting last year that had killed their little girl, old Thomas and Virgil, who lived next door and thought Karen was a pretty little thing, and Pat, celebrating an extra day off from his job over at the wharf. There were a few of Alicia's friends, a half-dozen people from Marina's building and neighbors from Shawntae's. Some came empty-handed, but others brought food, six-packs of soda or folding chairs from their long-unused porches. By two-thirty, more than forty people filled the side yard, mostly women, some children, only a few men.

That was the makeup of the neighborhood, Jamey acknowledged. Women trying to hold their lives and their families together without the help of the men responsible for those families. Men seemed to leave Serenity first. Kids left, too, if they grew up, if they weren't shot to death playing on their own front porch, if they didn't end up in juvenile detention or dead from drug use, abuse, gang violence or despair. But the women stayed. They held on. They kept trying.

Karen intended to stay, to hold on and keep trying. How long would it take him to accept that? she had asked. Watching her now with her neighbors—*neighbors,* in a place where before there had been only strangers and enemies—he knew. Unlike everyone else he had ever known, *she* wasn't going to give in, give up and leave him behind. She was making a place for herself here on Serenity, and she was never going to leave—not her home, not the street, not him.

Joining her on the veranda near the dessert table, he wrapped his arms around her from behind and pressed a kiss to one exposed ear. "You know how to throw a good party."

She smiled up at him, then, with a sigh, settled against him, her hands clasping his. "There are nice people on this street."

Years ago he had known that, but lately he'd needed the reminder. He had come to view Serenity as a place not worth saving, filled with people beyond saving. But everyone was worth saving. Everyone had some decent quality, some decent purpose. Well, almost everyone, he amended as the sound of slamming car doors drew his attention, and everyone else's, to the street. The Morgans' old Impala was pulled across the sidewalk, partway through the open gate, and Ryan, his brother, Vinnie Marino and Elpidio Rodriguez were lined up in front of the car, facing the crowd, looking every bit as dangerous as Jamey knew they were. "Tell the redheaded bitch to come on down here," Ryan shouted.

"Stay here." Jamey released Karen and started toward the steps, passing Cassie on the way. "Call the police and tell them the punks they're after are here and looking for trouble,'' he said quietly. As she quickly obeyed, Karen pushed past them and walked down the steps. The crowd parted, people leaving their chairs and food behind, the mothers gathering their children and edging away, leaving Karen in the open.

"You already forgot the rules for the parties," she said, her voice betraying no hint of the fear that Jamey was feeling and knew she must be. His blood was cold, his heart was barely beating, and his chest was painfully tight. "No weapons, no trouble, no bullies."

"I came for Alicia."

Jamey took the steps in one great stride and stopped in front of Karen. She stubbornly moved to his side. "She's not here," he said coldly, "but the police will be soon."

As a group all four young men moved forward a few yards. "Maybe I don't believe she's not here," Morgan responded. "Maybe I'll go inside and look around."

"And maybe you'll get off my property," Karen retorted.

"Where is she?"

"I don't know."

"Don't lie to me!" He moved closer still. "You've been telling her lies about me, filling her head with all kinds of stuff, making her think I'm no good for her. You took her someplace, didn't you? I want to know where."

"I don't know where she is." Karen's voice was strong, her words clearly and carefully enunciated.

"Then maybe this will help you remember." Morgan raised his left arm, extending it straight out, pointing the pistol he held directly at Karen.

Without taking his gaze from the other man, Jamey edged toward Karen, intending to pull her behind him, for whatever good it would do. The gun was a semi-automatic, no doubt loaded for a sure kill. At this distance, if he fired, he would probably succeed at killing them both.

"Where is she, bitch?" Morgan asked once more, his

voice deadly cold, all the more menacing for the lack of emotion it held.

Movement beyond Karen caught Jamey's eye. It was Reid, coming to stand beside her. It made Morgan smile. "You think I won't kill you, too, and enjoy doing it? You betrayed us. You were one of us until she came. You lived with us, you worked with us, you partied with us. You were just like us."

"I was never just like you," Reid denied mildly. "You're already in trouble, Ryan. You think killing us in front of all these people will make it better?"

"These are *my* people," he boasted, waving the gun in a broad gesture. "I *own* this neighborhood. I *own* these people. You think they'd talk to the police about me?" He spat out a curse. "They're scared little mice—scared of me. They know that if they don't do what I say, they'll be sorry. They'll be dead."

From somewhere behind them a strong voice spoke out in disagreement. "You don't own me, Morgan." Shawntae Williams separated herself from the crowd and came to stand with them.

As he moved close enough to slide his arm around Karen, Jamey glanced at Shawntae with equal measures of admiration and frustration. He appreciated the show of support for Karen's sake, but didn't the woman realize the danger? Didn't she realize that putting her life at risk wouldn't make saving Karen's any easier? Then her mother joined her, and admiration turned to amazement. Alicia's grandmother came, too, and old Thomas, Cassie, Marina, everyone, until a crowd had formed around them, with Karen at the center.

Uneasy with this turn of events, Morgan looked over his shoulder for guidance, and Trevor made an insistent motion toward the crowd. He was telling his brother to do something, Jamey knew, to take some sort of decisive action. There wasn't much, though, that he could do. Open fire or back down—those were his choices. He had to realize, even in his anger, that shooting into the crowd would seal his own fate—there would be no avoiding prison, maybe even execution—while backing down would cost him the respect of his boys and the grudging, fear-based deference of the people in the community. He would lose his stature as the meanest, toughest son of a bitch on Serenity. He would be giving in to—accepting defeat from—this ragged bunch of powerless, unprotected people whom he'd made a career of terrorizing.

In the distance sirens sounded, three, maybe four, distinct wails. Marino looked toward Decatur, then commanded, "Come on, Ryan, let's get out of here."

The young man whirled around. "*I* give the orders here!" he shouted, venting his rage on his friend. "*I* tell you what to do! I tell everyone what to do! Understand?"

Marino muttered a curse, started to turn away, then turned back with his own weapon pointed at Morgan. "Start the car, Trevor," he commanded, and the younger Morgan hustled to obey. "We're not following your orders anymore, Ryan. We're not going to jail because you can't keep your little girlfriend under control. You want to stay? Go ahead. But we're outta' here."

As the motor caught, Marino and Rodriguez backed away, through the gate, to the back doors. Morgan screamed obscenities as Trevor backed out, tires squealing, then gunned the engine. Less than three blocks away the tires squealed again, the noise ending in a terrific crash of metal against metal, followed by the dying warble of a siren. One of New Orleans's finest had just met three of the city's worst, Jamey thought with a hint of relief.

"I'll be back, O'Shea," Morgan said, keeping the gun pointed their way as he retreated toward the sidewalk. "I'll be back, and she'll be dead."

"She'll be waiting," Jamey replied. "And so will I."

At the sidewalk, Morgan tucked the gun in his waistband,

then took off at a dead run toward the end of the street. Moments later a patrol car raced by in the same direction. Maybe they would corner him on one of these dead-end streets or in an alley, Jamey thought. If they did, Morgan, being the punk he was, would probably force a standoff. Maybe he would get himself killed.

Beside him Karen gave a soft, heartfelt sigh, then wrapped her arms around his middle. She was shaking like a leaf in a hurricane, and he swore he could feel her heart beating in time with his. He held her tightly for a moment, then tilted her head back. "Are you all right?"

She smiled shakily. "Oh, darlin', I'm better than all right. Can you believe these people?"

Around them everyone was reacting—laughing, sharing fears, patting each other on the shoulder or arm. They were pleased with themselves for standing up to Morgan—proud of themselves for the first time in far too long—and it was Karen's doing.

She had been right all along. These people did need her—not as a social worker, not as a do-gooder, but just for herself. They needed her bright, Pollyanna outlook and her no-strings-attached offer of friendship, her unbroken spirit, her optimism and her dreams. Most of all they needed her extraordinary faith—in herself, in them, in the community as a whole.

He needed her faith. He needed her dreams. He needed *her.*

And as soon as they were alone, he intended to tell her.

The party broke up around six. Everyone pitched in to clean up, the women claimed their dishes, and Karen and Jamey said goodbye to them all. Quiet settled over the yard, the house and its three occupants as they relaxed on the porch. Jamey sat in the rocker, Karen on his lap, and Jethro, exhausted from an unaccustomed afternoon's play, snored underneath the bench.

This had been her best day since coming to Serenity, she decided as the floor squeaked in time to their rocking. For the first time she'd seen hard and fast evidence that she just might be able to make a difference here. Not only had her neighbors come out in force for the cookout, but they had protected her. They had faced down Ryan Morgan, their greatest nightmare, and he had fled. Other than that incident, everyone had enjoyed themselves—not even the interviews conducted by the police officers had been enough to dampen their spirits—and Jamey hadn't once mentioned better security, impenetrable walls, an alligator-filled moat or anything of that nature. He hadn't even objected when she'd suggested that they sit out on the veranda this evening.

She sighed softly, then remarked, "I saw you talking with Reid this afternoon."

"Yeah. He started your mural today." He rocked a couple more times. "He's going to move into the empty apartment next to mine."

She raised her head from his shoulder to look at him in the failing light. "Really."

"He's made enemies of his only friends, and he had nowhere to go, and the place has been empty for years, so…" He shrugged as if it were nothing.

Gently, she eased down again. "We might turn you into a father yet."

"I doubt it." After another brief silence, he added, "Maybe a friend."

Her smile was small and secretive, but its pleasure was no less intense. She hoped he and Reid did become friends, but she also hoped that someday they would find a familial relationship they could both appreciate. And she deeply, sincerely, desperately hoped there was a place in it for her.

"I have a suggestion."

She closed her eyes and breathed deeply of the rich, humid air. "What?"

"Ever since you looked at me on the veranda this afternoon and smiled—you know the smile—I've wanted to take you upstairs, undress you, lay you down on the bed and…" Ducking his head, he whispered in her ear wicked words that made her desire flare to life, that fueled incredible heat inside her while, at the same time, sending a shiver of goose bumps over her skin. Finishing his indecent proposal, he waited for her response, his expression improbably innocent.

"Come upstairs and tell me that again," she invited. "You can show me exactly what you mean." Wriggling free of his arms—causing him no small discomfort in the process, if the swelling under her hip was anything to judge by—she swung her feet to the floor, stood up and smoothed her dress. She bent to scoop up Jethro and was halfway to the door when the sound of a car stopped her. The engine was too finely tuned to belong on Serenity. This car purred like a powerful tiger and was sleek, long, black.

A limousine on Serenity Street. The sight reminded her of a silly children's book, about the fantastical sights a child had seen on a particular street, but she resisted the urge to smile. She could think of only one man who would come to Serenity in a limo, and there was nothing the least bit amusing about him.

Beside her Jamey stiffened and reached protectively for her. "Hold that thought, sweetheart," he said dryly. "You're about to meet the great Jimmy Falcone."

The driver stopped so that the back door of the car was perfectly in line with the gate. A burly, broad-shouldered man in a suit climbed out of the back, held the door for his boss, then swung the gate open. He and a third man followed Falcone up the sidewalk to the bottom of the steps.

Gangster, wise guy, mafioso, crime boss. Drug dealer, murderer, corrupter, destroyer. She neither knew nor cared which label he preferred. Probably businessman, she thought with disgust. She'd seen photographs of him before, but in person he looked different. He wasn't tall, several inches under six feet, and he wasn't oily. His suit was pure elegance and cost a fortune. So did the single ring he wore on his right hand. The tie was no doubt silk, the shoes Italian. But all that money couldn't buy class. It couldn't disguise evil.

His first words were addressed to Jamey. "You're O'Shea. I've heard about you."

Jamey offered no response whatsoever beyond a slow blink.

"And you must be Ms. Montez. There used to be a police officer here in New Orleans named Montez. He died a few years ago. You knew him?"

The son of a bitch *knew* she knew him. He probably knew everything about her. "He was my husband."

"I'm sorry. It was such a sad case—that poor girl. That man deserved to die."

She wasn't touched by his sentiment. "Why are you here?"

"I understand you've been having a little trouble with one of my employees down here—a young man by the name of Ryan Morgan. I understand the police have several warrants for his arrest. I want you to know that he won't be bothering you anymore. It seems he ran into a little trouble of his own this afternoon. His body was found by the river a short while ago. Someone shot him."

A few hours ago Karen never would have believed that she could feel shock, sympathy or anything other than fear and disgust for Ryan Morgan, but she would have been wrong. A great shudder swept over her, and she clutched the puppy a little tighter, making him squirm. "Why?" she demanded. "Why did you kill him?"

Falcone looked surprised. "You misunderstood. *I* didn't shoot him. *Someone* did. God knows, he had a great many enemies and not enough friends." The injured innocence vanished from his voice. "He threatened a lot of people, you included. He even turned on his own people, on Vinnie and the Donovan boy."

"He threatened your profits," Jamey said, his voice sharp and accusing. "Morgan used to boast that you didn't do business with anyone who couldn't control his territory, and you did a lot of business with him. So this is how you handle an employee whose performance suffers?"

Falcone ignored him. "As I said, Ryan Morgan had many enemies. The police will probably never discover which of them decided to take care of him once and for all. I should think that would make you happy, Ms. Montez. He won't be bothering you anymore."

"You'll forgive me," Karen said sarcastically, "but I don't celebrate *anyone's* death."

"Given the opportunity, he would have killed you without a second's remorse."

"Given the opportunity and the motivation, *you* would kill me without a second's remorse." She sighed heavily, feeling as if the world's cares were pressing on her shoulders. "If you came here expecting gratitude, you wasted your time. If you came for some other reason, kindly state it and leave."

"I just wanted you to know that Morgan is out of your life and there will be no further trouble. You leave my people alone, and you'll be left alone. That sounds fair enough, doesn't it?" He waited a moment, but when no response came, he nodded once, such a courtly gesture from a cold-hearted killer, and returned to his car, his two goons at his heels.

As they drove away, Karen closed her eyes and bent her cheek to Jethro's fur. She had no tears to shed for Ryan Morgan. She felt coldly empty inside, coldly guilty. She wasn't responsible for his death. All she'd done was come here, try to make a home for herself, offer a little needed advice to Alicia and a little desperately needed friendship to Reid. It wasn't her fault that Ryan had objected so furiously to her presence here. It wasn't her fault that he'd chosen to work for a man like Jimmy Falcone. It wasn't her fault that he'd died the same way he'd lived: violently.

"Come upstairs." With his hands on her shoulders, Jamey steered her inside and up the stairs to the bathroom, where he pulled Jethro from her arms and set the dog on the floor. "Take a bath. Cool down a little. I'm going to lock up, then I'll be back."

She followed his advice automatically, giving little thought to her actions. She bathed, shampooed her hair, put on a clean T-shirt—not Evan's ragged NOPD shirt, but one of Jamey's white ones—and went to stand at the bedroom window. She heard Jamey come up the stairs, followed by the sound of the bathtub filling again and, soon after, his footsteps behind her. She didn't turn, but continued to gaze at the sky, where heat lightning shimmered in the darkness.

"Maybe you were right," she said softly. "Maybe I should have stayed in Landry."

She heard a drawer open. In the last week he'd brought many of his clothes over, including a pair of red gym shorts that were his only concession to modesty these hot nights. They were boringly plain—cotton, faded, well-worn—but most nights she thought he looked sexy as hell in them. Tonight she didn't even turn to enjoy the sight.

"Do you think staying in Landry would have prevented Morgan's death?"

"It might have. He wouldn't have been so angry these last few weeks. He wouldn't have lost control of the neighborhood. He wouldn't have drawn Falcone's displeasure."

He came to stand behind her, picking up the towel she'd laid on the windowsill, using it to blot the water dripping from the ends of her hair. "Darlin', I don't know how to break this to you, but Ryan Morgan had been angry all his life. These last couple of weeks were no exception. He was a bitter, angry, resentful young man who'd alienated vir-

tually everyone in his life. You didn't change anything.
You didn't make matters worse. It was just easy for him to
blame you because you were new. You were an easy target
because you were smaller, more vulnerable, a woman, a
stranger. People around here wouldn't stick up for each
other. He never dreamed they would stick up for you.''

Thunder sounded faintly in the distance, and from somewhere across the room, Jethro shot across the floor and
wriggled his way between her feet. Balancing her weight
on one foot, she used the other to rub his stomach. ''Maybe
I should forget about Kathy's House. That was what Falcone was suggesting, wasn't it? That I could live here in
peace if I didn't try to change anything. After all, what
goes on in this neighborhood isn't really any of my business, is it?''

''Like hell it isn't!'' Jamey dropped the towel, gripped
her arms and turned her to face him. ''You came here to
help people, to reclaim Serenity, to take it from the punks
and turn it back into the community it used to be. Look at
what happened today, Karen. You wanted to work mira-
cles? Well, you got your first one today. Those people have
never stood up to anyone, but they stood up to Morgan and
his gang. You made a hell of a start, but you can't quit
now. What kind of message would that send? That when
things get tough, you give in and give up?'' He gave her
a frustrated little shake. ''They've already learned that les-
son, Karen. They've been giving in and giving up all their
lives. They need someone to teach them another way. *You*
can do that.'' He broke off, drew a deep breath, then finished, ''*We* can do that. You and me. Together.''

She stared at him, at the stubborn set of his jaw, at the
intensity that blazed in his blue eyes, and slowly the burden
that had settled over her started to ease. ''You sound like
a dreamer, Jamey O'Shea.''

He stared back. ''Maybe I'm becoming one. You know,

I've been spending a lot of time with this crazy redhead lately. She's making me a little crazy.''

A faint smile touched her mouth, then faded. "Exactly what kind of partnership are you suggesting?"

"The permanent kind. Always and forever. Till death do us part.''

Karen felt as if her heart had stopped beating in her chest for one long, stunned moment; then it started again, and she managed one more little smile. "I thought you'd given up on marriage.''

"I thought I had, too, until I met you. I'd given up on a lot of things until I'd met you." His hold on her arms became a gentle caress, relaxing, arousing. "What do you think, darlin'? Is there room in Kathy's House for one more?"

She twined her arms around his neck. "I don't know. I've got a pretty full roster of volunteers for Kathy's House. However, in *Karen's* house, there will always be a place for you."

He drew her close and kissed her, a slow, easy, all-the-time-in-the-world sort of kiss, then pulled back and gazed down at her, so heart-achingly serious. "I love you, Karen."

"I knew you did," she replied, feigning nonchalance, although her heart just might burst with the sheer pleasure of hearing the words. "I've just been waiting for you to realize it.''

His laughter was warm and sweet. "You're awfully sure of yourself, aren't you?"

"No. I'm sure of us. You and me. Together."

He kissed her again and again, each kiss a step closer to the bed. He lowered her down gently, drew her shirt over her head with utmost care, removed his own clothing and stroked, kissed, explored, caressed and loved her—oh, yes, *loved* her—so sweetly, so slowly, so thoroughly. Finally, when her skin was slick, when her muscles were quivering, when her heart was racing and her body was trembling, he joined with her intimately.

"You and me," he repeated between kisses. "Together. Tonight and forever."

* * * * *

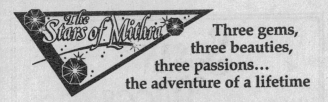

SHARON SALA

**Continues the twelve-book
series—36 HOURS—
in October 1997
with Book Four**

FOR HER EYES ONLY

The storm was over. The mayor was dead. Jessica Hanson
had an aching head…and sinister visions of murder.
And only one man was willing to take her seriously—
Detective Stone Richardson. He knew that unlocking
Jessica's secrets would put him in danger, but the rugged
cop had never expected to fall for her, too. Danger he could
handle. But love…?

For Stone and Jessica and *all* the residents of Grand Springs,
Colorado, the storm-induced blackout was just the beginning
of 36 Hours that changed *everything!* You won't want to miss a
single book.

Share in the joy of yuletide romance with brand-new stories by two of the genre's most beloved writers

DIANA PALMER

and

JOAN JOHNSTON

in

LONE STAR CHRISTMAS

Diana Palmer and Joan Johnston share their favorite Christmas anecdotes and personal stories in this *special hardbound edition.*

Diana Palmer delivers an irresistible spin-off of her **LONG, TALL TEXANS** series and Joan Johnston crafts an unforgettable new chapter to **HAWK'S WAY** in this wonderful keepsake edition celebrating the holiday season. So perfect for gift giving, you'll want one for yourself...and one to give to a special friend!

Available in November at your favorite retail outlet!

Only from

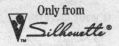

Welcome to the Towers!

In January
New York Times bestselling author

NORA ROBERTS

takes us to the fabulous Maine coast mansion
haunted by a generations-old secret and introduces
us to the fascinating family that lives there.

Mechanic Catherine "C.C." Calhoun and hotel magnate
Trenton St. James mix like axle grease and mineral
water—until they kiss. Efficient Amanda Calhoun finds
easygoing Sloan O'Riley insufferable—and irresistible.
And they all must race to solve the mystery
surrounding a priceless hidden emerald necklace.

Catherine and Amanda

THE Calhoun Women

**A special 2-in-1 edition containing
COURTING CATHERINE and A MAN FOR AMANDA.**

Look for the next installment of
THE CALHOUN WOMEN with Lilah and Suzanna's
stories, coming in March 1998.

Available at your favorite retail outlet.

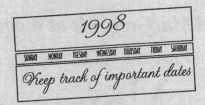

1998

SUNDAY MONDAY TUESDAY WEDNESDAY THURSDAY FRIDAY SATURDAY

Keep track of important dates

Three beautiful and colorful calendars that celebrate some of the most popular trends in America today.

Look for:

Just Babies—a 16 month calendar that features a full year of absolutely adorable babies!

1998 CALENDAR
Just Babies
16 months of adorable bundles of joy!

Hometown Quilts
1998 Calendar
A 16 month quilting extravaganza!

Hometown Quilts—a 16 month calendar featuring quilted art squares, plus a short history on twelve different quilt patterns.

Inspirations—a 16 month calendar with inspiring pictures and quotations.

Inspirations

A 16 month calendar that will lift your spirits and gladden your heart

Steeple Hill™

◆ HARLEQUIN®

Value priced at $9.99 U.S./$11.99 CAN., these calendars make a perfect gift!

Available in retail outlets in August 1997.   CAL98